PRAISE FOR MICHAEL LAIMO!

THE MAN FROM THE SHADOWS

Suddenly, a man emerged from the cover of trees at the darkened corner of the math building. Something seemed strange about him—the way he just appeared from the darkness, as if he had been hiding, the way he was walking, steadfast and strong, determined. Jamie looked around; although a few people were walking about in the distance, she was closest to the stranger.

He passed through the amber glow of a lamppost.

The dull gleam reflected dully off his bald head. And his sunglasses.

She stopped in her tracks, heart slamming in her chest. She took an indecisive step backward.

He continued to advance toward her at a hurried pace, passing under another streetlamp.

The image she beheld as the light from the second streetlamp showered the stranger could be described in a million different ways, but at this terrifying moment her mind could not calculate a single solitary word, as the horror was too excessive to comprehend. Her jaw slackened, her eyes bulged in her skull, a sharp fear-induced agony probed her brain: clear warning signs that screamed *get away!*

She looked again. The bald man was holding an odd-looking object in both hands.

It, his hands and forearms were *drenched* in blood.

ATMOSPHERE

MICHAEL LAIMO

LEISURE BOOKS NEW YORK CITY

A first book should always be dedicated
to the ones you love most. To my family.

A LEISURE BOOK®

September 2002

Published by

Dorchester Publishing Co., Inc.
276 Fifth Avenue
New York, NY 10001

ISBN 0-8439-5041-2

The name "Leisure Books" and the stylized "L" with design are trademarks of Dorchester Publishing Co., Inc.

Printed in the United States of America.

Visit us on the web at www.dorchesterpub.com.

ACKNOWLEDGMENTS

To avoid the risk of forgetting someone, I would like to thank all those writers and editors, not to mention my friends, who have shown support over the years. This book could not have been written without you all. I would also like to send a very special thank you to my editor, Don D'Auria, for believing in me and my work.

ATMOSPHERE

Chapter One

Shielding himself from the early morning rain, Detective Frank Ballaro of the New York City Police Department bent down, squinted and checked to see if it really was blood he had stepped in.

The showers, which had begun around six A.M. the previous morning, started out as just a sprinkle but strengthened as the morning gave way to afternoon. Throughout the day they paused at times—only to gather more strength before continuing to pour, leaving everything saturated in their wake.

He should have known that at least two inches of water would be awaiting his loafers when he stepped from the car; New York City's streets promised that. In the past he would have cursed out loud a few times, letting everyone within his proximity know exactly what it was he had done to himself. But this morning extreme exhaustion wore him down, and he accepted the slight mishap as simply another in a string of irks riddling his pressure-filled life.

Summer had been hot and dry all the way into October, the drought making it seem as if there would never be any rain to cool the city streets. When the weekend arrived, thousands would flock to the beaches on Long Island in the effort to escape the stifling heat. Some would seek relief from the fire hydrants. It was almost as if the city were a great sand castle built a bit too far away from shore, just out of reach of the ocean's foamy crescents.

But then summer segued into fall, and like magic the tide rushed in, transforming October into a cooling-off period: nearly twenty days of rain that pounded the skyscrapers and saturated the concrete sidewalks, flooding the labyrinth of subway tunnels after all the water tables had drunk their fill, causing streams of water to race along the curbs and rush around the corners in a seemingly endless circular flow.

The curb Frank stepped off of was no exception.

He hunkered down and rubbed a finger across the toes of his black loafers. Holding it beneath the dull incandescent glow of the street lamp next to him, he dabbed it with his thumb. Deep red. Thick like syrup. Indeed, Frank had stepped in blood.

He wiped his fingers on the rainy-wet lamppost, rinsing them of the red smear. He cautiously gazed about Fourth Street, his mental wheels spinning in search of a clue to the cause of the blood, purposely averting his gaze from his apartment building directly across the street to avoid the temptation of being lured there. The world played dead: empty sidewalks, not a vehicle riding the street. Shops closed and shuttered. Everything was steeped in darkness aside from the street lamps and the scattered glows from within some apartment windows. Not even a distant siren called out. The disorderly pace that usually thrived in this neighborhood had ceased to exist, making Frank feel like the last human on a world that had suddenly stopped turning.

He peeked at his watch, a simple act he had not performed during the past twelve hours. Four sixteen A.M. Again he resisted the urge to peek across toward his apartment. A very hard-earned three-day weekend awaited him. All he had to do was carry himself across the street, lock the door behind him and close out the rest of the world until Monday.

And to imagine: a very rare occurrence started it all off. Lucking into a good parking spot. Hell, why not? He deserved at least that much. He had spent the last twelve hours wrapping up the final paperwork on the Carrie Lindsay murder that he and his ever-annoying partner, Neil Connor, had slaved over the past two months. What a relief, to finally have the poor girl's older brother right where he belonged—behind bars—all the evidence needed to prove the case on paper, clasped

3

in a manila folder and locked in his desk drawer. The judicial icing on the cake, as he liked to say.

He sucked in a breath, tried to rub the looming headache from his eyes. For two weeks he had wanted nothing more than a good night's sleep. He always slept pretty well between jobs, when he didn't have to obsess about who, what and why, and with the closure on the Carrie Lindsay case clearing a lot of space in his head, that's exactly where he was: in between assignments.

But of all things, thirty-one-year veteran Frank Ballaro hadn't anticipated stepping in blood.

His detective's mind set itself in investigation mode. He had to know.

Swirling in the running water, the blood kept coming, carried by the ebbing current. It flowed with a smooth sensuality, spiraling down the gutter into a wicked design before reaching a bump in the blacktop, where it gelled into a ball behind a twig like an oil slick on a slab of flotsam.

Frank felt two of his three distinct personalities begin to do battle. The meek, weary, yet rational man in him tried desperately to ignore the blood and force himself to retire for the night, go shrug out of his stale wet clothing and into a warm bathrobe, have a bowl of hot chicken soup and sleep for sixteen hours. But that part—secondary and rarely listened to—succumbed to Frank's strongest personality: the brave truth-seeking N.Y.P.D. detective who had been commended with various honors over the years, the detective who was to retire in two years but still couldn't turn down a piece of challenging work when it presented itself, no matter what the circumstances, no matter what time it was.

The part that always piled on the grind, but somehow always eased him out of it.

Blood on his shoes? It was coming from somewhere. *Someone*. He *had* to investigate.

The early morning moon tore through a dispersing tapestry of blue-black rain clouds, adding a faint touch of light to the dull glow of the fading street lamps. Thin wisps of fog sluggishly advanced from around the buildings at the corner of Fourth and Mason like skeletal fingers, adding a cold sheet of humidity to the diminishing precipitation. A wind picked up and hurled a few wet leaves across the sidewalk.

Slowly and methodically, Frank paced along the edge of the curb, opposite the bloody flow, keeping his eyes glued to the hairline streaks of crimson wavering atop the stream of lapping rain water. He passed dark apartment buildings and storefronts on his left, cars parked alongside meters to his right.

A taxi turned the corner ahead and roared by, ripping through the silence, speeding past Frank down the block to Scudder Place.

From the gloom its former passenger appeared, footsteps approaching, tapping on the sidewalk. A girl.

Frank glanced in her direction. She sported green hair and a nose ring, wore a straightforward expression as heavy as an iron weight. Her jade eyes were catatonic, seemingly angry at the world. Frank thought of Jaimie, only nineteen years old, perhaps the same age as this confused girl. Dear God, how horrible would his life be if his baby came home one day adorned with electric hair and a pierced face? Or worse yet: a guy with the same embellishments. It was hard enough getting her to turn down the volume on that damn music she listened to. He couldn't imagine engaging in some futile lifestyle conflict with her.

He tore his eyes from the girl as she passed, returning his gaze to the gutter and the blood. He continued his pursuit of the wispy flow to the northwest corner of Fourth and Mason.

All of a sudden he heard a squeak and looked down to investigate. In the gutter a rat groveled on all fours, its pink tongue lapping urgently at a patch of blood congealing in the litter-clogged grill. Its oil-drop eyes were aimed at Frank, beady, paranoid, seemingly saying *come near my warm meal and I'll bite your little human finger off*.

Frank's weak and weary identity again begged him to turn around and head home, begged him to fight the sudden frivolous urge to pull out his .45 and pulverize the rat. Damn his third personality, that irrational part inside that always misguided his thoughts, tempting him to act foolishly and recklessly. The personality that would clearly get him into big trouble if he listened to it. Thank God this personality had never had the strength to coerce his body into action.

Take out the gun, pull the trigger, then slide

away into your apartment and start your three-day weekend.

The lunacy of these ill-advised thoughts sent his body to shudders. Chills swam through him like a school of fish. Clearly the fatigue was tearing his mind to shreds. But still, the rat's beady eyes, they just *stared* at him. And the whiskers, dappled with ruby droplets, tongue sliding in and out, in and out, lap, lap, lap.

He placed a hand on his gun. *C'mon, Frank, only one shot, that's all. Just one . . .*

Without a warning, a fierce scream ripped through the deadened silence of the night. Frank started. His skin crawled and he pulled his gun. The rat freaked also, squealing maniacally, darting into the sewer, leaving its tasty meal behind in a diluted puddle.

Frank jogged into the street. He saw a taxi racing up Mason, its headlights floating like two beacons in the ocean. He glanced quickly to the south and then back up the street, but saw only the approaching cab.

The scream sounded again, louder this time, more intense. Frank stepped forward, his eyes searching the street. Nothing, at first.

Then its source finally appeared.

A filthy man, completely naked, darted into the street a half block up, like a bat escaping the throes of hell.

Right in front of the cab.

The cab's wheels screeched. A jolting noise like a gunshot blasted. Frank thought the cab had blown a tire or backfired but soon realized with horror that the explosive sound was the result of the cab's cold hard metal striking the naked man.

Frank swallowed hard and clutched his gut in reactive pain as the man's waist caved into an accordion shape at the point of contact, the opposite side of his body tearing open like a piece of citrus fruit, exposing a red swamp of liver, kidney and entrails. The stricken man catapulted head over heels like a sailing gymnast performing an out-of-control cartwheel, struck the pavement and tumbled end over end on the concrete, pieces of his insides spraying about in a symphonic shower of red beads.

The cab screeched to a halt and the driver leapt out—just in time to see the body come to a dead rest fifteen feet away.

Frank raced to the body, hand cramping around his gun, finger wet on the trigger. The cab driver, wearing dark pants and a short-sleeved Hawaiian shirt, sprinted forward on long, chicken-thin legs but abruptly stopped a few yards away, steeling himself in a surrenderlike stance, arms in the air.

Frank focused on him, puzzled.

The cabbie started yelling, face taut with panic, accent thick. "Don't hurt me! I—I did not see him! He come from nowhere!"

Frank scrutinized the driver's defensive posture, his timid reaction, following his line of vision, which was aimed at his own shaking hand. The gun.

Ignoring him, Frank reached for his handheld radio but found only his empty belt. In the car.

He had removed it earlier and placed it on the seat next to him. His brains too it seemed.

Instead he gently brushed the young man's long stringy hair from his face, gazing at his empty features through the jagged headlight beams of the taxi. The man was barely more than a boy, in his late teens at most. His blue eyes were dilated and bleeding and virtually devoid of life, staring through Frank at an invisible blackness that could have been death itself looming over them. His sharp jaw trembled in syncopation with his entire naked body.

Frank peered down along the length of the young man's broken torso. A lemon-sized lump of guts emerged from the rupture in his waist.

But most unspeakable was the damage in his crotch.

Hellishly bloodied, his penis appeared to have been shredded, as if slashed at repeatedly with a straight-edged razor or knife. His testicles were shrunken, like two small raisins, drawn in. Blood pooled on the cement between his legs. Frank felt the gorge rise in his throat, and he had to force a swallow to get the bitterness out of his mouth.

Lightly pained whines escaped the victim's trembling lips. He appeared to be trying to say something, and Frank focused his attention on him, listening intently, hoping to hear something, any morsel of information that might clue him into a reason for the tragedy.

But nothing came except desperate wheezes. Shock was progressing upon him. His weak whispering pleas were most likely instinctive.

9

"I did not see him!"

Frank jumped and nearly shot the cabbie, who was now perching over him, arms wide in a plea, clearly less scared of Frank now and more concerned with his own ass than with the condition of the man he had just hit.

For the second time that night Frank had to control the urge to fire his weapon. He waved it in the cabbie's direction and the driver stepped back, cringing like a child warding off the blows of an angry parent.

"Call for help. Goddamn it! Move!" He felt a wave of frustration race along his nerve endings. The cabbie darted back into the cab and started shouting wildly into his CB radio.

Frank placed his free palm on the boy's forehead. Cold and wet. The boy's lips chattered uncontrollably, blue and chapped, devoid of moisture. His skin was now gray like cold fish. Frank swallowed a dry lump clinging to the back of his throat. It seemed there was nothing he could do to help him.

He still needed to find out what had happened.

He took a cursory glance around. Aside from the idling cab and the wild cries of the cabbie attempting to explain to his supervisor what had just occurred, silence dominated, just as it had only minutes earlier when he'd stepped from his car into the bloody water.

A breeze swept by, chilling the sweat on Frank's brow. It seemed to blow down past Frank, through the boy's blue stuttering lips, grabbing a single word from within.

"Atmosphere."

It emerged harshly, a barely audible whisper. Pained yet emphatic. Garbled but intelligible. But what did it mean? Was it possible the boy could be trying to reveal a reason for his naked insanity?

"What? What'd you say?" Frank's own words were as ragged as the injured boy's. They got no response. Suddenly he wanted desperately to feed his frustration, scrape at the boy's lips with his fingers and vainly attempt to pry out more information. But he did not, allowing the situation to unfold without any harsh interference. This left him only one option. Satisfy his curiosity with what he had: only one word. It was all he would ever capture.

The boy's eyes sealed shut, forever closed.

A police cruiser pulled up.

And Frank sat like a zombie in the wake of its madly twirling beacons, a dead body in front of him and a single word challenging his mind.

Atmosphere.

Chapter Two

The silent night surrendered to twirling sirens, lights and a whirlwind of activity. Four cruisers and an ambulance clogged the now cordoned off block. A few early morning enthusiasts watched from behind, craning their necks to get a good view of the commotion. Paramedics hunkered over the boy, working frantically, administering anesthesia, taping his injuries with sheets of gauze. A few policemen from the Thirteenth Precinct gathered about the medical team, watching inquisitively, while others casually leaned on the cruisers and laughed among themselves. Frank heard them cracking gay jokes about the victim.

"So, Smoky . . . what brings you out at this time of night?"

Frank recognized the voice at once. Smiling, he turned to face Captain Hector Rodriguez.

12

Frank had worked his longest tour of duty with Hector at the Thirteenth, nearly twenty years, before being promoted—and transferred—to the Twelfth, eleven years ago.

In 1968, his first month as a rookie cop, Frank had been posted at the corner of Bleecker and Third, three blocks from an open-air concert being performed by the Grateful Dead. Greenwich Village in the late sixties always offered a great deal of culture to look at: drunk and stoned kids roaming the streets, all living life to its fullest, sex, drugs and rock and roll. Frank was just a kid himself then and, being from Brooklyn, had had many friends participating in all the far-out activities thriving at the time. The day of the concert he had been perched at the corner watching the activity, wondering with a bit of envy what his life would have been like had he not chosen to become an officer of the law. He pictured himself dressed in bell-bottom jeans, a tie-dyed shirt, headband and John Lennon specs, a cigarette dangling from his lip.

As he daydreamed, a group of teens approached him, most of them proudly sporting marijuana joints. They jeered at him, and Frank—as young and naïve as they got—just stood there against a brick building, frozen like a snowman, while they all took turns blowing pot smoke into his face. He felt so helpless that they probably could have helped themselves to his gun. It was a good thing they didn't; he wouldn't be a cop today.

As it happened, the whole episode was simply a harmless prank on the part of the hippies, and as far as they had been concerned, they were simply spreading the "word," *love, peace and happiness, man*. Frank had gotten so stoned he needed to wait until the following day before he could write up a report on the incident. Of course by that time he had completely forgotten what any of the teens looked like. It was an incident that would haunt him for the rest of his career, and it was how he got the nickname Smoky.

"Please don't call me that, Hect."

"C'mon," Hector said, his voice rife with sarcasm. "I couldn't imagine calling you by any other name." He gave Frank a smile and a wink.

Ballaro returned the playful gesture with a grin of his own. It took effort, given the circumstances and the exhaustion racing through his veins, but Hector was a pal and deserved his respect. "Well . . . how about 'Frank.' That has a nice ring to it." He wondered how Hector, especially at his age, found the energy to be so vibrant at this early hour.

Rodriguez gave Frank a soft tap on the shoulder. "Okay. You got it. No more Smoky jokes . . . if I can help it." Another wink.

Frank took a good look at his old friend. Lines adorned every crevice of his face, around the eyes, nose, mouth. And his hair looked like vanilla frosting, white tufts escaping the brim of his cap. Lord, how time flies. He had to be pushing, what, fifty-nine, sixty?

"So what are you doing here? And when in God's name are you going to retire?" Frank pointed a thumb toward the paramedics, who were now racing the body on a stretcher along with an IV rig toward the ambulance. "You don't need this crap anymore."

"Can't, Frank," he answered succinctly, tipping his hat—a motion performed subconsciously. "This is my life. Call me crazy, but I love this, crap and all."

Frank knew quite well how Hector Rodriguez felt. He unexplainably felt the same way. It was something special deep inside, something that compelled him to seek out answers to every mystery. Take criminals off the streets, where they could threaten the innocent. He had no idea why all his life he'd wanted this. When he was growing up his parents never made any effort to steer him toward a career in law enforcement. On the contrary, they had painstakingly tried to divert his enthusiasm for becoming an officer, constantly pestering him about all the money doctors and lawyers made, assuring him that he'd quit his job as soon as he saw his first dead body.

That was nearly thirty years ago, and he'd seen many bodies since then, murdered ones, raped ones, kidnapped ones. Terrible encounters that tormented him with nightmares, migraines, an ulcer. But not once had he wanted to leave the force. It all seemed worth it when an opportunity arose to shut away a piece of filth, expunge all the crimes that he or she might have committed had they continued roaming the streets. It was almost like playing God: He could intervene, he could make a difference and put an end to one bad person's string of crimes. And as far as retir-

15

ing, well, every time he toyed with thoughts of packing it in, he would suffer sick visions of Jaimie in the grasp of some scum-of-the-earth, and he'd find the will to continue. "Takes a crazy man, huh, Captain?"

With this, Rodriguez asked the inevitable. "Speaking of crazy men, what the hell're you doing out here? What happened?"

Frank rubbed his tired eyes with a thumb and a forefinger. "It all happened so quickly." He went on to explain how he had worked late on the Lindsay case, parked the car, heard the scream. The cabbie, flailing wildly—it seemed he was good at that—was now telling his version to an officer who took notes on a small scratch pad.

"Must be something in the air," Hector said, watching the ambulance pull away from the scene.

"The time of year, Hect. Weather gets cooler, people get depressed and toss themselves in front of moving vehicles."

Hector pointed up Fourth Street. "You said you were standing on the corner when you heard the scream and came running?"

"Yes, I . . . wait . . ." Frank stepped away toward the curb. "There's something else . . ."

Hector followed.

"Come, look." Frank crouched down next to the curb. The rain had stopped altogether, and although the sun had not yet broken over the East River, it started to grow lighter out and he was able to see the blood more clearly than before: dried now, thin stains streaking along the gutter.

"This is what originally caught my attention. Don't ask me what made me look down, I just did. I stepped in it as I got out of my car." Frank stood back up, stretched out his right leg and displayed his shoe to Hector. There were crustlets of dried blood edging the sole. "Look, see?"

Hector peered down, his interest obviously piqued. "You sure that didn't come from the naked boy?"

Frank shrugged his shoulders. "Could've. But not while I was trying to help him."

"So you heard the scream, then stepped in the blood?"

"No, the other way around."

"So he'd been injured *before* the cab hit him."

"Yes, I'd say so. Assuming all this blood came from him. When I got to him, his genitals were badly mutilated. My guess is that *that* injury occurred *before* he fled into the street."

"Probably much before," Hector said. "It'd take time for the rain to carry the blood around the corner."

"That means the kid was tortured by someone."

"Looks that way. Unless it was self-inflicted, and I doubt that very much."

Frank locked gazes with Hector. "He must have been fleeing someone when he darted into the street."

Hector nodded. "Can you remember anything else?"

Frank closed his eyes, rubbed his chin, digging

17

through the cloud of fatigue shrouding his memory. "Well, after I stepped in the blood," he said, pacing along the curb, pointing, "I followed it to the corner." Both he and Hector trailed the veiny smears, which ran a few yards down Mason, then up the curb and across the sidewalk into a narrow alley. The two men peered wide-eyed into the dark of the alley like two young boys trying to drum up the nerve to descend into a darkened cellar.

"Hector . . . he came from here, the naked boy. I'm almost positive of it."

"You sure?"

"Hect, the blood. Look at it."

Hector Rodriguez turned around and silently motioned to one of his men with a wave of an arm. A young officer, maybe thirty years of age, trotted over. His badge read MULDOON.

"Officer Kevin Muldoon, this is Detective Frank Ballaro from the Twelfth." The two men exchanged handshakes and then Hector said, "Kevin, bring a light. I want to check out the alley." Muldoon jogged away and returned with a halogen flashlight.

"Kevin, we think the kid came from back there. We also think he was trying to escape from someone when the cab got him. Let's see if we can find anything."

Muldoon nodded, and the three cops entered the alley in single file, Muldoon in the lead, flashlight in his left hand. Frank kept a hand on his holstered .45.

They slowly shuffled forward, Frank at once

18

feeling closed in; the cramped buildings snuffed out much of the growing light—it was probably dark here at midday—and the ominous gloom nearly swallowed up the flashlight beam. Litter blanketed the ground; newspapers, flattened cans, broken glass, candy wrappers, everything saturated with rainwater. Their shoes squashed over everything.

Suddenly, from within the near-distant shadows, a pained whimper pitched forth.

Muldoon stopped dead in his tracks. Frank glanced over his shoulder. "You hear that?"

"Keep going, slowly," Hector said, pointing with his chin. He'd heard it.

All of a sudden Hector's belted radio squawked, ripping apart the silence in the alley like a whistling firecracker. He grumbled a *shit*, fumbling to turn it off. As soon as the silence was resurrected, a sickly moan loomed as if in answer to the radio's cry. The three cops stood in position, listening to it as it leveled for a moment, then tapered down into a gurgly cough before finally evaporating. The cry sounded like that of an animal with a leg snared in a hunter's trap.

Muldoon held the flashlight high to get a better angle, waving it around in ovals. "I can't see anything."

Frank tried to shove his lassitude aside, force some wheels spinning in his head. Throughout his career he had unwrapped numerous crimes clue by perplexing clue. But this? So far: blood led into an alley from which a naked, castrated young man emerged in an obvious state of alarm,

19

and ended up under the wheels of a cab. The poor bastard never so much as flinched before he was mowed down. And now, someone else here, hidden and hurt, someone who would no doubt provide another piece to an already intriguing puzzle.

They stepped forward, one step and then the next, slowly and carefully, Frank considering two possibilities: one, the moan came from the perpetrator, the individual guilty of the heinous castration, the presumed murderer. In which case extreme caution was necessary. Frank pulled his gun, finger gently touching the trigger.

Second, the unseen person could very well be a victim himself, requiring immediate medical assistance. This scenario, however, could not be trusted until an injured person in fact lay in their sights. Expect the worst, pray for the best.

They inched closer. In the beam of Muldoon's flashlight Frank could see a chain link fence separating a courtyard from the alley. From the shadows he saw a large tree growing just beyond the fence on the other side. A park bench sat a few feet to the right, under the tree. The crooked branches and leaves of additional trees swayed like ghosts in the distance, their wet dying leaves sending a staticlike noise through the air. To the right, four battered aluminum trash cans hugged the alley wall like barnacles on a ship's hull.

In the silence of the moment, Frank wondered if it could have been the fatigue shrouding his mind that concocted the pained cry—just as he thought it had conjured the blood on his shoes when all this started.

But then he heard it again, louder, more pained.

Frank stepped to the left of Muldoon. Shoulder to shoulder, they almost touched the alley walls. "Who's there?" Frank yelled, craning his neck but still unable to see the source of the moan.

Then, like a wicked alarm in the middle of the night, horrifying laughter sounded. It sent a dreadful chill coursing through Frank's body, as if a metal fork had been slowly scraped along a chalky blackboard. Shivering, Frank stayed motionless, feet rooted, listening to the shrouded cackle as it rose and fell. He tightened his grip on his .45. He and Muldoon looked at each other, nodded, then edged ahead, Muldoon in the lead. In his peripheral vision Frank saw Hector hang back and quietly radio for assistance.

Frank was about to shout a *come out with your hands in the air so I can see them* when Muldoon uttered "Jesus-H-Christ," in a quiet yet panicked tone. Frank quickly stepped forward, in front of Muldoon, looking to the corner of the alley, where Muldoon had the flashlight's beam aimed.

His heart trembled.

Flanking the right wall, a portion of the link fence had been peeled open from the bottom, exposing a hole large enough for a man to fit through. Between the hole and the last garbage can, two naked legs jutted out, covered with blood.

Chapter Three

"I need paramedics here now!" Hector yelled into his radio, a series of squawks and feedback breaking up his harried voice.

Frank and Muldoon stood opposite the body, unmoving, both men unsure of what to do. In this tentative state, Frank dug deep into his mind, tried to remember if he had ever in his thirty-one-year career seen anything remotely as grotesque, as horrible as the vision before him. He'd seen a great deal, but could not recall anything equaling this, and he simply did what his mind allowed him to do at the moment: stand frozen with fear and awe and amazement. And Muldoon—well, Frank could only assume similar feelings distressed him, perhaps to an even worse degree, given Muldoon's limited exposure to such things.

Muldoon remained immobilized as well, gun lowered, mouth agape, trembling.

It was quite a sight. A young man like the first sat naked in a puddle amid a ring of refuse on the alley ground. He leaned back crookedly against the building wall, his entire body trembling. At first glance it seemed he was staring up at them, eyes rolling wildly and unable to pin their target, but in reality his eyes were turned up into their sockets, the whites glistening, shot with ruptured circles of blood.

Just like the first boy they encountered, this victim also suffered gruesome wounds to his groin. The penis and testicles had been reduced to mere shreds of flesh. A flare of blood rose up from his crotch in a wavelike pattern across his entire upper body, across his face and into his hair—which was saturated and standing at odd angles. His thin arms, also coated in crimson, looked completely skinless, as if only raw veins and muscles were exposed.

When he was finally able to pull his gaze away from the blood, Frank noticed a small object locked in the boy's hands. It was about the size of a grapefruit, round with maybe a half-dozen circular, six-inch spikes emerging from it. As Muldoon tried to steady the flashlight's beam on the boy's trembling hands, Frank could see his bloody fingers gently caressing the object, smearing around the gore in finger-painting circles, exposing a dark shiny hue beneath the deep wet crimson. Frank thought the object was black, but couldn't be sure as it had so much blood covering it.

As shocking and as paralyzing as the whole vision had been, nothing could compare to what happened then. It tempted their minds with madness, taking them beyond all the carnage and into a more terrifying and disturbing lunacy.

The boy *smiled*. A wide grin, teeth ivory white beneath his red mask of death. A delineation of dementia gone overboard.

Frank's rational personality struggled desperately to convince himself to break away, to flee this terrible wickedness, and even though it was his own voice, it was not that of Frank Ballaro the adult, but that of Frank Ballaro the child, reminding him that something as profoundly terrifying as this was something not to be reckoned with—no matter what age he was, no matter what the circumstances might be. Frank realized for the first time in his life that in some situations, such as this one, the helpless child had more common sense than the rational adult.

But he resisted the urge to run. The strongest identity—the truth-seeking detective—again fought the child's voice and shut it down from making any weak decisions. It demanded answers, wanted to understand what had become of the young man before him, and it forced Frank to stay.

Something is very wrong, he thought to himself, *something here, in New York City, this Friday morning, October 21,* and he had unwittingly taken the first of many steps that would presumably lead toward an explanation to this madness, had scratched at the surface of an incredibly terrifying mystery. Its substance was now under his nails. It was too late to run.

The boy's chest rose and fell. The smile suddenly vanished from his face and his jaw dropped. A foul odor rushed out in an almost visible gush. Rushing footsteps approached from behind, flashlight beams flying like nightclub lights. Frank quickly turned and glimpsed a team of paramedics scurrying down the alley toward them.

"Freeze!" Muldoon suddenly screamed.

Frank leapt at the sound of Muldoon's shout, felt a lump form in the back of his throat. He spun and saw something . . . something so *alarming*, so quick and dreamlike and more frighteningly mysterious than the injured boy himself, that it at once became difficult to believe that what he saw actually happened right before his eyes.

A strange-looking man missiled into sight through the hole in the fence, perhaps six-two or -three, arms long and lanky, shoulders broad. His entire body was dressed in black, jeans, boots, jacket. His hands were covered as well, fitted with sleek gloves. Even his eyes were lost behind large dark sunglasses. Only the pearl white skin of his face and bald head were exposed to the growing morning.

With spiderlike finesse, the man stretched forward, grabbed the bloody boy beneath his arms and yanked him through the hole in the link fence, into the courtyard and out of sight around the corner of the building.

The air suddenly reeked of feces and urine. Hector screamed for backup, the quiet alternative of the radio serving no purpose now. In the commotion, Muldoon abruptly forced the EMTs against the alley wall, making room for additional police to squeeze through. One medic, a young girl with freckles and blond hair tied in a ponytail, screamed as she struck the brick surface.

Frank pressed himself against the wall opposite the EMTs, his three personalities engaged in a whirlwind of conflict. This battle, in combination with his semi-suppressed exhaustion, stunned him to the point where he simply couldn't make a move, and he remained frozen, allowing the oncoming police to engage in the pursuit while his mind chattered with itself.

What the hell just happened? Did some guy just reach through that hole in the presence of armed police officers and snatch a castrated man away in a second? Yes, it had to be. No level of fatigue could drum up such a bizarre hallucination.

Muldoon followed his counterparts through the hole in the fence. Frank finally convinced himself to move, and he and Hector followed.

The entire courtyard came into view. It was smaller than it had first seemed, perhaps only thirty feet across to the next building. It appeared from this angle that the only legitimate access to the yard was from the buildings themselves; all the other alleys were fenced off.

Frank immediately saw streaks of blood in the grass, like trails, the body clearly having been dragged away with the same quick determination as it had been scooped through the hole in the fence. Frank and Hector followed the messy streaks to a hole in the ground, where they stood circled about it, looking down inside and shaking their heads with utter disbelief. Muldoon and a middle-aged, mustachioed cop with tufts of black hair jutting from the sides of his hat were shining their flashlights down into the hole. Another officer was crouched on his knees, tugging at a manhole cover in the grass at the side of the opening.

The cop with the mustache, McGoldrick, spread his arms. "Bastard disappeared down the sewer."

"Did anyone see him go down?" Hector asked, jerking his head in all directions, including all the cops in the query.

"No . . . but there's blood all over the edge," McGoldrick answered, shining the flashlight around to confirm his statement. "And on the grass around it."

"Maybe he threw the body down there and fled?" Hector suggested, breath escaping his throat in anxious gasps.

"Captain, I don't think so. He would've been spotted heading across the courtyard. Cullen and Shafski went to check out the exits and the other alleys, but we're pretty sure he went down here."

Hector's face flushed red, as if the veins inside his head had exploded and let their flow seep beneath his skin. He shook his head, confusion bringing about a flurry of questions. One eventually came out. "Why hasn't anyone gone down after him?"

The cops stayed motionless, lips sealed and eyes blank, not the slightest bit of initiative present in their body language. Something had hold of them and kept them rooted.

"What? What's the matter?" Hector looked at Frank, eyes wide with disbelief as if to say, *You believe these guys, Frank? They're nothing like we used to be when we were young.*

McGoldrick stepped forward. "Captain, it's a cesspool duct. There's no ladder. It's nothing but cement walls and hook-eyes from here on down. You need equipment to get down there."

Muldoon nodded, confirming this.

Hector stared at him for a moment, clearly befuddled. "You sure?" Receiving four nods in unison, Hector removed his hat, frustration clearly getting to him. He swiped his forehead, then stepped forward, peering into the dark. Frank stood next to him.

"They're right, Hect. No way down."

"Except if you jumped."

"Must be, what, twenty? twenty-five feet? Can't be done without nearly killing yourself."

"Which means the bastard's still down there with a broken ankle or leg."

A crazy thought entered Frank's mind and he shuddered at its outrageousness. But it seemed to make some sense. "Unless . . ."

"Unless what?" Hector's mouth trembled and

his cheeks, even in the early morning light, started showing deep ruddy patches of maroon. He would listen to anything as long as he got a viable answer.

"Unless he used the body to break his fall." The option suddenly seemed all too realistic, and Frank could see Hector's frustration jarring almost every muscle in his face as he considered this possibility. It looked as if steam would start pouring out of his ears.

"Captain?" Muldoon interrupted. "He probably *is* still down there. It's a cesspool. There's gonna be a lot of pipes and ducts leading out, but no tunnels. None that a man could fit through, anyway."

Hector at once pulled his radio, placed a call into Special Teams. They'd have spelunkers here in half an hour, all geared up and ready to hoist on down. Holstering his radio, he asked, "If this is a cesspool, how come there's no stink?"

Still peering into the dark of the hole, Frank said, "I imagine it'd stink if you went down there."

Hector gave Frank a quizzical look.

Frank smiled and shrugged, fatigue making an effort of it. "That's why I'm a detective."

"The object," Muldoon suddenly said, bringing about a round of silence and a variety of perplexed looks. "The thing he was holding, remember, Captain?" He stepped forward. "The black thing? It was covered in blood and he was rubbing it with his fingers." He made a swirling motion with his hands.

Hector's eyebrows arched downward. Now he looked pissed, perhaps by the fact that he'd either forgotten about the strange object or didn't want to remember it.

Frank felt a chill sprint through his upper body at the mention of the strange piece. The sudden discomfort made him realize that this whole damn scenario was more than just a weird body-snatching of sorts. A plethora of mysteries surrounded everything, and he knew that somehow the object, the black thing with the prongs sticking out of it, held answers. Answers to secrets that were shrouded with a tenebrous black veil with poisoned talons hidden underneath so that they could no doubt scratch anyone who came near it in an attempt to lift it away.

Cullen and Shafski returned from their investigation, heads shaking. They hadn't found anything, not a drop of blood.

The bald guy did indeed go down.

"So did anyone find it?" Frank finally asked, his renewed strength now ebbing as fatigue once again caught up with him. Everyone shot harried glances around at each other, but there was no admission.

"What do you think, Frank?" Hector asked.

"I think it's what the guy was after."

The smile on Hector's face could have been one of incredulity. "What makes you say that?"

Frank thought about it for a moment and shuddered. He really couldn't answer that question with any form of truthfulness. *I just do* would have been the most appropriate response. Just "knowing things." It had been a dominant part of his inbred talent, the one trait that all three of his personalities willingly shared. He closed his eyes for a moment.

"I don't know for sure. It just seems obvious to me. I think it was the way the kid was holding it. Like he was . . . *caressing* it. Like it was something *special.*"

The statement hung in the silence, everyone clearly giving thought to it, their faces blank stares. Whether they accepted it as true was another story altogether.

Hector finally broke the silence, changing the subject, no doubt wanting his men to put their minds back on capturing the bald man. "Well, at this point there's nothing else we can do until the unit arrives." He tapped Frank at the waist. "Why don't you get some sleep, Smoky, and we'll talk tomorrow. Besides, it's all dirty work from here on in."

Frank stared at Hector. He felt slapped. What had he said? Was it that crazy an observation? Or was Hector cutting him a break, allowing him to go home?

Frank rubbed a hand along the side of his face and realized that everyone was staring at him. He probably looked like hell, eyes barely open, as pale as a ghost after a hundred years of haunting.

Hector nodded, gave him a quick, patronizing smile. "It's all right, Frank, go ahead. We'll be fine." He stepped next to Frank and whispered, "You and I both know I shouldn't have let you back here in the first place."

Hector was right. Legally, Frank could only be a witness to this crime and nothing more. He had been off duty, and although everything happened in his neighborhood, this wasn't his jurisdiction. Hector would be in charge.

But Hector was a dear friend. Tomorrow they would speak, and then Frank would get a small hold on things. . . .

Frank tried to smile but knew it looked like a grimace. Then he grunted, making his reluctance obvious, and turned away. As he dragged his feet, waves of relief suddenly washed over him like a rushing tide, rousing restless, anxious feelings that yelled *get home!* The prospect of getting into bed sounded so glorious all of a sudden, motivating that lesser listened to, rational personality to peek out from behind the curtain of his consciousness and take control of his bearings. He spun back, added, "I guess we'll be speaking soon then, right, Hect?"

"Of course, Frank. Very soon. You're a witness and we'll need your report."

Frank finally staggered away, crawling back through the hole in the fence and into the alley. Wet trash and dirty puddles sloshed under his shoes. The cool temperature locked the breath in his lungs. "So much for my long weekend," he mumbled as he passed a forensics specialist prepping the area for a sweep. He slowly followed the now nearly invisible streaks of blood past a police barricade at the alley's entrance, back around the corner, through all the activity and onlookers. He barely made it to his apartment.

Atmosphere

It wasn't until he was lying comfortably in bed a half hour later, up to his chin in sheets, that he remembered something else he should have mentioned to Hector.

Atmosphere . . .

Chapter Four

In the sleep that followed, Frank dreamed of babies, tens of thousands of infants dressed entirely in black. They stood like soldiers in a procession that went on as far as his eyes could see, their tiny bald heads a sea of pink texture disappearing into a strikingly colorful horizon. He stood on a platform before them, arms outstretched, he their messiah, they his disciples. They peered up at him with large black orbs—inhuman eyes—silently staring, waiting . . .

"Dad!"

Frank startled awake, his breath temporarily left behind in his dream, sweat dampening his body, the sheets enveloping him. Through filmy eyes he saw Jaimie's outline nestled in the half-open door frame, her arm extended into his room, the cordless phone attached to her hand.

"Oh, God, Jaimie . . ."

"You all right?" She arched her eyebrows into a perplexed triangle and swung the phone to her side.

Every time Frank got the chance to see his daughter—which hadn't been very often these past couple of months—he would take a few moments, no matter what the circumstances, to admire her beauty. She seemed to grow more and more attractive every day, like a flower in slow-motion bloom. Even now, through wearied eyes, she looked magnificent, her eyes as crystal blue as Caribbean waters, sienna brown hair and eyebrows perfectly fashioned around them in contrast to their wondrous beauty. And her skin—a silky olive tone that boasted her Italian half—made splendid use of the sun's rays on days she decided to indulge herself in its warmth. She might have gotten her mother's Irish looks, but her blood and skin were pure *Italiano*, something Frank, of course, was quite pleased about.

"Yeah. Sure. I'm fine. I was having a dream." He rubbed away the black blotches obscuring his eyesight.

"Sorry." She smiled weakly, a little embarrassed, it seemed, then raised the phone back up, holding it forward. "You got a call. Captain Rodriguez."

"Yeah. Okay." Frank groaned as he leaned over to grab the telephone handset from its cradle on the nightstand beside the bed. The bones in his back and waist popped and cracked, the sheets hissed under his body weight. He placed the receiver to his ear. "After last night you'd think I could grab a couple hours' shut-eye."

"It's two o'clock, Smoky. Or is it *Sleepy?*"

Frank rolled his eyes toward the clock on the nightstand. The digital readout glowed 2:07, bright red. He hadn't slept this late since he was in college. He hadn't stayed out all night since then either. No wonder Jaimie slept all afternoon on the weekends.

"Jesus . . ."

"It's a good thing I called."

"Not really. I'd rather be sleeping. As my daughter would say, I pulled an all-nighter."

"That her on the phone?"

"Would you believe me if I said it was my girl-friend?"

Hector chuckled and Frank wriggled up, adjusting himself into a more comfortable position, pillows propped up behind his head, legs stretched out beneath the sheets. His bones creaked again, different ones this time. "So what happened after I left?"

Hector hesitated, exhaling a long breath. He must have told the story a dozen times since the early morning and had no desire to repeat it again. Frank knew quite well that Hector wasn't supposed to share information with any outsiders, or witnesses, for that matter. Which of course didn't make a darn bit of difference as far as he was concerned. The stronger, stubborn detective inside, tired and all, would go deaf, dumb and blind until it got the rest of the story out of his ex-captain. Hector had no choice. He *had* to fill him in.

Hector's silence indicated clear exasperation. He wouldn't be able to play out this whole thing by the book. He'd have to give Frank a few inches.

Frank heard a shuffling of papers on the other end. "Well," Hector finally said, "the Special Teams unit arrived. A few men went down into the cesspool and found a tunnel." He paused for a moment, perhaps waiting for a response from Frank, which he did not immediately get, then said, "It had been dug out."

"Dug out?"

"Looks that way. Can't tell with what, though. A machine of some kind."

"Was there a body?"

"Don't jump ahead of me."

"Sorry. Go ahead." Frank felt a chill race down his back. His heart started beating faster and he gripped the phone like an eagle's talon around its prey.

"The tunnel led to an air duct in the R line terminal, on Broadway and Fourth—about four hundred yards from the hole in the courtyard. The kid's body was inside the duct, as dead and as naked as day, a few feet from where a vent had been popped out in a bathroom wall. We're pretty sure the bald guy escaped through it."

"He got away?"

"Yep."

"Any witnesses?"

There was a delay on Hector's end of the

phone, Frank heard him say "Thank you" to someone. "No. Nothing yet."

Frank felt staggered. The whole scenario—from the moment he stepped into the blood till now—was becoming more and more unbelievable by the minute—one which he wouldn't have bought for a second had he not been there to see it himself. "What in God's name is going on?" he asked, a fistful of sheets bunched in his free hand.

"I have no idea."

"And what is it all?"

"Damned if I can even offer a guess."

After a pause, Frank asked, "How wide was it?"

"What? The tunnel? Big enough for that bald goon to fit through—but barely."

"Then how did he drag the body through with him?"

"You saw him. He was a big guy. He made it fit."

"It must've been a mess."

"Yep. And I think you were most likely right when you said the body might have provided a cushion for baldie's fall. The kid's arms and legs were broken. Neck too."

The image of it made Frank's stomach curl with nausea. A young boy waking up innocently one day to have no life just hours later, his body mangled like a piece of highway carnage and left for the rats to feed on.

But this terrifying vision in his mind's eye was secondary to the knowledge that some wicked psychopath was still walking the streets with blood on his hands, and that no immediate solution existed for Frank to sever the maniac's bond with society. Frank realized at this very moment that he would find no rest, no peace of mind, until the guy was caught.

But with a terrible situation such as this, much more existed for Frank than just his commitment to society. An ever compelling need to grasp it demanded he draw himself close and refuse to surrender hold until he worked his way through to the very limit of its span. It consumed him, became an immediate obsession, and ultimately an art. Perhaps this compulsion surfaced through a shifting of chemical balances, perhaps a simple psychological tendency drove him. Regardless, it inspired his very existence.

Given the current circumstances, he doubted the settling down period he'd anticipated after the Carrie Lindsay case had been put to rest would come to pass. This mystery would be just as it was during the brutal weeks he sweated the perplexities of her murder.

Life-consuming.

He had nearly driven himself to hallucinations speculating on the events leading to the poor girl's dying moments, time and time again asking himself the same unanswerable questions: How had she been seduced by her brother? Had she trusted him, agreed to play his game? Or was she snatched against her will?

Regardless, the facts were alarming. The sixteen-year-old had been raped and sodomized repeatedly during the last moments of her life, beaten and bloodied beyond recognition. When the police found her, her entire body bore a mottling of angry blue blotches and bruises, had been swathed in blood. She had no broken bones, but virtually every inch of skin, every muscle and every tendon had sustained damage. Frank remembered seeing the body for the first time, practically folded in half like a piece of paper and stuffed in a large overnight bag, hidden away in a closet in the Park Avenue apartment.

"Frank?"

"Yeah?"

"You still with me?"

"Hect ... I'm sorry. I'm still tired." He smoothed the sheets with his hand, thinking about how torturous Carrie Lindsay's last moments must have been. The images of death, *her* death, seemed so surreal and impossible. *Dear God, how terrible it must have been. . . .*

"When you get your old self out of bed, I'd like you come in and give a statement. Outside of the cabbie, you're our only real witness, and it's important I see you, preferably sometime today."

This was the last thing Frank expected on his day off, but strangely enough, the first thing he wanted now. "Hect ... the first kid. Any ID on him? Any connections to the second kid?"

Once again Hector blew into the phone. It hurt Frank's ear and he had to pull away from the receiver for a second. "Frank, I can't have you playing detective right now."

"Why not?"

"You're a witness, and frankly I can't waste any

more time. I need to get your statement. Afterwards we'll talk. I promise."

Frank licked his lips. Frustration. The detective in him wanted all the facts, wanted to start piecing the clues together right away, pronto. "Okay, I'm a witness," he said, rolling his eyes. "But remember, I'm a damn nosy one."

Frank agreed to meet Hector at the Thirteenth at four o'clock. After hanging up, he crawled out of bed and spent a half hour in the bathroom, commiserating with the nearly unfamiliar face watching him from the mirror as he shaved. Fifty-three years old. Jesus, it seemed just yesterday that Jaimie was born, and that was nineteen years ago. Five years had already passed since Diane left him. Hard to believe.

That had been real hard on him. After twenty-eight years of marriage, Diane—who had spent most of her time watching her diet and getting fit at the Midtown Health Club—selfishly felt that she had aged much more gracefully than he, and came to the rash decision that a thirty-year-old "kid" would make a much better lover than old Frank Ballaro.

It was the shocker of his life. He had never suspected for one single moment that she had been having an affair. She simply picked up and left with a few of her things, leaving only a Dear John letter behind to Frank and Jaimie.

Frank refused to put all the blame on her for leaving. He had spent his whole life trying to be the finest detective New York City had to offer, neglecting their marriage—and their sex life. Although the manner in which Diane ended things was clearly unacceptable, he still wished to this day he had made an effort to divide his duties in life, half for Diane, half for the NYPD. Perhaps she still would've been around if he had, regardless of his inability to perform regularly.

He showered, got dressed in a pair of khaki pants, a navy cotton sweater and sneakers. He went to the kitchen where Jaimie sat studying, a variety of textbooks and papers fanned out on the table before her.

The one good thing that had come out of Diane's departure was the growth of his relationship with Jaimie. She had been fourteen at the time, certainly old enough to understand what had happened. They both read the letter, holding each other for comfort. Tears of resentment sprang from their eyes, but somehow the sadness strengthened the bond between them, became a pledge of security that would last through the subsequent five years. Frank wouldn't take anything in the world—even Diane's return—in exchange for the relationship he now had with Jaimie. Some things were sacred, and this was one of them.

"Good morning."

Jaimie smiled. "Good *afternoon*. Can't believe you outslept me today. Rough night, Frank?"

Frank reached into the refrigerator, grabbed a corn muffin and a can of Coke. "You could say that. And please call me Dad." He sat at the three-seat rectangular table flanking the cutout wall in the small kitchen. The smallest room in the two-bedroom apartment, it barely allowed enough standing room for both of them, making things difficult when they decided to prepare a rare dinner together.

"What are you studying?"

Jaimie placed her pen in the crook of the open textbook, blew up a puff of air that sent her bangs against her forehead. "I have an exam in finance."

"Takes a lot of studying to make money, huh?"

"More than I ever expected." Jaimie rubbed her eyes. "Oh, you got a call earlier this morning, from Neil. He said it was important, but I didn't want to wake you since I knew you were off."

Frank let out an exasperated sigh. Already his partner was starting in. What the hell was so important that he felt the need to call him on his first day off? Frank thought he had made himself very clear, reiterating throughout the entire investigation that he planned to spend a few days away from the precinct when the investigation came to a close. And now that he finally made it—although there were times when he thought he wouldn't—here was Neil Connor calling first thing. "Thanks, hon, you did the right thing."

Jaimie picked up the pen, put the capped end in her mouth, then stood and grabbed a bag of pretzels from the cabinet above the sink. She wore a pair of faded Levi's and a tie-dyed T-shirt, reminding Frank a bit of the hippies who had given him the business on the street corner in Greenwich Village back in '68. Damn thing still haunted him. The only difference was that she had no joint in her mouth. Good thing too. Frank would freak.

"So why are all these people calling you on your day off?"

He took a bite of the muffin, washed it down with half the Coke. "Something came up. I have some work to do this afternoon."

She stuck a pretzel in her mouth. "What is it now? I *thought* you were taking a few days off."

"I thought so too." He paused, thinking for a moment of the castrated boy in the alley, then said, "Jame, something happened last night, here in the neighborhood. A couple of kids were murdered."

Jaimie's eyes widened as she swiped a sip of Frank's Coke. "God. What happened?"

Frank retrieved his stolen soda. "Long story. But they were two boys about your age."

Jaimie rolled her eyes. "Dad . . . I'll be fine."

Frank locked gazes with his daughter. "Please. Be careful. There're a lot of crazies out there. Kids with earrings in their noses."

She picked up the pen from her book, grinning. "Haven't we been through all this before?"

Nodding in agreement, Frank wondered to what extent he should reveal the events of the early morning hours. Of course he had no desire to itemize every weird detail. It would only scare her, and that was something he didn't want to do. Never in the past had Frank revealed to Jaimie the finer details of his investigations, but he always believed it would be wise to teach her some street smarts, let her in on what really went on day to day in the streets of New York. Sure, newspapers shared the outer surface of crime—murders, mayhem (Jaimie had done a fine job of keeping up to date with the Lindsay murder, letting him know exactly what *she* thought), but there was so much more hidden beyond the headlines—burglaries, muggings, thefts, assaults. People ended up in the hospital daily, with injuries sustained in these so called "petty crimes." Frank wanted to make sure his daughter didn't become a victim of them.

For now, he decided to tell her nothing more. It would only distract her from her studies.

Smiling, he said, "Someday you'll be a parent . . ."

". . . and I'll understand," she finished. "I know. Listen, I have to finish up. I have a test in two hours."

Frank stuffed the rest of the muffin in his mouth and stood up. "Okay, okay, I get the hint," he said, raising his arms in surrender. They exchanged smiles and he placed the soda can in the recycling bin under the sink.

He moved to the living room, sat on the couch and dialed Neil at the precinct before he could persuade himself to do otherwise.

"Connor . . ." His voice was harried and rushed.

"Neil. Frank."

"Frankie. We have a problem."

Talk about cutting to the chase. Oh, that Neil and his tendencies. Frank always taught himself to never accept Neil Connor's panic quite seri-

45

ously. His partner had a habit of raising red flags as soon as something struck him as an inherent problem. Most of the time those flags never amounted to much more than casual inconsiderables, leaving Frank flustered and annoyed. Amazing that Neil Connor achieved as much success as he did; Frank always felt he was too panicky for the job.

"Neil, I'm off. This better be good."

"Actually, it's bad. Bobby Lindsay made bail."

All of a sudden Frank felt as if the good Lord had struck him with one of those big lightning bolts He carried around with Him. Two months he'd worked on the case, days twelve hours or longer, slaving and sweating to discover the proper evidence to put the bastard away.

And to think he had known from the onset that the eighteen-year-old had sexually maimed his sister.

But he had had to find the evidence to prove it. That had been the hard part.

Bobby Lindsay's methodology had been cunning and conniving, his attack well thought out and executed. As a result, hardly any circumstantial evidence turned up—at least not enough for the police to work with. No fingerprints were found at the scene of the crime, the suitcase in which Carrie was found, her clothing, skin, everything—printless.

In addition, no hair evidence showed up, not a single fiber. Coincidentally, Bobby claimed during an interrogation to have joined some unnameable religious order prior to the murder and had shaved every hair from his body, toes to head. Even his eyebrows.

Additionally, the kid possessed a paranoid demeanor that had surprised Frank and Neil all throughout the questioning. For Frank Ballaro, the lack of evidence pointed all fingers to no one but Bobby Lindsay. But how to implicate him?

As they waited, wondering just that, something broke. And Frank got his man.

With all Bobby's clever planning, his detailed formulations, his perfect crime had a crack in its armor. He made a mistake.

He bought the wrong condoms.

Although the girl had been raped and sodomized repeatedly, there was no semen present. When the coroner's report came back, they found large traces of non-oxynol 9 in and around Carrie Lindsay's genitals. The report went on to explain that non-oxynol 9, a generic name for a common over-the-counter spermicidal lubricant, was also found to be used in the manufacture of some condoms as a secondary precaution in preventing pregnancy.

The search of Bobby's room had found a box of Trojan Ultra Ribbed condoms with non-oxynol 9 in a drawer next to his bed. There were five missing. The next day a video showed up of Bobby Lindsay purchasing the same brand of condoms from a convenience store two blocks away from his home. The grainy surveillance tape was dated June 2, two months before the murder.

They had their man.

"Frank? You there?"

Frank broke his paralysis. A film of sweat had formed on his hands. "Who in God's name set bail for him?"

"Judge Mathews. My guess is, she didn't think his folks would show any sympathy, and honestly, I didn't either. Heck, it's not even his real father. But the two of them just waltzed right in to the City Courthouse, arm in arm, and plunked down a mil cash. That ain't no kitty litter. I'm telling you, that Jo-Beth Lindsay must have her rich husband wrapped around her finger like a gold ring."

"Why the hell did Mathews set bail?"

"Well . . . I figure it's like this: If he makes bail, he can't go anywhere because they tag him with a homing bracelet. It'll send up a million red flags if he places one foot out of the door. If he tries, they shoot him full of holes, and the city gets the dough. Beats the hell out of spending all sorts of bucks to keep him in jail while deciding whether the creep gets the death penalty. Higher-ups won't 'fess it, but it's the truth."

Frank scoffed inside, even though it really made sense. "Neil . . . where do you get these ideas?"

"It's the truth, Frank, I'm tellin' you. And another thing. I don't think she's buying all our evidence. Kid's pleading innocent. They hired some hotshot Jew lawyer from the Upper East Side. Gonna be a real uphill battle." He took a deep breath. "Nevertheless, he's out, and we got to keep an eye on him and his folks. Us too, kiddo. There's going to be a shitload of pissed off people when this hits the papers tomorrow."

Frank ran a hand through his thinning hair. "It's gonna be a nightmare. Thanks for letting me know, Neil."

"Wanted to fill you in before you heard it on the 'News.' "

"I appreciate it." Wanting to get off the phone, he blurted, "Listen, Neil, I gotta head over to the Thirteenth." He suddenly realized he had spilled something he had hoped to keep secret—at least until the news broke about his involvement in last night's adventure.

"The Thirteenth?"

"I'm going to pay Hect a visit. Haven't seen him in a few. We're gonna grab a bite." Dodged that bullet.

"Ah . . . send Hect my regards. Sorry to be the bearer of bad news, Frankie. Try to have a good weekend."

"No easy feat."

After Frank hung up, Jaimie appeared from the kitchen with her books cradled next to her chest. She now had her hair tied back in a scrunchie, and Frank thought she looked more beautiful than an angel appearing from the heavens. She dropped her books on the couch and put on a blue windbreaker she retrieved from the closet next to the door. "Gotta run."

"Good luck on your test."

"Thanks. Oh, I almost forgot. Some of us are going out for dinner tonight. After the test. I won't be home till later."

"How late?"

"Dad . . ."

Frank had a feeling he wouldn't be home for dinner either. "Okay. Have fun. And be careful," he said, standing, smiling.

"I will."

"Maybe we'll have dinner together this weekend?"

She smiled. Beautiful. "Okay. I'd like that." Then she left.

And Frank felt utterly alone.

Chapter Five

The bald man entered the long hall. It looked just as it did the first time he was here: dark and gloomy. Yet somehow, even through the sunglasses, he could see everything clearly. It wasn't as if his eyesight had improved; he just knew where to go, as if his thoughts had been attuned to an outside force that invisibly guided him to this place, this place that he not only needed to be, but that would provide him with answers to all the questions suddenly speeding about in his head. Questions like: what is life? And what purpose do I serve?

Dressed entirely in black, he wore jeans, a T-shirt beneath a leather biker jacket, gloves and sneakers. The gloves, caked with blood and dirt, hung at his sides as he stared straight ahead and carefully eyed the lengthy corridor. Impulsively,

51

*he lifted his arms and dragged his soiled finger-
tips along the smooth ebony walls as he traversed
the length of the hall, leaving streaks of brown
and red upon them like sand trails from a snake
in the desert. As he did so, his thoughts and memories evaporated, leaving a blank slate behind in
his mind. Still he tried to remember something
about himself, what he had been called before he
was summoned to this place and became the person he was now. But as his thoughts ricocheted
around inside his head, stronger, darker impressions surrounded and subdued them like a virus,
pointing out to him quite clearly that it really
wasn't necessary to know anything about who he
used to be before this moment, that nothing else
mattered so long as he had guidance from the
Giver.*

*Unexpectedly, he reached an impasse at the
end of the corridor. He stood there, confused at
first about what to do, but quickly he allowed his
thoughts to collect themselves and find an answer
to this dilemma. They told him to enter. Yes, enter. Something important waited on the other
side and he knew his purpose at this very moment
was to access it. He searched for a means to venture forth. A knob, perhaps? Or a switch? But he
found nothing. Still, he identified this impasse as
a door of some fashion.*

*He gently placed his gloved right hand on the
smooth, inky surface. Like a sudden shot of static
through a stereo speaker, a ghostly electronic
storm emanated from within the shiny blackness
in front of him, as if it were alive, seeping through*

his gloves into his pores. The wall evaporated, unveiling a vast room, allowing him access into its reach. He stepped forward and found himself within a great span of blackness, faraway walls enveloping him as if he were an embryo inside a great black egg. This place seemed familiar. He had been here before. Yes. This was the place where he first received the Atmosphere. Oh, yes, the Atmosphere. He wondered for a brief moment how he knew it was called that. As usual, he could not answer his own query. He simply accepted the fact that he just knew, as if the knowledge of the object had been buried in his mind all this time and had been empathically called forth by the Giver.

He spun his body, looking around. The room was round, like an amphitheater, entirely black and glossy, the walls, ceiling and floor like the finish on a brand-new car. Ever so slowly, he walked toward the center of the vacuous room. The squeaky footfalls of his black sneakers echoed hollowly amid the quiet, careening off the curved walls like an invisible pinball. He finally stood at what he perceived to be the middlemost point, placing his hand in his jacket pocket to make sure the Atmosphere was still there. It was. He had done this so many times before, even on his way here—in the street, on the subway, in the tunnel—because he knew it was crucial that he not misplace it. It was the Atmosphere, and the Giver had chosen him to carry out its requirements.

He waited for what seemed a very long time

before the Giver made its presence known. A slight humming sound filled the room, then quickly grew into a pulsing that radiated from the walls like a distant explosion. It permeated his skin, deep into his bloodstream, bearing a euphoria with it that he could neither explain nor define. It eclipsed the pleasures of any drug he had used in his past life. It surpassed the gratification of the heady rush he felt while listening to the pulsating beats and rhythms of ambient and techno music. He closed his eyes, permitting the sensation-filled droning to douse his mind and body like a rapid wash of warm water. He felt himself smiling and truly hoped that it would last a long, long time.

Suddenly he felt himself getting hard, the pulse now reaching into his crotch. The vibration sped up. A tingling raced through his bloodstream. It felt wonderful. He wanted it to last forever. He wanted to see its magic, and when he opened his eyes, he found a faint bluish color illuminating the room. He immediately felt as though he were swimming miles beneath the ocean, spelunking in a warm limestone cave where shimmering stalactites washed their ghostly natural phosphorescence over his body. This, in combination with the bodily resonance, brought on a higher feeling, a miraculous awareness. This perhaps was Nirvana. This was what the Suppliers felt. Yes, it would be his pleasure to bring it to them again and again. Now if only the Giver would allow him to supply someday!

He stared into the light, eyes wide and tearing.

Now all the walls glowed, brighter than before, a sea of neon blue swimming through the room. Then, like magic, the walls became translucent. Colorful shapes flowing beneath their surface, intertwining amid one another in a jubilant frenzy. Microbiotic creatures orgied into a great tapestry of surreal hues. He raised a palm to the fluid shapes. "I am yours," he managed to whisper, the pulse in his body reaching orgasmic proportions. The shapes moved within each other, growing brighter, as the seconds passed. Suddenly brighter more magnificent colors emerged: greens, purples, yellows, oranges. All glowing, fusing with the dominant blue like sucklings on a mother. Again he said, "I am yours," more than a whisper now.

"Do you have the unit?" the emphatic monotone voice boomed, a guttural computerized airing. Yet it was incalculably alive, breathing.

The bald man brought his hand down, searched in his jacket pocket for the Atmosphere. For a terrifying moment he thought it would not be there, that he had lost it as he feared he would. But his fingers felt its smoothness and latched onto the six spines emerging from the domed surface. He pulled it out, careful not to drop it, holding it close to his chest as if it were a baby kitten.

The colors spoke, swirling madly with every utterance: "Place it at your feet."

He felt jewels of sweat dappling his forehead. Oh, how it hurt to give it up. He pulled it away from his chest, held it in front of him so he could gaze at it again, the Atmosphere. Oh, the Atmo-

sphere. Again he tried to recall if the Giver had ever used this term in his presence, but his thoughts swam aimlessly within his mind. What did it matter, anyway? In his mind this object was indeed an Atmosphere. It needed no explanation. It was a wonderful, blessed thing.

He slowly crouched down and placed it on the smooth jet surface. At once, the bottom of the object appeared to meld with the floor, its black exterior a perfect merge with the surrounding environment. The six tubular spines on the domed crown, standing out at odd angles like the spines on an anenome, started to sway, bathing in the vigorous lights as if in empathic communication with them.

Suddenly a small door appeared in the wall ahead, much like the entranceway to this place— like magic. It revealed an opening no bigger than a shoe box. From within its darkness a gyrating appendage emerged, slithering forth like a sentient tentacle, but no more natural in its embodiment than anything else in this stark place. Black and lustrous like the walls and floor, the segmented extremity tapped chitinously against the hard flooring as it writhed forward. It reached the object at his feet, stopped alongside it, then wrapped itself around the fused base like an attacking snake suffocating a mouse. Once secure, the end attached itself to one of the prongs, like a nozzle on a hose. A whining noise ensued, circling the room like a scream escaping a lost soul, drowning out the unremitting resonance.

"The unit is full," the electronic voice droned.

The whine stopped and a high-pitched shrill re-sounded in its place. It continued for as long as the whine transpired, then stopped, at once returning the room to its eerie, resonating pulse. "The unit has been evacuated."

The bald man nodded, understanding the Giver.

"Harbinger, what is your purpose?"

The bald man perceived an odd sensation in his head, as if a switch had been turned on to reveal an appropriate answer to the query. "To seek out Suppliers."

"Harbinger, what will you do if an Outsider discovers you?"

"Kill them."

"Harbinger, what will you do if an Outsider overcomes you, or escapes?"

"Kill myself."

"Harbinger, take the unit. Seek out new Suppliers."

"Yes, Giver," he answered automatically.

The room went black, relinquishing the colors, restoring the darkness. He leaned down to pick up the Atmosphere, the very feel of it sending tiny jolts of electricity through his fingers. He returned it to his jacket pocket, allowing his fingers to again roam the spines, wondering what it must be like to become one with the Atmosphere just as the Suppliers had—the fortunate ones on whom he had bestowed its magic. He so badly desired the opportunity to supply. But he had been afraid to query the Giver. Perhaps next time. Yes, next time, when he returned the Atmosphere

for replenishing, he would request that he be-
come a Supplier.

He turned and left the way he had come,
through the ebony corridor, into the long tunnel
and back into the subway. Eventually he made it
outside and his memories returned—his name,
his purpose, his thoughts and beliefs. The sun-
light pained his eyes; even with the sunglasses,
they hurt. No matter. He would go home and hide
until the sun went down. Then he would set out
and share the pleasure of the Atmosphere with
new Suppliers.

Yes, indeed. Perhaps next time the Giver would
allow him to supply.

Chapter Six

Four o'clock approached. Friday afternoon. New York was a maze of dips and recesses, buildings and subway entrances. The sky was cloudless, warm rays of sunshine extending across Queens, Brooklyn, Jersey. Taxis fired by, horns blaring. Buses gridlocked the street corners. Innumerable people, anonymous within the chaos, shifted in every direction imaginable, mazing their way to destinations unknown, their thoughts unquestionably in as much disorder as the environment surrounding them. People yelling. Children shrieking. Complete chaos, yet somehow systematized in its entirety. A typical day in the city.

Climbing the concrete steps leading to the Thirteenth Precinct, Frank felt winded and lightheaded, as if he had just run a race. The trek from his apartment was only six blocks, less than a ten-minute walk. But still he felt tired.

Sometimes, weather permitting, he would walk to his office at the Twelfth, which took nearly thirty minutes, and he usually felt fine, sometimes invigorated. But today he had trouble simply keeping up with the traffic. *One bad night will kill you*, he thought, figuring it would take at least two days before he felt like himself again. He paused for a moment to catch his breath, one hand gripping the handrail, one hand instinctively feeling for the gun in his belt.

The outer appearance of the Thirteenth looked exactly as he remembered it from his last visit two years before: chipped brickwork, the weather-beaten arched doorway basking in dull green paint, a big metal *13* fringed with rust identifying the station.

He entered and immediately smiled, the work environment triggering instant memories of the past. Some things never changed.

The first things he noticed were the community policing charts and robbery beat maps, still posted in the same places they had been for the last twenty years: to the left, on the dull-as-dull-can-be gray walls. As a matter of fact, everything in the precinct possessed the same sallow flavor. Ceiling to furniture to floors, as if the room itself was ill and all the color had been drained from its veneer. The sickly gray hue gave him the impression of the shade a body retains after rigor mortis sets in. And then there were those scary art prints hanging crookedly amid the charts, faded and seemingly untouchable, like petrified fungi growing on a tree trunk. They'll be there in another twenty years, Frank thought, recalling the somber feelings the environment elicited when desk duty ran overtime; it always felt like *he* were being institutionalized.

Beyond the phone system and the recent addition of computers, the Thirteenth Precinct remained virtually the same as it was when he last worked here eleven years ago.

Frank quickly thought back to the summer of 1990, when he and Diane had vacationed in California. He took a few hours to pay a visit to his telephone acquaintances at the Seventy-first in Los Angeles—friends he made while researching a murder case he'd worked on the previous year.

Frank hadn't believed his eyes when he first laid eyes on the working environment in L.A. It was as if he had just stepped into a country club. Polished floors, clean walls, organization comparable to that of a library. And the technology—*unbelievable.* Radar maps of the city; computerized composite programs storing over six thousand simulated facial features; infrared tracking devices. And unlike the crusty coffee pots at the Twelfth, those lads in L.A. had a nifty cappuccino maker complete with brass pots and gourmet coffee. No comparison. The stations in New York were slums compared to those in Los Angeles. But in Frank's opinion, all that polish—yellow walls, cushiony furniture, espresso—it kind of softened the ethic of those who worked in it. Certainly he didn't think less of them—it wasn't *easy* being a cop in L.A. But it took a real tough, hard-as-nails guy to work as a cop in New York.

The case that had earned Frank friends in L.A. resulted in all his New York associates nicknaming him "the psychic detective," a moniker that lasted a good two years. A tip from Inspector Morris of the L.A.P.D. revealed that a local businessman named John Douglas, who had had a very public, ongoing marital dispute, hadn't shown up at work for a week and was eventually reported missing. Inspector Morris' research revealed that Douglas had flown to New York's JFK two days before his wife left for business in Manhattan. Morris notified Frank at the Thirteenth, who subsequently looked into it. As details developed, Frank found out that Douglas had stalked his wife while here, following her upon her arrival at the airport to the New York Hilton, and later all around the city as she went about her business. He eventually discovered her capping off her second night in town snuggled up in her hotel room with a business associate.

He had murdered them both, shooting each of them three times with a semiautomatic.

Although he'd been assumed to be hiding somewhere in the city, there had been no immediate sign of Douglas's whereabouts following the murders. Frank, listening to his instincts, put a stakeout on a pawn shop in which the owner claimed a man fitting the suspect's description had purchased a semiautomatic the day before the murders. Unbelievable as it seemed, Frank figured that Douglas's execution had been planned, that the guy had intended to go into seclusion, therefore needing every penny he could get his hands on. The very next day, Douglas tried to return the gun to the pawn shop and get his two-hundred dollars back. Just as Frank had guessed.

Instincts, he bragged. Not psychic. They needled him anyway.

A visit to any precinct in the Big Apple would unquestionably find a flurry of caged decadence within its walls: restless teenagers sporting handcuffs, fidgeting in their seats as desk officers questioned their activities; prostitutes with prune-sized bruises on their faces claiming they were just "hanging around"; scofflaws screaming at the tops of their lungs, emphatically insisting their innocence. Today was no different at the Thirteenth. They were all there, a movie re-run for the thousandth time, a front-row seat for Frank. If he had gone to work today at the Twelfth, he would have found much of the same.

Suddenly the doors to the precinct slammed open behind him. A shirtless vagrant appeared, scraggly beard crawling halfway down his chest. Two cops had him by the arms, wrists cuffed behind him—Frank's sharp memory recognized one of the officers from the crime scene early that morning. The vagrant was screaming in a raspy voice about aliens from outer space who were trying to steal his empty deposit cans. Frank shifted aside, watching curiously as the cops shoved the bum forward, forcefully leading him through the office to the back room. Every precinct had a back room, a row of cells where criminals were detained for a short period until they were either sent off to jail or released on their own recognizance. Lovely place. Always lots to see.

A half-dozen metal folding chairs ran along the perimeter of a small waiting area. A frail-looking elderly man with an unkempt beard and one clouded eye occupied one. He used his good eye to gaze up at Frank. Behind a sign-in desk, a middle-aged desk sergeant sat thumbing through a stack of paper.

"Help you?" he asked, eyes glued to his paperwork.

Frank stuck his detective's badge under the cop's nose. "Frank Ballaro for Captain Rodriguez."

The cop looked up. A show of regard livened his face. "Ah, Detective. Captain Rodriguez told me to expect you. I'll tell him you're here."

"Thanks." Frank glanced around. A few cops were laughing out loud, making cracks about the crazy man; his pleading cries about aliens were still audible even from behind the closed door of the back room.

"He's right, you know . . ."

Frank twisted his neck toward the voice. The man with the clouded eye still gazed at him, straggles of hair escaping the worn Yankees cap he wore. "Pardon?"

"The aliens. They *are* here." His voice sounded like a distorted stereo speaker, and as he spoke drool dribbled from his toothless grin. "And they're covering it up," he whispered, pointing to the offices where the police were working.

Frank raised an eyebrow. "I'll have to keep an eye out, then."

"You do that." The man smiled, wet lips flattened against each other like two slimy worms.

"Shut up!" the cop behind the desk said. "Sorry 'bout that."

Frank placed a hand on the desk. "He's harmless."

"He's nuts. Like the rest of them. Been here three times this month." He leaned forward, smiling. "Said the aliens are here."

"Must be catching."

"Huh?"

"The guy they just brought in."

The desk sergeant laughed. "Yeah, they're a dime a dozen. By the way, nice job."

"Sorry?"

"On the Lindsay case."

Frank smiled halfheartedly, nodded. "Thanks." *Damn*, he thought. Bobby Lindsay, out on bail. It had escaped him for a moment. Being reminded of it now suddenly triggered the vexatious, irrational side of his personality, the same one that had crept up on him early this morning, tempting him to splatter the rat in the gutter. Suddenly he felt the need to get a grip, keep himself from leaping over the desk and choking the desk sergeant. Last night he'd blamed this illogical anger on fatigue. But today?

He was starting to scare himself.

"Frank!" He heard Hector Rodriguez yell his name from across the room. Frank saw him standing in his open office door at the rear of the precinct. "Come back," he motioned, waving.

The desk sergeant nodded as Frank passed him. He wormed his way through the maze of desks. Twenty or so cops milled about, some busy at work on computers, others questioning disgruntled folk whose expressions clearly indicated that this was the last place they wanted to be.

Frank reached Hector. They shook hands. "How are you?"

"Tired," Hector said. "Been going nonstop since I last saw you."

They entered the office. Hector shut the door behind them and added, "You don't look so hot."

"I feel like *I* was the one who was hit by a taxi. Too old to pull them all-nighters."

"I bet. It must be tough sleeping 'til noon." Hector smiled.

"Two. How quickly you forget. Must be old age."

Hector grimaced; then, as always with him, it was right down to business. Motioning with his hand, he said, "Have a seat."

Frank stayed standing, and with no hesitation threw out his first question. "Anything new come up?"

Down to business—two could play that game.

Surprisingly, Hector didn't give him the runaround. "The first kid's dead too." He sat down behind his desk. "Stayed alive another ten minutes or so but was DOA at Mercy Hospital. Looks like we got a double murder here."

"Did he say anything?"

"The kid?"

"Yeah."

"EMTs reported nothing. You know . . . I was going to ask you the same question."

"Actually I was hoping you would." Frank stepped to the watercooler against the wall, pulled a plastic cup from the attached dispenser and filled it. "Before anyone else showed up, he did say something." He took a mouthful of water, then tossed the cup in a pail next to the cooler. "This is going to sound strange, Hect, and please don't think I'm crazy or that I was tired, because I'm sure I heard it correctly."

Hector waited, hands folded beneath his chin. "Yes?"

"Atmosphere."

"Pardon?"

"That's it. Atmosphere. He said just that one word, one time." Frank gripped the back of the chair facing Hector's desk and leaned forward slightly. "I was kneeling over him, trying to get him to talk about what had happened. At first he said absolutely nothing, just groaned a lot, and I thought I'd never get anything out of him. But then, right out of the blue, it just slipped from his lips, almost as if he had no control over it. I tried real hard to get him to say something else, but he was hurting real bad, and I got nothing. He said just the one word, one time. That was it."

Hector rubbed the stubble on his chin. To Frank he seemed to be pondering the word and its potential significance. "That's all he said, huh?"

Frank nodded.

"What do you make of it?"

"No clue," he answered, shrugging his shoulders. His muscles felt tense.

Hector grabbed a pen from the cup on his desk, jotted down the word on a piece of stationery. "Frank, as you already know, I need a statement from you. But I'd also like you to make yourself available in case I need you. We're definitely treating this as a double murder, and the bald guy is our only suspect right now. We have witnesses, but your testimony will be needed first since you saw everything from the very beginning."

"Sure, no problem. Listen, Hect, I really want a piece of this. . . ."

"Frank . . . please," Hector said, holding up his hands. "Don't make this difficult. You know very well that I can't put you on the case. We'd have to arrange for a temporary transfer, get signed authorizations from Captain Klein and myself. All at my request. And then the paperwork. C'mon, Frank, by the time it all goes through, Baldie will have a few more notches on his bedpost to brag about."

Frank grinned defensively. This was Hector, tried and true, everything by the book. But his shell was thin, and crackable.

"C'mon, Hect, I'm not talking about dealing our cards faceup, you know that as well as I do. I can help, and you know it, so don't give me any of your by-the-book bull crap." Frank felt a vein in his head start to throb. He was getting excited. "Let's cut to the chase. Let me in on this."

"Frank, I understand this happened in your neighborhood . . ."

"That has nothing to do with it."

"Look, you're a dear friend, and I have the greatest respect for you, but the fact of the matter is that even though I *know* you could help, and that I would love to work with you again, we have fine detectives here, all of them with egos that don't take too kindly to outside interference. Think about how *you* feel every time someone from the FBI shows up, invading your territory."

Twinges of frustration started to well up in Frank's throat in the form of a hot burning ball. He wanted to tear at Rodriguez's collar, shake some sense into him, convince him that he was the best man for the job.

"And," Hector added, "I'm sure you have plenty to do at the Twelfth."

"I've got a few days off. Hect, c'mon. You'd want the same thing if you were in my place." He knew he was starting to sway Hector, playing him just the right way, nice and easy does it.

Hector smiled, half a grin of agreement, half cut partially in frustration.

"Couldn't you come up with anything better than 'by-the-book bull crap'?"

Frank smiled. "Hect . . ."

"I'll tell you what," he said, his breathy tone clearly expressing a settling against his better judgment. "Before you go inside to give your report, I'll let you in on what we already know. If in your spare time you hear something you think we ought to know, I'm all ears. Just keep it quiet, all right?"

Frank smiled. Indeed, if the situation had been reversed, Hector *would* have behaved in the same manner, would have picked at Frank's skin until he got his way. Frank felt like a great weight had been lifted from his shoulders. Good ol' Hect, showing his professional respect for Frank, letting him do a little under-the-table work.

Now they could get down to business. Frank finally sat down and leaned forward, elbows on his knees, heart suddenly pounding with excitement. "Thank you. Now what about Baldman? Anything?"

Hector grabbed a yellow clasp envelope from the right side of his desk. "What do you think?" He pulled a sheet of paper from the envelope, showed it to Frank.

Frank looked at the page. An artist's composite sketch of the sunglassed bald man stared back at him. A fine representation, chin sharp, slit for a mouth, nose a mere drop of cartilage and skin. "That's him."

"Yeah, pretty good, huh? It's going out tomorrow morning, local press first. If nothing comes up, we'll go national; first the precincts, then public if we have to. It'd be nice if his face came up in a database somewhere. Meanwhile, I've got someone searching ours right now. Keep your fingers crossed."

Frank handed the sketch back to Hector. "Can I have a copy?"

"Sure." Hector slipped it back into the envelope. "Actually—take this one." He handed the envelope with the sketch back to Frank.

"Any ID on the two kids?"

"The first kid had nothing on him. All we've really got is what you already know. Male, Caucasian, eighteen to twenty-two years. Exact cause of death right now unknown—until the coroner's report comes back. Should have something in twenty-four hours. We're guessing trauma due to blunt force. Toxicology results will be back before that, tell us if he was under any influence. In the meantime, we've got someone checking out calls on missing persons."

The image of the dying boy haunted Frank. He shook his head and rubbed his eyes.

"Something wrong?"

He looked at Hector, watched him come into focus through the fading blotches in his vision. "The whole thing is bugging me. It was so damn . . . unusual. You know? The kid, being naked and all, seeing him getting hit by the car. And then afterwards, when I looked into his eyes, they were so glassy. Spaced out. It could've been shock, could've been drugs, but I got a strange impression there was something else. I can't put a finger on it, but I know it's something we should be looking into."

"Like what?"

"Well . . ." He hesitated, not exactly sure what it was he wanted to say.

Hector leaned back, put his hands behind his head. His leather shoulder holster stretched across his chest like a giant shoelace. "Don't get too worked up over it. It's probably all drug-related. I'll let you see the toxicology report when it comes in. Don't waste your energy on something that's unlikely."

Frank stared at Hector. The captain's eyes were unmoving, seemingly waiting for Frank to either shock or amuse him. "Look," he said, frowning defensively, "I can't say for sure what happened out there, but I do know that that kid was terrified of something. He ran like hell from the alley. *Naked.* I'm telling you, I don't think he cared what happened to him as long as he got away from whatever it was that had him spooked. And then when I saw his face, the *fear.* Believe me when I tell you that I've never seen anything like it, and it's something I'll never forget. Honest. It was *weird.*"

Hector lowered his arms, took a mouthful of coffee, grimaced. Must have been cold. "You want my honest opinion, Frank? I think the two kids were all doped up having some sort of sex in the alley when Baldie jumped out of nowhere, surprised them with a knife and sliced away their dicks. One kid almost got away. The other didn't. *That's* why your boy was afraid, Frank. You'd be too if someone did a Bobbitt on *your* pecker."

Frank felt droplets of sweat trickling down his back. "Did you find a knife?"

"No. Baldie must've taken it with him."

"How about the thing the second kid was holding on to? Find that?"

"No."

"Well, one thing I am positive about: That

thing, whatever it is, is what the bald guy was after. Bad enough to risk his own ass in order to get it."

"I thought about that," Hector confessed, "after you mentioned it this morning. But there's no evidence to confirm that right now. We searched the entire area, the tunnel, found nothing. We don't even know how the damn tunnel was dug out. That's a mystery in itself."

"What about the other kid? ID?"

Hector shuffled some documents on his desk, picked one up. "Had a school ID on him. Patrick Racine, nineteen, student at the Fashion Institute. No prior arrests, good grades, nice family. They've been notified. I'm gonna have them interviewed either later tonight or tomorrow."

"Gee, Jaimie goes there, F.I.T."

"This is all a little too close to home, huh?"

"Real close."

"Why don't you ask her if she knows Racine, about his lifestyle, anything that would warrant his being out late or in the neighborhood."

Frank nodded. "Sure." Then he said, "Let me go on the interview."

"Frank, please . . ."

"I *have* to be there." Anxiety ripped at his heart.

"I'll give you a transcript."

"Hect, please. I just want to listen. I won't say anything. I just know I can pick up a lot if I'm there."

"I'll give you a tape and a transcript. End of story." Hector stood. "I think we're done for

Michael Laimo

now." Clearly Hector was starting to lose patience, not necessarily with Frank, but with the whole situation. "Why don't we get your interview set up with Sergeant Simmons?"

Frank stayed seated, frustration tickling his nerve endings. "You hear about Bobby Lindsay?"

Hector placed his fists on the desk. "Yes. I'm sorry."

"It'll be front page again."

"You did what you could. All you can do now is let the system do its job and everything will work out. Kid'll get his."

Hector's phone beeped. He hit the speaker button. "Rodriguez."

"Captain," a tinny voice blared. "I think we found something on the bald guy."

"I'll be right there."

Frank stood, gave Hector a grin. Action.

Hector walked around his desk. "Let's go check it out, Smoky."

74

Chapter Seven

Jaimie waited on the platform thirty minutes before she felt a slight stirring breeze springing up from the tracks, alerting her to the F train's approach. With her Eastpack knapsack fastened firmly to her back, hands gripping its straps, she leaned over the edge and peeked into the tunnel as the train's headlights floated in from the darkness like widening searchlights. Cursing the MTA, she stepped back while the train roared into the station and screeched to a stop. Along with a number of other passengers, she quickly squeezed into the train before the doors rang shut.

She quickly gazed at the train's interior and its usual variety of occupants: people from many walks of life, many countries, students, workers, all on their way to determine their net worth in the world. A few open spaces segregated the seated riders. She planted herself between an old Korean woman reading her country's newspaper and a man in a business suit who fiddled with the tiny dials on his watch. A number of people remained standing, holding on to the poles.

She loosened her knapsack, then looked at her watch. Already 5:12 P.M. She had left the apartment early, hoping to spend at least an hour in the Institute's library to get in some last-minute studying. But the train—unpredictable as always—ran late, virtually stranding her. Now she would have just enough time to rush to the lecture hall, settle in and take the exam.

The train made its next scheduled stop at Eighth Street. A few more passengers boarded, filling the remaining seats. The Asian woman sitting next to Jaimie departed and a young guy about her own age wearing a black T-shirt and headphones with a loud, relentless beat inside took her place.

The door-closing warning bells rang out. An announcement was made, alerting the passengers to the next stop—Fourteenth Street.

Just as the doors began to close, a mangy homeless man squeezed through, stumbling.

He coughed, then leaned against the side of a seat occupied by an elderly man. He was breathing heavily, as though he had run a long way to catch the train, but more than likely he had bronchitis or some other belligerent infection or virus.

Jaimie gazed at him: dirt and whiskers covered his face like a mask; clothes hung upon his body like oily rags strewn atop a service station pump. In one hand he gripped a battered laminated document, in the other a tin cup. He staggered to the center of the car and haphazardly pirouetted, gazing at the passengers, eyes wide and wild. Those near him inched away, allowing themselves as much personal space as possible.

Suddenly the homeless man began to yell, raspy voice cutting through the air as though laced with razor blades. "Ladies and gentlemen, may I have your attention—I am very hungry and in pain and would appreciate you giving to the homeless shelters of New York." He held up the battered certificate as if it were a legitimate license to solicit funds from strangers; it probably was for *someone* at some point. "Anything helps, a penny, nickel, or dime. Please help." Then the vagrant held out his rusty cup to the riders near him, shaking its measly contents as if to say *I need much more than what's in here to survive*, which was probably the truth.

Jaimie looked away from the vagrant, suddenly realizing that the train had not yet pulled out of the Eighth Street station. She anxiously looked at her watch. Her exam started in twenty-five minutes. Her blood started to race, her heart pumping restlessly. Not only was the threat of her being late for the exam quite real, but now a smelly bum was about to shove his dirty tin cup under her nose.

She hated when this happened—which seemed all too often lately—and in the past she discovered that the best thing to do was pull a few coins

77

from her pocket and send the vagrant on his way. She dug into her jeans, but no coins jingled out. Only two tens and her school ID. The train started to inch forward slowly. A few riders voiced their complaints to no one in particular. And while others turned their backs on the staggering bum, some dropped some coins into his cup, earning themselves a guttural, tired "thank you."

Changeless, Jaimie would have to avoid eye contact.

She peered down, aimed her sights at a gray, flattened circle of chewing gum on the dirty floor, trying to think only of exam topics: open to buys, cost averages, profit margins.

Footsteps slowly approached, thump . . . thump . . . thump. They ceased; dirty laceless boots covered the circle of gum she stared at, filthy swollen ankles protruding like weird overgrown fungi.

The cup jingled.

It suddenly seemed as if she had been sucked into some weird dream sequence in a movie. Her father had warned her time and time again to never give anything to these creeps, just go on her way as if they aren't there. They were diseased individuals, always being brought in for crimes: assaults, muggings, robberies, even killings. They prowled the streets like wolves in the night, looking for a ticket for their next meal, drink or fix.

But as much as Frank loathed these creatures, Jaimie always felt sorry for them. They were human beings, after all, people who perhaps had

had a chance in life to succeed but due to unforeseen circumstances were not allowed the opportunity to participate in society. Now nobody cared. But they deserved *some* respect.

"Change, miss?"

Jaimie raised her head and looked at him. Gooseflesh crawled along the length of her body. The skin of his face was horribly wrinkled, like a crumpled paper bag that had been smoothed out. Tangles of hair and whiskers reached out wildly from his head and chin, unidentified scraps of food nestling within the brown and gray growth. And he smelled like the Jersey Shore at low tide. Jaimie shuddered. At the same time, her heart bled. She reached into her pocket.

Suddenly his hand stretched out and grabbed her wrist. It felt rough, as if it had been dipped and dried in cement. She winced, her heart pounding. The man in the business suit next to her took notice and stopped fiddling with his watch, seemingly readying himself should the contact go any further. The guy with the headphones on her left had his eyes closed, lost in his own rhythms.

Then the bum spoke, eyes unblinking, rancid breath hitting her face like a cloud of steam.

"Watch out for *them.*"

The sudden ringing of the train doors broke Jaimie from her paralysis. The bum released his hold on her and quickly fled the car before the doors slammed shut. She turned and watched him lurch away into the R train waiting on the opposite track. She saw him inside the other

79

train, his face a horrible mask looking back at her through the windows as the train pulled away.

She rubbed her wrist where the bum had grasped it, as if trying to wipe away whatever dreadful disease he might have left behind. What did he mean? Watch out for who? And why did he tell *her*? Could he know something? *No.* Jaimie shook the irrational thought from her head. There could be no conclusion other than that the bum was distraught, an individual suffering from mental illness, his behavior a random act of lunacy. She couldn't assume that she was in any form of imminent danger.

Unless he really knew something . . .

No use wasting any more time thinking about it. She couldn't have anything distracting her now. She had an exam to take.

And besides, a more critical issue loomed. The train. It sat motionless.

She looked around. Passengers were grumbling over the standstill, pulling on their sleeves and looking at their watches. Everybody seemed to be in a rush. What else was new?

Jaimie followed suit, again looked at her watch. 5:25. The exam began at 5:45. Surely students were already there, seats taken, books open in front of them, squeezing last-minute details into their heads.

The doors to the lecture hall would be locked as soon as the exam had been handed out. If she were late, she would be locked out and given a makeup in a few weeks. That would be unacceptable; she'd studied a great deal; all the details were freshly crammed in her head. To wait a few weeks would be devastating. And makeups were always given in essay format, a bitch compared to the multiple choice tests given in class.

The train started to shake forward, inches at a time. Peering through the corner of her eye, she watched the passengers around her. Techno boy on her left, eyes still closed, head bobbing to the beat of the music in his headphones. Businessman on the right, back to tinkering with his watch.

She gazed forward for the first time since the bum had grabbed her. She noticed a new passenger: a strange-looking man wedged in the middle seat of a three-seater. Bald, he wore sunglasses, and was dressed entirely in black—a leather jacket, jeans, T-shirt, gloves, even his sneakers were black. Although it appeared he was looking at her, she couldn't tell for sure as his sunglasses sufficiently masked his eyes. Averting her eyes, she peered above to the ads lining the wall of the train just below the ceiling. Dr. Geraldo Alvarado smiled down at her, his pearly white caps telling his tale: *dentisto, hablo español.* In another ad, two healthy men frolicked with a shapely woman in a swimming pool, the picture having nothing to do with the cigarettes the ad claimed they smoked.

She looked back down to see the bald guy shifting in his seat. An elderly man seated next to him squirmed like a salted slug, brow furrowed, evidently uncomfortable at the bald guy's invasion of his personal space.

81

Suddenly the bald man spread his lips wide and smiled, the whites of his teeth almost a match to those of Dr. Alvarado. But it wasn't the sort of grin a person makes when he suddenly thinks of something funny, or a flirtatious smirk directed at a pretty girl. This grin had ulterior motives, perhaps a trace of underlying unbalance.

Positive that the unwanted gesture had been cast in her direction, Jaimie directed her gaze back to the piece of chewing gum on the floor, then checked her watch, then went back to the gum. With her good looks, she was used to displaying indifference to the men who constantly came on to her.

But she wasn't positive that the bald guy was actually hitting on her. The smile seemed too eccentric. Like the bum, he looked as though he had motives other than just trying to get her attention. She suddenly felt that no matter what she did to discourage him, he would still grin at her.

The train halted its crawl, the dark of the tunnel the only view through the windows. She peeked up and saw the bald guy digging into his jacket pocket.

He started to pull something out.

She prayed it wasn't a weapon.

Technoboy suddenly intensified his gyrations, the music inside his headphones no doubt reaching a crescendo. Slightly uncomfortable with *him* now, Jaimie warily peeked from the corner of her eye in his direction.

He was staring directly at the bald guy, unwaveringly, as if their gazes had been tethered together with a string.

The train inched forward, blackness still in the windows.

The lights inside the car started to flicker. A female groan of panic rang out from the other end of the car. A series of Hispanic utterances followed, complaints, no doubt, from their indignant tone and manner. Jaimie warily glanced back at the bald guy. He held an object in his hands; not a weapon, thank God. It was black, shiny, oddly shaped. He used his gloved thumbs to gently caress it, as if it were a pet.

His smile stretched even wider, as if he were experiencing a sexual feeling, his head tilted not at her but at techno boy one seat over.

The train finally started moving again, at a snail's pace but moving nonetheless.

Techno boy was now rocking feverishly, head bobbing and weaving, shoulders rolling so that they started knocking into Jaimie, unnerving her slightly. She took a deep breath, wondering if something could be wrong with him, if he might be having a seizure. He was totally strung out, skin flushed, eyes wide open, tears running from them like raindrops. The Walkman was held in a white-knuckled grip. His actions seemed too extreme for just an overenthusiastic response to the music in his head, and she wondered briefly if she would have to run for cover in order to avoid an elbow in the gut.

Jewels of sweat formed on the bald guy's domed head, each one shimmering beneath the flickering lights like simulated stars on an astronomical globe. Techno boy, still heaving to and fro, started to moan, ghostly snivels emitting from his lips. The bald guy rubbed the object harder, as though masturbating. A few riders started to notice the peculiar exchange going on and restlessly shoved off toward the doors, seemingly in hope of escaping the train as soon as it pulled into the Fourteenth Street station.

Jaimie's discomfort grew. Acid bubbled in her gut in response to a sudden premonition that something unsettling was going to happen. Listening to her instinct, she quickly rose and stood near the other riders by the doors, tightening her knapsack around her shoulders. There was safety in numbers, she thought, deciding she'd rather walk the last six blocks than spend any more time on the train.

Light appeared through the windows. The train was finally pulling into the station.

Just as the light of the station seeped into the train, techno boy leaped up from his seat and grabbed the black object from the bald guy's hand, jostling some standing passengers. A few screams erupted. The train stopped and the doors slid open. Techno boy shoved aside the group of people exiting the train and fled through the open doors, taking the object with him. A man in a suit and tie fell down on the platform. A few women screamed, one yelling obscenities in Spanish. Jaimie clutched her beating heart and watched with dismay as techno boy fled into the subway station and lost himself in the crowd.

The man in the suit and tie stood up and brushed off his clothes. Jaimie stepped away from the action and poked her head around, checking to see if the bald guy had hung around.

Gone.

She repositioned her knapsack, looked at her watch and cursed the MTA again. Then she darted up the stairs out onto Sixth Avenue.

Taking a deep breath, she ran. In order to make it to her exam on time, she'd have to try real hard to avoid knocking someone over between here and the Fashion Institute six blocks away.

Chapter Eight

Frank grabbed a chair from an unoccupied desk and rolled it next to the desk of Detective Phillip Martin. Martin was a third-generation detective. He possessed a perfect combination of inquisitiveness and ruggedness that not only streamed in his blood but demonstrated itself in his appearance. He had silver hair, blue eyes, a handlebar mustache, eyebrows almost as thick as his mustache and ruddy cheeks that looked as if they were filled with bullets. Every station house had a cop like Martin. Frank was reminded of Detective James Riley from the Twelfth. Red-faced, with an abrasive demeanor, a real Irish toughnose perfectly fitted to frighten all those first-offenders in the station on their inaugural visit.

Standing at Martin's right, Hector leaned a respectful hand on the detective's shoulder. "What did you find?"

Martin rubbed the left side of his chest, using his right hand to guide the mouse alongside the computer on his desk. The monitor flashed— charts rolling, windows collapsing and changing as he loaded up what he wanted to show Hector. "Something really interesting, that's what. It took a while to get the ball rolling at first, but once I found what I was looking for, everything dominoed right into place."

Cracking his knuckles, he repositioned himself in front of the keyboard, inching his chair forward. "I started out by searching our database of police sketches. I entered *white, male, bald* into the search engine." He peeked over at some notes he had scribbled in an open notebook on his desk. "One thousand, seven hundred and fifty three instances occurred."

He demonstrated, utilizing the mouse to click the search button. The computer hesitated; a small hourglass flashing on the screen signaled its attempt to explore the hard drive. Martin bit his bottom lip, urging the computer on, uttering "C'mon . . . c'mon." Finally, as Frank started getting antsy, the hourglass vanished from the screen and was replaced by a small window showing the search results: the same figure Martin had mentioned.

"There we go. Same total as before. Our artists sure are busy fellas, huh? Lots of faces in there." He started running through the sketches, each one taking perhaps ten seconds to load onto the screen. "I spent a while going through them, one by one, but soon realized, as you can very well see, that I'd be here for days trying to come up with a fairly close match to our guy. Bald guys, lots of 'em."

"Shaving must be the trendy thing to do before committing a crime." Frank grinned, thinking uncomfortably of how Bobby Lindsay had shaved his entire body.

"So then I thought," Martin said, apparently ignoring Frank, "what if I refine my search to . . ." He typed in *white, male, bald, sunglasses* into the search box. "Watch this." He hit ENTER.

The hourglass reappeared, flickered on the screen for a few seconds, and then a new window popped up, displaying the search results: *17 hits.*

Frank, rubbing the emerging shadow on his chin, felt his heart pump. Excitement. Adrenaline racing through his blood. This was getting good. He wanted to scream at Martin, rush him along to get to the meat of the matter.

Clearly, though, the detective didn't want to excavate his find in slabs. He wanted to take it all nice and slow, spell it out for his boss piece by piece, exactly the way it had been originally uncovered, as if he had excavated his gold mine with a putty knife. *Smart*, Frank thought. *The bastard's adding suspense.* Typical detective, showing off for the boss. Frank would've done it precisely the same way.

"I pulled up the first sketch, and here's what I found."

Martin grabbed a disc from the desk, slipped it into the computer's A drive, directed the mouse to open the file. The computer produced a faint grinding noise, the monitor flashed, and then a face appeared, a sketch of a bald man wearing sunglasses, small nose, slit for a mouth—the man from the alley. Or so it seemed.

"Holy shit—that's our man," Hector said, rubbing Martin's shoulder, smiling at Frank.

"Looks just like the sketch you showed me." Frank scratched his chin.

"It's not the same sketch, though," Martin added. "This one was drawn up two months ago, at the Seventh. And get this: This guy's a kidnapping suspect."

"Uh-oh. We have to find him," Hector remarked.

"Shouldn't be too difficult. We've got him on file." Martin aimed the mouse pointer to the edge of the window and dragged it to a split screen, revealing a mug shot of the same man, minus the shades.

Frank smiled inside, felt a warmth of relief spread through him like a spray of bathwater, easing the adrenaline tensing all his personalities and bringing about a calming effect, like a fix of drugs to his puzzle-solving addiction.

"Well . . . who is he?" Frank asked, licking his lips, almost salivating.

Martin retrieved the file on the suspect. The screen went blank and then a row of fingerprints appeared, running along the top edge of the screen. Below, a front- and side-view mug scrolled into view, accompanied by the mystery man's vital statistics:

Harold Gross, Height: 6' 1", Weight: 195,
Eyes: Brown, Hair: Shaved (Brown)
DOB: 2/18/70
Current Address: 435 East 108th Street, Apt.
6J, Bronx. Telephone: None

"Nice Jewish boy," Hector said.

"Jewish, yes." Martin grinned. "But not so nice. Check out his rap."

He aimed the mouse pointer to a button at the upper right of the screen and clicked it. The photos and fingerprints disappeared and were quickly replaced by a laundry list of convicted crimes committed by Harold Gross. "Seventeen arrests dating back to January of Nineteen ninety-one. Started out small—petty theft, public disturbance. Later he graduated to the bigger stuff, mostly aggravated assaults. Nothing too out of hand, though. Never did more than a month's time." Martin clicked the sketch and mug shot back to front.

Frank tilted his head slightly, observed the sketch and photo more closely. The grainy shaded lines of the portrait carved a frighteningly perfect match to the face in the photo. "Amazing likeness. It sure as hell looks like him." He ran a hand through his hair. "But how can we be sure that this Harold Gross is *our* bald guy?"

Hector made a small *hmph* sound as if to second Frank's query.

Martin nodded. "I knew you'd ask that. Remember I mentioned before that Gross had been a kidnapping suspect? Well, not too long ago, only a few weeks back, he apparently spent some time hanging around with a kid from the Bronx named Andrew Knowles—who's now nowhere to be found."

Hector grumbled.

Martin nodded, pulled his notebook close to the edge of his desk. "On record, we know that Andrew Knowles was seventeen years old. A problem kid. High school dropout. Arrested twice for drug possession, once for disorderly conduct. Parents reported minor domestic problems to the police a couple of times. In July, Knowles's parents filed a missing person's report. Says here he befriended a 'Harold Gross' three weeks prior to his disappearance, had unexplainably started spending all his time with the stranger, nearly twenty-four hours a day until he just stopped coming home altogether. Detectives from the Seventh went to Gross's place, and what do ya know?" He looked up from the screen and peered at Hector. "Their report shows no evidence to warrant even an association with Knowles."

"So then we don't know for sure that Gross actually had anything to do with Knowles's disappearance," Hector said.

"Well, we have no evidence to corroborate his guilt. As far as the report is concerned, Knowles is simply missing, a probable runaway."

Leaning forward, Frank said, "I think our foremost concern now is whether Gross is our man from the alley."

"Indeed. But we can't assume he's our body snatcher until we actually question him." For the first time Martin turned and looked at Frank. His cheeks were turgid, his lips dry, his blue eyes two sapphires set in stone. He no doubt spent way too much time in front of a computer. Frank returned the stare, wanting to set a fire under his desk chair. As systematic as Martin was, his diligence slowed him down.

"But who's to say he wouldn't have made the two kids in the alley just 'disappear' if we hadn't shown up?"

Martin smiled cockily, not ready to let Frank show him up just yet. "Hold your horses—you're getting way ahead of me. I thought of that, and had no doubts about our bald guy being Gross." He turned back to the computer. "I mentioned earlier that my search resulted in seventeen hits. Well . . . I had completely forgotten about the other sixteen after spending so much time researching Gross. When I saw that I still had sixteen other faces, I went back and checked those out too, thinking all along that I had lucked out and found our man on the first try."

Martin clicked the mouse a few times. "You won't believe this."

An amazing sight appeared on the screen before them.

Sixteen miniature police sketches, four rows and four columns, all bald men wearing sunglasses. All creepily similar to one another—like the sketch of Harold Gross.

Frank's mouth dropped, but Hector said "Holy shit" a moment before Frank could.

Martin said, "My sentiments exactly, only I repeated myself a dozen times as I checked each one out." He turned a page in the notebook, then looked up at Hector. "You might want to sit down for this, Captain."

"Try me," Hector challenged. Both he and Frank leaned forward, reading along with Martin as he ran down his findings.

"Out of the remaining sixteen sketches, three were armed robbery suspects, one of whom wore a bandanna on his head." He pointed to the third sketch down in the first column. "Two were mugging suspects, one a rapist. The rapist is in jail, as are two of the bandits. The other three are out on parole." He placed small Post-It notes over the faces of the six criminals.

"That leaves us with ten bad boys," he said, hesitating.

"Yes?" Hector urged.

Martin tapped the monitor with the eraser of his pencil. "These sketches were drawn up from eyewitness accounts during a series of supposed kidnappings that ran all the way from eastern Long Island to Manhattan, Jersey and Rockland."

Frank wiped a film of sweat forming on his brow. "Jesus."

Martin looked at Frank. "Wait, it gets even weirder." He gripped his left cheek with his thumb and index finger. "Each case dealt with disappearances of male adolescents ranging in age from fifteen to nineteen. Every report had been filed by at least one parent, and on all of them there were claims that the victim grew suddenly reclusive, careless with his appearance just weeks before his disappearance, each and every one leaving home for long periods of time only to return home at night for a few hours' sleep and a meal."

Frank raised an eyebrow. "Sound familiar?"

Hector nodded. "Knowles."

"Yep." Martin added, "And these sketches? Six were given by parents, the other four by friends of the youths . . ."

"Reliable sources," Hector finished.

Frank asked, "Is it possible that Gross could be responsible for the disappearances of all these kids?"

Martin spun his chair around, toward Frank and Hector. "I've always felt that if it seems too obvious at first glance, then it probably is. Given *these* glaring circumstances, I had to check it out." He leaned forward. "You know what I found? It's too obvious."

Hector finally pulled up a chair, sitting to Martin's right. He rubbed his eyes, clearly growing weary. Frank shifted in his chair to allow the blood to flow more freely to his legs, which had started to grow numb. Being wholly absorbed in this unfolding of clues, he hadn't changed his position since he'd sat down nearly twenty minutes earlier.

Martin spun back to face the monitor. "The

first thing I wondered was why on earth there wasn't some intense public investigation on this guy. Recurrent similarities in ten diverse descriptions of a supposed kidnapper who is making teenage boys vanish would demand a huge manhunt. And it would be a big-time media event, not unlike your Lindsay case, Frank." He took a sip of coffee and grimaced. "Well, there isn't anything remotely close to an investigation on file. You know why? Because the FBI led the investigation and kept the whole damn thing under wraps. And they had not one, but *two* guys under scrutiny. Neither of whom were Gross."

Again, Martin turned a page in his notebook. He must have been up all night with this, Frank thought, knowing exactly how it felt to obsess over a treasure hunt.

"The first guy they went after was named James Hilton," he noted, pulling up a mug shot of a middle-aged bald man with a scar running along his left cheek. "Forty-seven years of age, a long history of small crimes under his belt, as well as one armed robbery and one grand theft auto. He was the lead suspect in the investigation of three missing boys, ages sixteen, seventeen and eighteen." He shifted the mug shot over to the right side of the screen and pointed to one of the sketches. "See the scar?"

"Not Harold Gross, but James Hilton," Frank observed.

"You bet. And more of these are likely to be Hilton."

"And the other guy?"

Martin shifted the mouse and brought a second photo to the forefront of the display. Again, a male as bald as Gross and Hilton. "Edward Farrell. Thirty-three, past record similar to that of Gross and Hilton. Was at the center of an FBI probe last year concerning the disappearance of four teenaged boys."

Hector shifted forward; his chair creaked like a rusty door hinge. "I'm at the edge of my seat, Phillip, don't keep me hanging."

"According to the report *we* have, both Hilton and Farrell were found dead, apparent suicides."

"Bullshit," Frank insinuated.

"Seems like it, huh?"

Hector said, "You said it yourself. If it seems too obvious, then it probably is."

"So then what *did* happen to Hilton and Farrell?" Frank asked.

"The only thing we know for sure is that they're dead."

Frank leaned back, placed his hands on his head. "Seems to me we can't be certain about anything other than the facts we have, that we've stumbled onto something really fucked up. Sure, thanks to Martin we have a good deal of information, but clearly no definitive answers. We're still in the dark. Think about it: We've got at least three bald guys wearing sunglasses going around snatching teenaged boys, two of whom are dead. And we have no details of an investigation on record other than some trivialities that the FBI decided not to keep under lock and key. If that ain't fucked up, then I'll turn in my badge."

Martin rested his chin on his fists. "So the question is: Where do we go from here?"

"Hect?" Frank asked.

Hector Rodriguez stood, stretched a bit, then picked up the phone on Martin's desk. "Ernie, I'd like to see you in my office in five minutes. Yes." He hung up, then said, "Phil, first off, cancel the national data search, and don't release the sketch of Gross. We've got enough to go on for now. I'd like you to find out anything you can on Hilton and Farrell; their pasts, where they hung out, what they did for a living." He scratched his head and admitted, "I agree; I don't necessarily think we're getting the entire story regarding their deaths. The FBI knew something and kept it quiet. Perhaps they wanted to avoid mass hysteria among parents, but that doesn't seem feasible. These were teenagers, young adults who willingly went with their abductors. You know, come to think of it, try to contact some of the parents of the missing kids, find out anything you can about the details surrounding their disappearance, and their relationships with Hilton and Farrell."

Martin nodded, then Frank interjected, "Hector?"

He looked at Frank.

"If I can make a suggestion . . ." He waited for Hector's approval, which he received with a weak nod. "It seems too coincidental that Gross, Farrell and Hilton had such similar records. Perhaps an inquiry should be made as to whether any similarities existed among the missing kids."

Hector nodded his agreement. "Can't hurt. Phillip?"

"Can't hurt."

"Very well, then. Frank, come." He paced away, then stopped and turned. "Oh, and Phillip?"

Martin turned from his computer screen. "Captain?"

"Nicely done."

"Thank you, Captain."

Rodriguez pulled Frank aside. "I think I'd like to get that interview with Racine's parents taken care of tonight. If we can confirm a prior association with Gross, we'll get a warrant to search his apartment in no time. Then maybe we can find out what the hell is going on here."

Frank stood silent, arms folded in front of him, waiting like a child next in line to receive a prize.

"Yes?" Rodriguez asked.

"Don't mess with me, Hect."

"You have a statement to give."

Frank stood mute.

"Isn't there something else you'd rather be doing than this crap?"

Half of him wanted to say yes. The other half said, "No."

"I hope I don't regret this. C'mon." Hector walked to his office, where Detective Ernie Barba waited inside. "Before I change my mind."

Frank smiled. "Crap. C'mon Hect, you can do better than that." He tapped Hector tenderly on the shoulder and squeezed in front of him into his office.

Chapter Nine

Jewels of sweat dappled Jaimie's brow as she circled the final answer on the last page of her exam. She could not recall any of her answers for sure now that the exam lay folded closed on the desk in front of her. As a matter of fact, even though she *knew* she had just completed the exam, she couldn't remember actually *taking* it, much less how she decided on the answers circled on its pages. The past two hours had passed as if she had functioned solely on autopilot, independent from cognitive thought.

She remembered times in the past when she'd experienced a similar sensation, borrowing her father's car and driving out to Long Island to spend some time with her friends at Jones Beach. A quasi-hypnotic state seemed to shroud her awareness as she rode along Ocean Parkway, her mind signaling a physical response from her body only upon her arrival at the exit for the beach.

Perhaps if she hadn't had the run-in with the homeless man on the subway, or witnessed the strange exchange between techno boy and the bald guy, her mind would not have been distracted and she might have gone into the exam with all her acumen intact. But as it turned out, she had suffered a mental blow that seemingly sucked away a good part of her concentration, leaving her infatuated with the strange experience.

Taking a deep breath, Jaimie shouldered her backpack, rose from her seat and walked to the front of the lecture hall where Dr. Lougeay sat reading a textbook. He looked up briefly as she placed her exam atop the growing stack on the table in front of him.

She felt a surge of relief wash over her as she turned and walked away, her exam finished and handed in. It felt wonderful to be rid of the anxiety that all those hours of studying had wrought upon her. Now all she had to do was wait and see what grade she got and pray it wouldn't be too bad.

Her footsteps carried her slowly back through the lecture hall. Glancing about in a dreamlike state, she noticed that approximately a third of the students still pored over their answers, most presumably doubling back on responses left blank or guessed at earlier. Before reaching the exits at the rear, she stopped to see if any of the remaining students wore distressed looks on their faces. Misery loves company.

Instead she saw something else, something so unexpected it made her freeze with fear.

One particular test-taker, a male, was staring at her. Or so she guessed, since he wore dark, impenetrable sunglasses.

He was completely bald.

Jaimie felt a moment of panic as she tried to decide whether this was the same person as the man on the subway. Had he followed her for some sick, insane reason? Dear God, she prayed not.

She took a tentative step forward, legs wobbling as she returned his gaze. She could see that *this* bald man's features were different from the last: the nose bigger, the body stouter, the lips fuller. And his clothes were different too. Although dressed entirely in black like the man on the train, this stranger wore pants instead of jeans, and no leather jacket.

Different person.

But so frighteningly similar.

Then she caught sight of something else, something so bizarre that it scared her for *real* this time, and she gripped her gut. Truly, she was unable to tear her eyes away from the strange picture before her.

Still staring directly at her—or so it seemed— the student had a pencil gripped in his right fist, fingers wrapped tightly around it. He was haphazardly running it back and forth across the surface of the exam booklet on his desk, creating a dark blotchy layering of lead that virtually covered the entire front page like a glossy paint.

He grinned, viciously wide, seemingly in response to the tremble in Jaimie's bottom lip.

Like the man on the subway.

She found the strength to tear her feet from the carpeted floor and headed for the doors, feeling two vicious eyes boring holes in her back. Before finally escaping through the exits, she willed herself to look back one last time, to convince herself that the eerie image was indeed real and not dreamed up within her imagination. The student was still there, shorn head reflecting shinily beneath the dusty neon lights—just as she had seen him seconds earlier.

However, to her surprise—and relief as well—his stare had not followed her. Instead, he remained in the same seated position, camouflaged eyes watching the spot she had just vacated. Apparently he hadn't been looking at her.

So who was he staring at?

Following his gaze, Jaimie beheld a familiar sight.

Another male student sat amid a circle of empty seats, pinned by the glimpse of the bald student. A freshman by the looks of him, his exam lay folded neatly on the desk in front of him. He wore a sweater, jeans, and had a pair of Walkman headphones wrapped around his neck. Undoubtedly unaware of his surroundings, he returned the catatonic gaze, eyes glossed with moisture.

Shivering at the familiar yet unusually eerie

sight, Jaimie finally fled the confines of the lecture hall.

A wash of neon fell upon her eyes, the brighter lights temporarily blinding her. Squinting, she hurried down the hall, around the corner to a small student lounge where she had plans to meet Tracy Shueler and Barbara Hall. Arriving there, she leaned against the back of a chair, breathing heavily, watching over her shoulder just in case . . .

A hand gripped her elbow from her other side.

Jaimie leaped, yanking her arm away with a gasp. She spun, backpedaling.

"Whoa," Tracy said, raising her hands defensively. The black sweater she wore hung on her skinny frame like a loose curtain on a rod. "You a little tensed up today?"

Jaimie relaxed her shoulders, clearing her face of a wave of hair that escaped her scrunchie. She loosened her knapsack, placed it on the orange vinyl couch next to them and sat on the armrest. "You scared the shit outta me," she said, blowing out a lungful of air.

Tracy smiled, however weakly, placing the black canvas bookbag she carried next to Jaimie's knapsack on the couch. A tear in the tough fabric separated them. "Didn't mean to set a fire under your feet," she offered, laughing lightly.

"Hey, guys."

Jaimie looked up and saw Barbara approaching. She wore a pair of worn jeans not unlike the ones Jaimie had on, and a green turtleneck. Her long blond hair sent spiral curls wriggling down her shoulders like a cluster of tentacles. She threw herself on the couch behind Jaimie, arms stretched out as if she'd just crossed the finish line in a marathon. "I just spent the last two hours in behavioral psych watching Tom Parello's muscles bulge beneath his shirt. I'll never learn a damn thing if he keeps showing up for class."

"I thought you had the hots for Dom Celso, the guy from Humanities Two?"

"Oh, I still do."

"So who's gonna win the trophy, Dom or Tom?" Tracy asked, smiling.

"Both, if I can help it."

"And some other guido she hasn't met yet," Jaimie threw in.

Giggling, Tracy stepped around Jaimie, sat next to Barbara on the couch. The vinyl squeaked beneath her jeans. "Not to fear . . . Babs'll keep us up to date with all the Italian scuttlebutt. No dark-haired beauty's ever gonna get by without us getting a report, right?"

Barbara said, "Speaking of hair, some guy in my psych class—he was actually kinda cute . . ."

Tracy rolled her eyes and Jaimie smiled.

". . . but he went and shaved his head. Bald and shiny like a cue ball."

The smile left Jaimie's face and she leaned forward. "Barbara, you serious?" Suddenly a part of the conversation, she wanted to hear more.

Barbara smirked and twisted her head slightly, raising an eyebrow. "Yeah . . . why? You know something about him?"

"No . . . I . . ." She placed a hand to her forehead, instantly embarrassed by her outburst. "I'm sorry, I'm feeling a little spent from the exam," she said. Spooked by today's events, she felt she'd be better off not mentioning anything about it in an effort to distract herself from what was probably nothing at all.

"You're not bailing out on us tonight, are you? Happy hour at Danford's, Jame! Men everywhere!"

She smiled. It would do her good to get out as she had planned. Her day had taken a turn for the worse and she probably needed a few drinks, a few laughs. That would certainly steer her toward a more enjoyable evening.

"No, of course not," she said, forcing a smile. "I've been looking forward to this all week."

The girls stood up, stretched, all of them smoothing out their clothes at the same time.

"Shall we?" Tracy asked, grabbing her bag and leading the way, Barbara and Jaimie following in her footsteps.

"By the way, how'd you do on your test?" Barbara asked.

"I'm not sure," Jaimie answered, wanting so badly to ask Barbara if the bald guy in her class wore sunglasses. Instead she glanced behind her, watching students come and go along the hallway, of keeping a wary lookout for bald men.

Chapter Ten

"Nice neighborhood," Detective Ernie Barba said.

Frank and Barba unlatched their seat belts as Hector skillfully parked the squad car alongside a fire hydrant between a black Acura and a green Accord, near the corner of Fifty-seventh and Park Avenue—just down the street from the house where the Racines lived.

The neighborhood, on the Upper East Side, undoubtedly bragged of residents who were upper echelon types. Doctors, lawyers, celebrities, none of whom made less than a half-million a year. All big shots who shelled out the bucks to live in three-story private houses with grandiose architecture, fireplaces and no fewer than three bathrooms.

"Where do you live, Ernie?" Frank asked as he slid out of the car.

Barba got out on the right passenger side, shut the door and stepped around the back to catch up with the senior officers. "My wife and I just bought a home on Long Island. Melville. Used to live in Forest Hills, but the apartment got a little cramped when we had our daughter."

Frank remembered when he and Diane bought their first home, also on Long Island, in Plainview. They ended up lasting about three years there, the two of them sharing the long list of duties that came along with owning a house. Yard work, cleaning, shopping, maintenance, the list was endless. And although the two of them had sufficiently fulfilled their responsibilities, Diane's efforts were grudgingly done in haste. Soon her complaints escalated relentlessly. She was tired of the housework and the food shopping and the commute to her job in Manhattan. Eventually, after months of pleading, she insisted they move into the city.

Frank hadn't wanted to raise Jaimie—who was only an infant at the time—in Manhattan, and he had been vehement against moving. Quite familiar with the New York City public school system, with the arrests and the drugs and the crimes that popped up all too often even in the elementary schools, he didn't feel her chances for an education there—much less her safety—were equal to those in Nassau County. Stuck between a rock and a hard place, he didn't know how to please

Diane—whose arguments, although cutting, were justifiable and attractive—other than to simply give in.

So he did just that, and they moved to the Upper West Side into a town house apartment where the maintenance was virtually nil, a cleaning lady could be hired for thirty bucks a week and the groceries could be delivered. Additionally, without the commute, Diane had three extra hours a day at home raising Jaimie, whom they eventually enrolled in a private school.

After many initial arguments, life in the city ended up suiting them just fine, until their separation years later.

"Nice area," Frank said as they walked briskly along the sidewalk.

The sun had taken refuge far behind the skyline, veiling everything in dusk. Just as Frank realized how quickly the day had turned to night, the sodium-vapor streetlights lining the sidewalk came on, lending illumination to the growing darkness. A young couple approached from the opposite direction, snuggling arm in arm, both wearing leather jackets and jeans. Frank felt a chill and shivered as they passed. It seemed the evening brought along some cold weather with it.

"You know the area?" Ernie asked.

"Sure, used to live in Plainview—years ago."

"Too bad. We could've been neighbors." A short plume of cool breath spewed from his smile.

Ernie Barba reminded Frank of himself when he was that age—nice Italian kid, wife, house, kid. The young cop seemed to have a promising life ahead of him. Hopefully none of those years would be spent alone, like Frank's last five had been.

Well, Frank thought, *as long as he doesn't suffer the same problem I do: His wife won't leave.*

Frank thanked God every day that he still had Jaimie living with him, and although he didn't see her very often, her company brought a smile to his face, reminding him that someone in this world still loved him. He would have gone nuts a long time ago if she hadn't been around.

The three of them continued their pace along the sidewalk, passing iron fences and gates riddled with ivy. Halfway up the block, Hector slowed, then stopped in front of a home with a brass *456* attached to the eave above the doorway.

"This is it," he said. He reached through the gate bars and pressed a button on a metal box attached to a post just within reach.

A tinny, somber voice returned. "Yes?"

"Captain Rodriguez, NYPD."

The gate buzzed, allowing them entrance to the steps leading to the door.

Leonard Racine appeared at the threshold. He wore a pair of khakis and a long-sleeved sweatshirt, both of which looked as if they had been slept in. Red streaks laced the whites of his eyes like tiny tree branches, and his light brown hair had messy tufts jutting out at odd angles. No doubt he'd spent the last twelve hours running his hands through it in frustration.

"Mr. Racine?" Hector said, climbing the steps. "I'm Captain Hector Rodriguez from the Thirteenth Precinct. These are Detectives Ballaro and Barba." They exchanged handshakes and entered the house.

The three of them were led down a hall past the living room, into the dining room. Frank took notice of the oak table, the Louis XIV chairs, the cut-glass chandelier. The Racines were collectors of antiques, it seemed. Expensive ones too, and Frank was immediately impressed. They sat, Leonard Racine at the head of the table, Frank and Hector facing Ernie.

"Can I get you gentlemen anything to drink?" Mrs. Racine walked in, a handkerchief knotted in her hands. She too looked disheveled, as though she had been wrestling on the floor with her husband. Judging by the fine decor and cleanliness of the place, the two of them hadn't looked this unkempt in years.

"This is my wife, Amanda," Leonard said, barely looking up from the polished grain in the table. Everyone nodded, pleasantries were exchanged, but nobody offered a handshake—Amanda Racine included. This wasn't a welcoming situation, only painful, and amiable congenialities became unnecessary. The three men kindly declined her offer of a drink and she sat down opposite her husband at the other end of the table.

"Mr. and Mrs. Racine," Hector said, "we'll try our best to make this as short and as painless as possible, but please let me make this understood.

We need your utmost cooperation if we are to find your son's killer."

"Yes, of course."

Amanda nodded weakly, dabbing the handkerchief at her nose.

Barba placed a microcassette recorder on the table and pressed RECORD.

Hector stated, "For the record, let this be known: Friday, October Twenty-first. Time, seven-fifteen P.M."

Frank took a small notepad from his jacket pocket, prepared to record his observations.

"Mr. Racine, your son was how old?"

"Nineteen."

"Did he have any enemies?"

"No, no. He was a good kid, never had any trouble with anyone."

"Friends?"

"Some, but not many. Seemed to get along with them fine."

"Had he any other kind of trouble that you know of? With the law, school or someone else?"

"No, of course not."

"Definitely not," Amanda Racine added, shaking her head.

"He work?"

"Part-time, two days a week in the Garment Center as an assistant designer. He just started bartending on weekends maybe three weeks ago."

"Where'd he tend bar?"

"Honestly, I don't even know. I never asked. He just said he was tending bar, and I really didn't think anything further of it. I assumed it was at one of the college places he hung out at with his friends. He had talked about doing it so he could see his friends and still make a buck. As I said, he only started three weeks ago." Leonard stood up, pulled a napkin from the baker's rack in the kitchen, and wiped his forehead. "Obviously now I wish I knew. You think it could have been someone from the place he worked?"

"Maybe. Maybe not." Hector leaned over to Frank. "You thinking the same thing I am?"

Frank scribbled on the paper: *Designer + Bartender=Gay?* Hector's theory suddenly came back to him, that the two boys indeed might have been having a homosexual rendezvous in the alley when the bald guy attacked them. Perhaps the bald guy was gay himself and attacked the boys in a jealous frenzy. Or just the opposite: he could be a gay basher.

Hector pulled back from Frank, rubbed his chin. "Mr. and Mrs. Racine, was your son gay?"

Both their mouths dropped open, either because they were surprised or appalled. Regardless, their shock was evident in their faces.

Mrs. Racine spoke first, her mouth trembling at the effort. "Do you know something about our son that we don't?"

"Right now we don't know much of anything. That's why we're here."

She nodded, looking at her husband, who sat back and shook his head.

"Yes, of course," Leonard said. "No, our son is not gay."

"Girlfriend?"

"Not at the moment, that we knew of."

Hector said, "If you'll both pardon my saying so, it seems that you aren't up on a good deal of his personal life."

Leonard blew out a breath, lines of guilt furrowing his brow. "My wife and I have been very busy. I'm a broker; Amanda's an antiques dealer. I've been spending a lot of hours at the office of late, and Amanda travels quite a bit with her job. So to answer your question straightforwardly, no, we haven't spent as much time as we would've liked to with Patrick. But to be frank, I'm not sure he had much time for us either. Between school and work, he was as busy as we were."

Gesturing at all the expensive furniture, Hector said, "It doesn't appear that Patrick really needed to work two jobs."

Amanda replied, "We made a deal with him: We would pay for school, but he had to earn his spending money. Leonard and I agreed that we didn't want him becoming too dependent on us."

Hector nodded, as did Frank. They understood. The Racines were honest, hardworking people who, although quite well off, never spoiled their son.

"Does Patrick have any siblings?"

They both shook their heads. "He was an only child."

A tremendous darting pain ran through Frank's body, a burning sensation that felt as if a hole had been seared right through his chest to the center of his heart. He had forgotten that they

113

were talking about the sudden death of this family's child. The harsh reality of it struck him like a boxer's unexpected blow to the midsection as he became aware that Patrick had been their only child.

As Jaimie was his.

God forbid. If he ever lost Jaimie to something as tragic as this, the devastation would be unfathomable, incalculable, nightmarish. Without doubt he knew he would never be able to live through a single minute in such dire agony. His body would collapse in shock. He was amazed by the fortitude the Racines had, to be able to sit here and converse about this tragedy less than a day after it happened.

Suddenly, and unexpectedly, he felt a slight twinge of anger rise up in his blood, as if something had indeed happened to his daughter. It was Frank's irrational side starting to swell up from within. He took deep, careful breaths, quietly calming himself, finding the willpower to suppress the outrage, the fear. Thankfully, his inquisitive detective self had resumed control, had become the stronger identity of the moment. No battle would be waged—for now.

"Do you know where Patrick might have gone last night?" Hector asked.

They both shook their heads. "We were out to dinner with clients of mine," Leonard said.

"Working, maybe? At the bar?"

Leonard shrugged. "I don't think he had class until later on Fridays. So sure, he could have worked. But he also could have gone out."

"Did either of you notice any strange behavior of late? Him becoming reclusive, withdrawn?"

"No," Leonard answered.

"No, you didn't notice, or no he hadn't changed?"

"No, he was fine," Amanda offered. "As a matter of fact he was spending more time out. I assumed he was either working or studying at the library."

"When was the last time either of you spoke to him?"

Amanda and Leonard traded glances with one another, and it appeared to Frank that they were both trying to figure out exactly when they *had* last spoken to their son. Leonard said to her, "You saw him on Monday, right? Remember? You told me he came home late from the library, looked like hell. You said his eyes were all watery and bloodshot."

"So it was Monday night, then? Three nights ago."

"Yes," they both said in unison. Amanda suddenly asked to be excused, stood and shuffled off to the kitchen. They heard her run the water and then blow her nose. She returned with four glasses and a pitcher of ice water. Frank helped himself, as did Hector. Barba remained stoic and silent, watching the counter on the tape recorder.

"Did your son use drugs?" Hector rubbed his thumb in the condensation forming on his glass of water.

Again the Racines looked shocked. "No," Leonard responded.

115

"Are you positive?"

Leonard leaned back in his chair. His face went red and he looked across at his wife, who dabbed at her eyes again.

"I won't say for sure that Pat hadn't experimented socially, simply because I'm aware that most kids do it nowadays. Pot, some coke maybe, although I doubt Pat did anything more than puff on a joint."

"You said his eyes were bloodshot and watery. Sounds like drug use, no?"

Leonard clenched his fists. "Captain Rodriguez, my son was not a druggie. If my wife believes he was just tired, then he was just tired. Nothing else."

"Mr. Racine, please, I only ask for investigatory purposes. We're simply looking to rule out certain possibilities, one being that his murder could be drug-related."

Racine nodded, frustration clearly eating him alive. "I understand. But you also need to be patient with us. This has been a very difficult day."

"Of course." Hector moved right on to the next question. "Had he made any new friends that you know of? Any phone calls, from someone unfamiliar?"

Leonard shrugged again.

"As a matter of fact . . ." Amanda said, "I remember receiving a phone call from someone who asked for Pat, about a week ago. I told him that he was at school. I took a message and left it on the message board by the phone."

She pointed toward the kitchen. Adhered to

the wall alongside the phone was a rectangular cork board with a number of messages pinned to it. Frank rose from his chair and examined them more closely. Three messages; two for Amanda, one for Leonard, each signed by someone named Emily.

"Do you remember the caller's name, Mrs. Racine?" Hector asked.

"No," she said, shaking her head apologetically.

"Where's the note? Could it still be around?" Frank asked.

"Patrick probably took it. Could be in his room."

Frank raised an eyebrow at Hector. He couldn't help but notice the dark half-moons forming below the captain's eyes. He looked real tired.

"We'd like to take a look in his room. Is that okay?"

Leonard rose shakily from his seat. "Sure, fine. Hon?"

"Yes, of course."

The five of them rose from the table. While Amanda cleaned up, Leonard led Frank, Hector and Ernie down a hallway lined with Victorian art prints. Frank quickly admired the prints, each exquisitely displayed in finely carved oak frames, each one different from the next but all similar in size and design, as if exhibited as part of an artist's collection.

They stopped at the second door on the right, Patrick Racine's room. Frank noticed at once that

117

the room had been kept as meticulously as the rest of the house; the bed neatly made; furniture dusted; rug vacuumed. A desk sat beneath the room's only window, and a bookshelf ran the length of the right wall. It held a variety of Patrick's things: a few textbooks, novels, a CD player and plenty of CDs.

Frank walked over and fingered through some of the CDs. He saw the names of what he assumed to be bands, ones he had never heard of before: System 7, The Orb, Eat Static, Andromeda. Further on, Plastickman, Carrier Waves, Abduction. *Of course* he had never heard of them before. This collection of CDs represented a teenager's taste in cutting-edge music, nothing like the oldies he himself enjoyed so much. He looked further. At the end of the shelf were some CDs, titled *Techno Explosion*, *Ambient Space* and *Alpha Waves*, all claiming to be compilations of various bands. Thinking back, Frank had heard Jaimie use the term *techno* at times when he begged her to turn down the volume on her stereo. Yes, she herself listened to this "music" sometimes, though to Frank it sounded like repetitive nonsense, as if a needle was skipping on a record.

Seemed Patrick Racine was quite the techno music enthusiast.

Frank turned and looked at the desk. A computer and printer took up half the desktop, with papers cluttering the rest of the work area. He went over and flipped through a few sheets of paper but found only class notes.

"Mr. Racine," Hector said, "do you have a maid?"

"Yes. Emily. She cleans every day between three and five, usually before we arrive home."

"When was the last time you spoke to her?"

"I rarely do. My wife speaks to her a couple of times a week." He leaned out into the hallway. "Hon?"

Footsteps sounded and Amanda appeared in the threshold. She looked worse than she had when they first arrived, tears streaming down her face.

"Mrs. Racine, can you remember the last time you spoke to your maid?"

"On Tuesday. I paid her."

"Did she mention anything about Patrick's room? Anything even slightly out of the ordinary?"

Amanda tilted her head in thought. Frank imagined that it must be difficult for her to capture memories when so much chaos stormed inside her head. "She did say that Pat's room had been cleaned. That the bed had been made. But that wasn't unusual. Sometimes he would help her out, 'do a few things to make her job a little easier' he would say. I used to tell him that she got paid for what she did, but he felt sorry for her. I just assumed he cleaned his own room. He'd done it before."

"Is it possible your son hadn't been home since the last time Emily cleaned his room?"

Again, looks of amazement crossed their faces. "At this point, anything is possible." She buried her face in her hands and rubbed her eyes.

Frank, still standing over the desk, opened the top drawer.

His heart started to pound. Hard.

It was there.

A note to Patrick, signed 'Mom.'

Harold called. He'll call back.

Frank picked it up, showed it to Hector. Ernie glimpsed it too.

They all nodded to one another.

Time to pay Harold Gross a visit.

Chapter Eleven

Run, run, need to run . . .

David Traynor decided today, unequivocally, he needed to run. Never in his nineteen years had he felt a comparable desire to move his legs in such a rapid fashion. To take deep regulated breaths, to watch intently as frozen breath puffed from his mouth. The thrill of it captivated his being, clenched all his thoughts and commanded his motivation.

He *needed* to run; at the moment nothing else existed in life but to do just that.

Run.

Why had he become so absorbed with this desire to run? He knew that answer—logical explanation, no doubt—had to exist somewhere deep within him. But he also knew that his need for a reason had become overshadowed by the yearning to satisfy the urge. That the answer was secondary to his immediate desire.

As long as he ran.

Run, run, need to run . . .

Suddenly, after nearly two hours of pushing his body, after coercing it to withstand such intemperate discipline, another question slithered forth from deep within his consciousness.

Where?

Where had he been going all this time? For two hours his legs demanded he run—although now he could manage not much more than a labored jog. Now the answer to *where* seemed all the more timely and pertinent.

He needed a place to go.

Where do I live?

As he searched his memory for a location, the walls inside his head collapsed for a fleeting moment. Suddenly a new sensation came into play: fear. The fear of being lost in a world with no place to go, with no one to help. The fear of being completely out of control, guided by an unseen force so powerful that visions of the world coming to a disastrous and painful end seemed quite viable.

As quickly as it had collapsed, it once again assumed control.

And again David Traynor wanted to run.

But during the shockingly brief interlude in which David had been free of the bond that held him captive, a multitude of memories stormed within his head. Who he was, where he lived, his age, his likes and dislikes, the music he listened to. Simple things about himself that he once again no longer possessed the ability to grasp. They had all been there for a moment. Inside his head. For him to realize, to feel.

He set his mind to thinking. Prior to the brief moments of coherence, he had asked himself a question.

Where do I live?

Now, because his mind had allowed a pinhole opening into his consciousness, he had the answer.

He gazed about his surroundings. Dark monolithic buildings surrounded him, shadowy streets intersecting at all sides, grainy pavement greeting his footsteps, invisibly escorting him toward his new destination.

Home.

Street signs marked his location, useful only to the mind held captive deep within his head. The portion of his mind now controlling him carried only those thoughts necessary for the task at hand, and brought forth direction—a mental map leading the way home.

So his feet again carried him, weaving him haphazardly through the darkened neighborhood, in and out of deserted streets and unlit alleys, through empty courtyards, in between parked cars, avoiding sight by those few pedestrians milling about beneath the moon's beams.

Familiar sights soon came into view. The evacuated lot where an abandoned tenement building had been torn down; the elevated platform where he sometimes caught the train; and, oh yes, his building.

Home.

Dragging his feet in exhaustion, he entered through the front doors of the building, climbed one, two, three flights of stairs, tripping along the way, hands grasping blindly at the graffiti-marred walls, his breathing loud in its weariness. Shuttered doors lined the hallway, but only one ignited his memory, as if an entity perched just beyond its threshold, emitting waves of psychic thought in an attempt to lure him in. He stopped in front of the door, staring at the steel barrier, the rusted *3F,* trying to convince his mind to formulate his next strategy.

Keys.

The voice, although not his, came from within. Wishing to unfold the mystery, knowing very well that he had no alternative but to obey the command, he allowed his mind, the voice, to lead the way.

He blindly fished for the keys in his jeans pocket, pulled them out and entered the apartment.

Although he knew that this was indeed his home—his mind told him so—nothing here triggered any memories of the past. Four walls, sheathed in dust, paint chipped and faded; worn furniture, drawers pulled out, wrinkled clothes escaping from within; piles of magazines, the girlie kind, many of their pages torn out and left astray. And music tapes, scattered all over, their protective covers long lost to the litter demons on the floor.

He moved forward, wearied feet pushing through the clutter. He sat on the bare mattress, its bulk set crookedly on a metal bed frame. He ran his shaky, sweaty fingers along the headphones cradled around his neck, feeling the plastic curvature, the soft ear pads, the wire leading down, down, down, across the hard plastic features of the Walkman tape player clipped to his belt. He fingered the buttons, the volume dial, the clear plastic window displaying the tape beneath.

He put on the headphones.

Music boomed forth, a relentless, hypnotic pulse of synthetic tones.

Suddenly, his mind allowed another remembrance, of something else . . .

Excitement.

Yes! He remembered! His purpose. With the aid of the music, his mind revealed a purpose for his actions.

He had been asked to supply.

Moving his hand from the Walkman to his jacket pocket, he felt for the object. His fingers touched its smoothness, ran fluidly about the six circular spines jutting from its surface, about the slopes at their base, within the hollowed-out crevices at their pinnacles. He felt a warmth emanating from its infrastructure, from its *body*. It kissed his fingertips, tiny tingles slowly wandering the length of his fingers like a swarm of gentle electric charges.

How he knew that this object had been meant

for him, he could not fathom. But the moment the Harbinger on the subway graced him with its presence, its *existence*, he knew he had to become one with it.

He knew at that moment, somehow, that he was to supply.

He pulled it from his pocket.

Beautiful. Its ebony, shining brilliance emitted an unsullied blend of emotions, a perfect intermingling of love, hate, sex, death, anger and ecstasy. It was . . . sacrosanct.

It was the Atmosphere.

He ran his thumb along the perimeter of the base. At his gentle touch, vivid colors appeared on the black veneer like a deep swirling oil slick shimmering on the surface of nighttime water. Instantly, his eyes turned up in his skull, his teeth clenched, and a series of remarkably vivid visions paralyzed him into a state of utter delight. Colorful leaves in sudden death, falling from a great tree, entombing him in their gentle embrace. A spray of mist, a million beads in a spectrum of hues, bonding into a striking, penetrating whole, washing over him in a shower of euphoria. A great night sky, billions of faraway stars twinkling, gossamer strings of lights tethering them together into a phenomenal latticed web.

He rubbed the piece harder. Friction gloved his fingers, then his hands and wrists. The object suddenly felt spongy, its marblelike exterior yielding as if it had been transformed into an amorphous, moving skin. The softness returned his embrace with a million gentle pinpricks of energy, each and every one a single entity in itself, abandoning its ebony domain and entering the world of his body and soul.

It felt good. It made his penis hard.

A bell sounded.

He dropped the object. It hit the floor with a thud and came to rest, nestled in a dirty shirt.

Ring.

His eyes slowly rolled from within the recesses of his skull, his jaw untensed, relaxing itself. His euphoria dissipated. Through blurred eyesight and muffled hearing, he sought the source of the bell.

Ring.

It came from inside the room—his unfamiliar home—straight ahead. He rose from the bed, ignoring the dropped object, and walked slowly, warily, toward the sound.

Ring.

Pushing aside a pile of porno magazines, a dirty T-shirt, a pair of shorts, he found it. Although the object seemed as unfamiliar as everything else in the room, his mind directed him to act in a correct and proper fashion.

Ring.

He picked up the scoop-shaped part, removed his headphones and placed it to his ear.

A voice—the voice that was in his head—emerged from the object.

"Supplier?"

His heart pounded ferociously. He hesitated, then said, "Yes."

"I am Harold. Your Harbinger."

*   *   *

Harold Gross stood at the corner of 189th Street and Wilson Avenue, his gaze, hidden behind sunglasses, aimed three floors up the side of the shadowy tenement building, watching the lamplit window of the room that the current Supplier now occupied. His left hand squeezed the filthy telephone receiver, pressing it sharply against his ear; his other hand restlessly sought balance against the free-standing phone post. Activity brought stimulus, which brought a somewhat pleasurable yet unpredictable skewing of his equilibrium, and he had to keep in control of himself at all times, reserved, discreet and most assuredly secure.

He soon heard the pulse emanating from the phone, a signal that the Supplier had finally discovered his purpose, and the rhythm of the Atmosphere. The time was right, and Harold could now prepare for harvesting.

This would be his fifth.

He could hear, no, *feel* the new Supplier's steady breathing—rhythmic, pulsing, charmed—and he knew for certain that the time had come for the process to begin. He smiled inside, knowing that he had done quite well with this selection; there didn't appear to be any resistance.

So far.

"*Yes,*" the Supplier answered.

"I am your Harbinger," he repeated. His heart slammed in his chest. He could only fantasize the pleasure the Supplier must be feeling in this moment of discovery.

"Yes, I know."

"Do you have the object?"

There was a brief interlude in which the Supplier's breathing faded. A slight shuffling sounded. In a moment's time, the breathing returned, but no voice spoke.

Harold asked again, "Do you have the object?"

"Yes, now I do. And it feels so . . ." The Supplier's breathing rose to a sharp, staggering hum. A scraping noise sounded, and it appeared to Harold that the Supplier was having trouble gripping the phone.

The process. Yes, indeed, it was starting.

"Stay where you are!" Harold found himself yelling, adrenaline racing through his body, excitement through his veins. "I'll be with you shortly," he said, trying to make it sound as if he *needed* to be there.

One particularly crucial piece of information the Giver had injected into Harold's consciousness was that he should never under any circumstances interfere with the filling process, that he should wait until it had run its course completely before he went in to harvest the Atmosphere. From the very beginning, when he had been retained to harvest, this message, sharp and clear, floated on the surface of his mind like a beacon drifting in the night sea—an ongoing warning against any form of interruption. But the fervor of watching, of experiencing the very act of supplying firsthand, thrilled him to a point surpassed only by the Suppliers themselves, culminating in a craving so strong that turning away had become virtually unthinkable.

Little had he known at the time—when he allowed himself to behold the process—of the risk involved, even if he heeded the Giver's warning. Yes, the experience of witnessing the process in the alley last night had been extremely rapturous, but in making himself a spectator, he nearly revealed everything and jeopardized his privileged status as a Harbinger.

The two boys had been easy catches; most anyone in the club would have been, well attracted to the pulse. This had made his selection simple and uncomplicated.

The hard part had been keeping away. Once he released the Atmosphere into their possession, he immediately felt the allure, so intrigued that he had no alternative but to witness the act of supplying for himself.

Ten days ago, while harvesting his first Supplier, he had behaved much as was expected of him: responsibly, with discipline. He'd allowed the process to unfold naturally, just as the Giver demanded he do. As a result, everything had worked out beautifully. But the charge of ecstasy he felt following the filling process—when he retrieved the Atmosphere—caused a conflict of interests in seeking new Suppliers. He suddenly found himself in a bind, and eventually with no alternative but to answer his own selfish desires, to press past the Giver's requirements and become part of the process.

He knew that he had done something wrong

by allowing himself access to the alley when the two began to supply. Although their concentration had been wholly centered on the pulse, his presence distracted their focus, and they periodically broke the rhythm. In minutes, the two started to fight one another for sole possession of the Atmosphere. He interceded in an attempt to restore equilibrium, but that further disrupted everything, and one of the Suppliers escaped, racing from the alley.

In a vain effort to salvage as much of the filling as he could, Harold reinstated the Atmosphere in the hold of the remaining Supplier and waited until the process had finished. Thankfully the Outsiders stumbled onto the scene only after all was said and done—albeit just moments after. His only problem at that point was retrieving the Atmosphere, which had turned out to be a rash but necessary move.

He couldn't fathom the punishment the Giver would have given him had the Outsiders taken hold of the glorious Atmosphere.

His dreams of supplying would never come to pass.

Of course, immediately following the near disaster, he understood why he should have kept the two boys under wraps, led them to supply behind closed doors. He hated himself for giving into his urge to witness, leaving them susceptible to discovery.

He promised himself that he would not make the same mistake again.

That all seemed so long ago now.

Easier promised than done.

As soon as he heard the pulse on the phone in combination with the rapturous breathing of the new Supplier, he knew keeping himself out of the picture would be impossible. He needed to witness, needed to supply for himself.

He couldn't live without it.

"Supplier?" he said into the phone.

The breathing was still there, but no reply came. The Atmosphere's pulse was growing stronger. He could feel it emanating, filling the room.

It sounded *awesome.*

"Supplier . . . wait for me. I am coming to be with you."

At that tense moment, the breathing stopped. Then the pulse faded.

Something was wrong.

Harold dropped the phone and ran toward the building.

David Traynor dropped the phone at the second mention of the Harbinger coming to join him in his ecstasy. As far as he was concerned, no possibility existed for him to share the Atmosphere with anyone, his mind screaming *no, no, no!* over and over. And he listened to it, just as he did when it insisted he run, just as he did when it led him to this building, made him open the door and perform every move that carried him to this very moment.

Now it insisted he leave, again run far away to another place where he could be alone to relish in the pleasures of the Atmosphere, answer its inducement. He exited the apartment through the fire escape, down the side of the building, fleeing undetected from the advance of the Harbinger, into the night.

Run, run, need to run . . .

Harold repeatedly slammed his body against the door. A young black man peeked out from behind a chained door down the hall, barked a weak, meaningless threat but advanced no farther, undoubtedly unnerved by Harold's insane demeanor.

Waves of distress screamed inside his body, forcing sweat out of the pores in his brow, his chest, his back, soaking his shirt. The fear—the *knowing*—that the Supplier had just lammed—well, it simply murdered every inch of him, tormented him with a terrible anguish, as if a demon were inside his body maniacally rearranging his organs and veins.

He slammed harder against the door, clawed at its surface like a crazed cat trying to escape its travel cage. The door started to break free of the jamb. The metal hinges loosened; a screw popped free.

Pain screamed in his shoulders, and he hurled himself against the door in one last fit of rage. His urgency prevailed.

He broke through.

Oh, no . . .

The room was cold and empty and desolate. A breeze blew through its only window.

The Supplier was gone.

Chapter Twelve

Another fine parking job by Hector had the cruiser set between two cars, their makes unidentifiable under the hack-and-slash body work and paint jobs they had acquired over the years. The three detectives left the patrol car and paced up the sidewalk on Third Avenue, just south of East 108th Street in the Bronx.

The demographics of the two neighborhoods they'd visited that night couldn't have been more different. This part of town—although only five miles away, a thirty-minute drive in city traffic from where the Racines lived—might as well have been on the other side of the planet. Whereas the Upper East Side boasted town houses and classic architecture, doctors, lawyers and stockbrokers, the Bronx, famous for Yankee baseball and its zoo, exhibited cookie-cutter, low-income housing projects overcrowded with families dependent on welfare and other assistance, parents working menial jobs to put food in their childrens' mouths.

For a change, Frank's three personalities shared a common bond: he'd be much better off if he avoided visiting this neighborhood again, especially at night.

They turned the corner onto 108th Street, keeping their conversation to a minimum, leaning on intuition instead. Many animals lived in this jungle and would no doubt try to take a bite out of any adversary if the potential for a meal existed.

They kept on their toes—even though they carried weapons.

"Here, this is it," Hector said. Frank gazed at the small yet intimidating structure, trying to swallow his sudden uneasiness. His weak, reticent personality started to inch forward. Not many times in the past had he needed to probe such a residence in this type of neighborhood—one that was overcrowded, rundown and rampant with disease and crime. Now his emotions plagued him, and he felt that at any moment some maniac could very easily jump out of the shadows and blindside him, or knife him, or shoot him, or . . .

Perhaps he *was* getting too old for this shit.

Although no immediate cause for alarm existed, he placed his hand on his holstered gun as they approached the tenement, not sure which part of his personality—the meek tentative one, the truth-seeking detective or the hot-headed aggressor—was responsible for doing it.

They ambled quietly across the stretch of littered pavement that led to the building.

A pair of iron benches paint-marked as territory for some small-time gang served as a gateway to the tenement's entrance.

Frank peered up and sighted a row of destitute children gazing through a set of broken windows three floors up, their cold eyes seeking answers, like hungry wolves stalking prey in hope of one more night of survival. From the curious expressions on their dirty faces, he could tell that they were wondering why the three of them had arrived here tonight, had chosen to enter their home—even though the appearance of police officers in this community of distress was commonplace. He pulled his gaze away, and the three cops continued along the pavement into the ominous moon shadow of the building.

They set foot through the graffiti-embellished entrance. Their footsteps echoed in the hallway like drops of water in a cavern, the cadence of their strides periodically interrupted as their shoes sliced through garbage and grime. Frank shuddered, wondering how big the rats and cockroaches might be, hiding in the shadows nearby.

"Hey . . ." a voice shot out from the shadows, deep, raspy.

The three cops stopped, turned and saw a homeless man squatting on the floor in the front corner of the hall, knees pulled tightly into his chest.

"You be coming for the man in black?" he asked, eyes glowing in the shadows, wide and lolling. " 'Cause if you is, I gots to report it to the leader of the troops!"

Curious, Frank stepped forward. "The man in black? Who do you mean?"

The vagrant stood up awkwardly, nearly falling back down in the process. His clothes hung in tatters like strips of skinned animal flesh. "I don't know his name, but he's with *them*, and they's got to be stopped. That's what the leader says."

Frank smiled curtly. "Who is this leader?"

The man staggered toward the door. "Jyro! That's who. Now you jus' watch for the men in black. There's one here. They's the bad guys, working for them. The radio people."

Under normal circumstances Frank would have completely ignored the bum—he always insisted to Jaimie that she do the same—but now he felt compelled to listen, to try to pry out information. The bum looked crazy, but he also seemed to believe what he was saying.

"Who are the radio people?"

"You jus' go home and put on your radio. You'll know it when you hear 'em!"

Then the vagrant ran out of the building, trailing his odor behind.

Frank faced Hector and Ernie. "The men in black? Radio people? What do you think, gentlemen?"

"Just like the rest of them, Frank. Mentally ill."

"Them?" Frank asked, smiling. He had hoped to get a serious answer from Hector, but got

mostly what he expected—a shrug. He'd be best off doing the same thing right now. It wasn't time to play on gut instincts. They had other business to attend to.

They moved to the elevator, once again silent, the lack of conversation increasing Frank's discomfort. It was an . . . *apprehension* hanging in the air, and Frank could feel it. Judging from the uncertain looks on his companions' faces, Hector and Ernie did too.

I don't know his name, but he's with them. . . .

Suddenly Frank remembered something. When he'd first walked into the Thirteenth Precinct earlier that day. The one-eyed man sitting in the chair.

He's right, you know . . .

The aliens. They are here.

They. Them?

Frank shook off the insane thought.

The small elevator waited for them. They got inside and it began to rise, but a terrible image unnerved Frank: the elevator crashing down, leaving the three of them abandoned and helpless on the ground, the local scavengers helping themselves to their belongings.

"Frank?"

Frank shook the daymare away.

"You joining us?" Hector was smiling slightly, he and Barba standing on the landing at the sixth floor, waiting for Frank to emerge from the elevator.

Frank stepped out and joined the others.

"Still tired, Sleepy?"

"All right, Hect, cut me a break."

They walked the length of the empty hallway. A baby's incessant wails issued from an apartment toward the end of the hallway. A pair of Hispanic shouts did battle from behind the closed door of another. The violent pounding of rap music worked its way up from the floor below. A variety of odors commingled in the air, some from dinners, most from neglect and uncleanliness.

"How can anybody live in a place like this?" Frank wondered aloud.

"Poverty doesn't discriminate," Hector said firmly.

"No shit," Barba added, wiping his brow and looking around.

After passing five doors, Hector stopped. The door he stood in front of was unremarkable and gray, making it simply one in a long row of doors. Here we are, 6-J. Harold Gross's place."

Hector nodded. Barba knocked.

No answer.

He repeated. Again, no answer.

Frank instinctively reached for the knob and twisted it. The door clicked and swung open about two inches. "Uh-oh," Frank said quietly. "Didn't expect that."

He looked at Hector, who pinched his lips in thought, then whispered to Barba, "Ernie, what time was it when you called in for the warrant?"

"Seven forty-five, around there. They said it'd take an hour."

Hector glanced at his watch: 8:20. "Mark the

139

time in your minds gentlemen. Eight-fifty."

Nodding, gun now drawn, Frank gently placed a hand on the door and pushed. It slowly opened. If Gross was inside, he would know he had visitors.

Ernie entered first, gun stretched out in front of him. He spun from right to left. Frank immediately followed suit, racing in to the left, swinging his weapon, seeking even the slightest bit of movement. Hector immediately raced to the bathroom. He returned, shaking his head.

All was quiet at Harold's place.

The three men took a moment to catch their breaths, re-holstering their weapons, still glancing about alertly. Harold's apartment was in utter disarray, as if someone had burglarized the place, although the likeliness of that occuring—even with the open door—was minimal, as the lack of valuables here wouldn't so much as tempt even the most novice crook. No phone, no television, no radio, only worthless items: scattered articles of clothing, old magazines, newspapers, broken plates left out with food scraps from meals long eaten. A tattered couch, foam bursting through holes in the fabric like out-of-control fungi. A moldering rug, buckling under their feet, acting as a graveyard for cigarette butts. An age-old bar stool and a beverage crate, centering the room with no particular direction. Paint chips falling off the walls like a peeling sunburn.

"I'd rather be a guest at the Racines'," Frank said.

"No kidding." Barba removed his hat and

wiped his brow. It appeared their sudden entrance into the apartment had him a little shook up. He'll get over it, Frank thought.

"Well, we're here," Hector said, pacing around, shifting a pair of jeans on the floor with his shoe. "Let's see if we can find anything."

Never in his twenty-eight years had Harold Gross felt so lost, so out of control. He kept telling himself to get a grip on reality, but chaos stormed in his mind, and he kept slipping farther and farther away from sanity. With the Supplier and the Atmosphere now gone, he could no longer rely on the section of his mind that had mastered his actions so sufficiently over the past two weeks, that had guided his every step, his every move.

Yes, Harold Gross was indeed very lost.

Bursts of memories kept breaking through, thoroughly confusing him. He remembered so many things about himself that had been completely shuttered: that he had been abandoned as a child twenty years earlier, forced to live in foster homes. That he graduated to juvenile halls when he discovered that a quick buck could be earned by just taking it. He worked menial jobs, flipping patties at burger joints, washing dishes at diners, street cleaning. He spent a total of 256 days in jail, the rest on parole or under supervision. Arrested seventeen times—deserved many, many more. He'd dealt drugs, stolen, burglarized, mugged a few people.

But never had he *killed* anyone.

Or had he?

With holes in his mind now breaking open to accept waves of reason, he reflected back on his memories of the Atmosphere. It had felt so glorious, so incredibly satisfying to simply have it in his possession, and to share it with others—so long as they gave it back when they were through. It was as if he had been a chosen one, a unique individual to spread its glory to the world. And perhaps he had.

But for reasons he now understood to be malevolent.

He had been deceived.

Tears sprang from his eyes, of emotions forcing him to choose one of two different paths. He could seek out the lost Supplier and the Atmosphere, retrieve it and allow it to carry him back into the untruthful yet blindingly stimulating state of consciousness.

Or he could shed his skin of the unknown evil and begin his life anew.

That would be too damn hard.

This is what a junkie must feel like when he's aching for a fix. . . .

Harold looked up at the building in front of him. He'd been pacing the streets for an hour or more, trying to bring himself back to reality. He stepped forward, walking the littered pavement, kicking an empty beer can as he made his way to the entrance.

What better place to sit and make a decision?

Home.

* * *

Frank, Hector and Ernie spent thirty minutes picking through Harold Gross's meager belongings. Just as their first impressions had revealed, nothing of any monetary value seemed to exist here, only garbage. Newspapers, weeks old, yellowed and tattered. Magazines, stained and swollen to the size of the Verizon Yellow Pages. A small three-foot refrigerator, sitting crookedly below the apartment's only window, its paltry contents barely edible. Dirty clothing strewn about, not a drawer for them to rest in.

They did, however, find a few interesting things.

Hector showed Frank something he noticed when he first entered the bathroom. The sink. It held six inches of dirty water, clogged from an abundance of hair. On the floor to the left of the sink three disposable razors lay scattered like dead animals, their blades clogged with hunks of brown hair. Tiny droplets of blood dotted the edges of the white porcelain sink and the dirty mirror hanging on the wall.

"I figured he was just bald all the time. Naturally, you know?" Frank said.

Hector placed his hands on his hips. "Seems as though he likes to keep himself up to snuff as far as his head goes."

"Not much else, though. Guy's a damn slob."

"Captain?" Ernie called from the living room. "I found something."

Frank and Hector exited the bathroom. Ernie had moved the couch away from the wall and was hunkered down by a small rectangular hole in the wall. Beside him on the floor lay a metal vent that presumably had covered the hole at one point.

"I saw that the edges around the vent were a little worn, so I kinda played with it and it just fell out. Look at this." He aimed a penlight inside the hole.

Frank and Hector crouched down and looked inside.

"Holy moly . . ." Frank said, nearly speechless.

First they saw the money, a big pile of it wrapped with rubber bands. Hector gently removed the stack and thumbed through it. Ones, fives, tens, twenties, some crisp, some not, but a nice accumulation nonetheless.

"It's his goddamned life savings," Frank observed. "He's a miser."

"There's a brown paper bag in here too," Ernie said. "Captain?"

Hector nodded. "Please."

Ernie reached in and grabbed the bag. "Whatever's in it, it's light." He handed the bag to Hector.

Hector unfolded the top, peeked inside, then reached in and pulled out the contents. A pile of small papers appeared, some tumbling to the floor.

Frank picked one up. "This is a store receipt for jeans. There's a return tag attached to it."

"They're all store receipts. Clothes . . . music . . . electronics, and get this—almost everything here has been returned." Hector scratched at his mustache. "The Gap . . ."

"He has good taste," Frank said, thumbing through a few more.

". . . Fifth Avenue Electronics . . . Rock and Soul Music. He bought a hat at Jerry's Bargains and returned it a week later."

"Macy's. Bought and returned two shirts."

"Here's one without a return. A place called Village Clothing, on Union Street. Wow, big purchase. Listen to this. Three hundred sixteen dollars. Pants, leather jacket, gloves, sunglas—"

"Hect!" Frank dropped the receipts.

Hector looked at Frank momentarily, smiled. "—sunglasses, socks, shoes. This is our probable cause."

"The icing on the cake."

"Captain?"

"Yes, Ernie," Hector said, still looking down as he quickly fanned the remainder of the receipts.

"We've got company."

Hector and Frank looked up.

Still wearing the same black clothing from the alley, the leather jacket, the jeans, the sunglasses, Harold Gross stood in the doorway, looking at them.

Harold became immediately paralyzed at the sight of the Outsiders in his apartment. He tried to get himself to move but could only stand frozen like a mannequin, an intermingling of emotions—much different ones than those the Atmosphere conjured—thwarting his every effort: fear, indecision, confusion, anger, all integrated to form a single complex state of awareness, complicating the battle of thoughts inside his head.

As the three Outsiders stared at him, he offered a glare of his own, trying hard to decide exactly what he should do given the dire circumstances. He forced himself to dig down deep within his consciousness, try to come up with a solution to his inaction. But no thoughts came, and both parties remained in deadlock for what seemed an eternity, though perhaps only a few seconds passed.

Then suddenly, an answer came forth, not one from his own mind, but of another origin—a voice, the voice of the one and only entity that could indubitably provide him with a reliable answer. The only one he could trust at the moment.

The Giver.

It was as if the force field holding back his thoughts had vanished, releasing the solution to Harold's dilemma, loud and clear.

Kill yourself.

Frank, Hector and Ernie, now unexpectedly face to face with Harold Gross, couldn't decide what to do. The man was dangerous, unstable, probably armed, and needed to be handled like a crate filled with china: gently. Go easy at first, then throw the punches if need be. That would be the best course of action.

Hector dropped the receipts he held. The couch blocked a clear pathway toward Harold. He took one step to the right, in front of Frank and Ernie.

"Harold Gross?"

Harold immediately raced off down the hall. Ernie leapt over the couch, yelling "Freeze!" Frank ran past Hector, following him, Hector on his heels. Frank remembered the feeling of paralysis he'd experienced in the alley when he first encountered the mysterious bald man who had turned out to be Harold. He hadn't the energy or the gumption to pursue him through the fence. This time, he swore to himself he'd shoot him before he let him get away.

He only prayed that this time there wouldn't be any holes for Harold to escape into.

Once in the hall, Frank saw Harold racing past the elevators. Ernie was ten steps behind, keeping pace with him. At once Frank noticed the absence of an exit sign and turned quickly in mid-pace to see one over the security-barred window at the other end of the hall, half its face cracked and missing. "Are there any steps over there?" Frank yelled.

"I don't think so." Hector's words were nearly lost in his labored breaths.

With horror, Frank saw that Harold showed no intention of slowing. *Dear God.* "Ernie! Be careful!"

Ernie slid to the tiles when he realized what Harold was going to do. He covered his head with his arms, shielding himself from the inevitable.

Harold hurled his body into the window, shoulders first. Glass shattered everywhere, raining over Ernie, who crawled away from the bursting fragments.

But what Harold hadn't realized was that the windows were barred, and he slammed forcefully into them, jarring them a bit, but not enough to give him his freedom. He fell to the floor in a river of glass, his face—sunglasses now thrown askew—a sudden bloodied mask, jagged shards of glass sticking out from his cheeks and forehead. He staggered up, wobbling like a marionette, then screamed sheer lunacy, an animalistic howl, started pulling frantically at the bars, seeking escape as if his life depended it, banging his forehead against the top of the window frame, one, two, three, four times, over and over again. Blood flew from his wounds in an amazing spray.

Ernie scrambled up, gun pulled. "Freeze, motherfucker!"

Harold continued to yank on the bars, screaming, crying hysterically, tears lacing through the blood on his face in pink rivulets.

Frank, gun pulled, said, "What the fuck is he doing?"

Hector moved alongside him. "You've got three guns on you, asshole. Get away from the window."

Harold, still pulling, finally turned to face his pursuers. Tears and snot washed down his bloody face in a pathetic stream of agony. His eyes were two glassy black orbs. *"Please,"* he cried. *"Please kill me . . ."*

Finally, with Hector holding the gun on him, Frank and Ernie wrenched Harold away from the bars, tackled him to the glassy ground and cuffed him. Hector called for backup.

A squawk emanated from Ernie's radio. With one hand on the back of Harold's head, his knee in his back, Ernie answered the call.

"Captain?"

Hector faced him.

"The warrant. It was just issued."

Chapter Thirteen

Today's happy hour at Danford's was no different than it was all the other afternoons Jaimie joined her friends for what they termed a cleansing, which meant the washing away of the day's studies with a few cold beers. Of course none of the girls were of legal age to drink; many of the students here hadn't reached twenty-one. But somehow, the college hot spot always managed to get away with allowing a few university students in to release some pressure, as long as their drinking didn't get out of hand.

"If you smile at the bouncer, he'll let you in." This was Tracy Shueler's philosophy, which had always worked for her, although Jaimie would rarely try this on her own. She hardly felt comfortable riding Tracy and Barbara's coattails into the bar, which she found herself doing much too

GET UP TO
4 FREE BOOKS!

You can have the best fiction delivered to your door for less than what you'd pay in a bookstore or online—only $4.25 a book! Sign up for our book clubs today, and we'll send you **FREE* BOOKS** just for trying it out...**with no obligation to buy, ever!**

LEISURE HORROR BOOK CLUB

With more award-winning horror authors than any other publisher, it's easy to see why CNN.com says "Leisure Books has been leading the way in paperback horror novels." Your shipments will include authors such as RICHARD LAYMON, DOUGLAS CLEGG, JACK KETCHUM, MARY ANN MITCHELL, and many more.

LEISURE THRILLER BOOK CLUB

If you love fast-paced page-turners, you won't want to miss any of the books in Leisure's thriller line. Filled with gripping tension and edge-of-your-seat excitement, these titles feature everything from psychological suspense to legal thrillers to police procedurals and more!

As a book club member you also receive the following special benefits:

- **30% OFF all orders through our website & telecenter!**
- **Exclusive access to special discounts!**
- **Convenient home delivery and 10 days to return any books you don't want to keep.**

There is no minimum number of books to buy, and you may cancel membership at any time. See back to sign up!

*Please include $2.00 for shipping and handling.

YES! ☐

Sign me up for the Leisure Horror Book Club and send my TWO FREE BOOKS! If I choose to stay in the club, I will pay only $8.50* each month, a savings of $5.48!

YES! ☐

Sign me up for the Leisure Thriller Book Club and send my TWO FREE BOOKS! If I choose to stay in the club, I will pay only $8.50* each month, a savings of $5.48!

NAME: _____

ADDRESS: _____

_____

TELEPHONE: _____

E-MAIL: _____

☐ **I WANT TO PAY BY CREDIT CARD.**

☐ VISA   ☐ MasterCard   ☐ DISCOVER

ACCOUNT #: _____

EXPIRATION DATE: _____

SIGNATURE: _____

Send this card along with $2.00 shipping & handling for each club you wish to join, to:

Horror/Thriller Book Clubs
20 Academy Street
Norwalk, CT 06850-4032

Or fax (must include credit card information!) to: 610.995.9274. You can also sign up online at www.dorchesterpub.com.

*Plus $2.00 for shipping. Offer open to residents of the U.S. and Canada only. Canadian residents please call 1.800.481.9191 for pricing information.

If under 18, a parent or guardian must sign. Terms, prices and conditions subject to change. Subscription subject to acceptance. Dorchester Publishing reserves the right to reject any order or cancel any subscription.

JOIN NOW!

often lately. Her father would have a fit if he found out his daughter was using her good looks to get into a bar.

Sitting at a booth in the crowded pub, they shared large portions of buffalo chicken wings and french fries, washing the munchies down with light beers. Tracy and Barbara took turns commenting on a few of the guys strutting their stuff around, while Jaimie smiled along, pretending to agree with their commentary. Her taste was more for the smart-sexy type—tall, dark and lean, wearing glasses perhaps, and articulate—as opposed to the meaty, brainless, self-absorbed guys her girlfriends adored so much. These meatheads were a dime a dozen, right off the factory belt, and much too common for Jaimie's taste. Sometimes when they spewed their pickup lines at her, she would feel as if she needed a deep hole to hide in until they went away.

A guy holding a beer brushed by the booth, earring dangling from his lobe, his head mostly shaved, a farm of stubble texturing his dome. Although his eyes had not been shaded by sunglasses, Jaimie felt a surge of discomfort at the sight of him, and she shuddered at the spooky reminder of that afternoon.

"What's with all the guys shaving their heads nowadays?" Barbara wondered aloud, shoving a fry in her mouth. "They look ridiculous."

"Seems to be a new thing. I don't like it, though." Tracy motioned her hands in front of her as if she were giving someone a shampoo. "I like to run my hands through long, wavy locks."

The conversation prompted strong images of Jaimie's unusual experience, and she felt compelled to bring it up. "You know, I saw a couple of strange-looking bald guys today. One on the subway, one in class. They both had the same kind of clothes on, all black. Sunglasses too." She smiled in an effort to cover her discomfort, hoping that either Barbara or Tracy might have seen a similarly dressed guy and would comment.

Barbara wiped buffalo wing sauce from her mouth with a napkin. "Yeah, they're all over Greenwich Village. It's a gay thing, 'cause I can't see any girl in her right mind finding that attractive. They dress for each other, you know?"

Jaimie sipped her beer, at once wondering if she might have let her thoughts get carried away. Maybe it *was* a gay thing; she wasn't too familiar with much pertaining to that lifestyle. Perhaps both of the bald guys she saw today had behaved normally as far they'd been concerned, and were simply trying to attract other guys, as strange as it seemed. But then what was that odd black object the bald guy in the subway held in his hands? And why did the other guy steal it?

Like spectators at a zoo, a couple of guys wearing jeans and F.I.T. sweatshirts suddenly emerged from the crowd and approached the girls' table. Jaimie cupped her hands over her ears, attempting to tune them out, but still managed to hear them comment on how beautiful the three of them were. Each had enough muscles beneath their sweatshirts to blanket a ship's hull, but it didn't make up for the blank expressions on their faces, dumb, one-dimensional, a clear indication of limited intelligence. God rarely gave out equal amounts of brains and brawn.

This was an ideal time for Jaimie to excuse herself to the bathroom. The alcohol hadn't done a very good job of helping her forget the day's events—only in pressuring her bladder—and she wasn't in the mood to be social with these meatheads. Barbara and Tracy would just have to wrestle the pests on their own—which Jaimie knew would be quite fine with both of them.

Battling the crowd, she wended her way to the rear of the crowded bar. Upon her arrival at the rest rooms she found a line circling out from the ladies' room around the corner, reaching almost to the kitchen, at least fifteen girls waiting. It'd take a good half hour before she got in. She spun away in an angry huff and worked her way back through the crowd. From a distance she saw the two meatheads taking residence in the booth alongside Barbara and Tracy, each trying to swing their hooks around the girls' shoulders.

Returning to the booth, Jaimie retrieved her backpack from beneath the table. "Line's too long. I'm gonna use the bathroom at the math building, then probably go home."

"Jame," Barbara said, ignoring her comment, "this is Dan." Her cheeks glowed bright red, probably a combination of beer, hot chicken wings and the delight of her new company.

Dan smiled. He had blond hair and nice shoulders, but crooked teeth. *Meathead.*

"He was just telling us that an F.I.T. student was murdered last night."

Jaimie shivered as she shouldered her backpack, her fluster suddenly frozen. "My, God. Who?"

Dan shrugged but didn't say a word. Apparently his vocabulary was limited. He smiled again, showing those gnarly teeth, then redirected his efforts back to Barbara. Clearly Dan couldn't give a hoot about the dead kid. He wanted to get laid, and to Jaimie, his aspirations couldn't have been more visible. *Nice way to start a conversation, Dan.*

Barbara smiled. "He doesn't know. Just heard it himself."

"Well, I'm going home," Jaimie said. "If you find out anything, let me know." She received nods and good-byes from her friends, who seemed quite content with their new acquaintances. After a struggle through the crowd, Jaimie found the door and went outside.

It felt good to breathe in the cool night air, as if she were clearing out all the impurities inhaled in the smoky bar. She quickly paced back toward the campus. A hundred yards away, the Walton Math Building's lights glowed like beacons in the center of the ocean. The amber spray from the lampposts guided her along the campus walkway as she gathered a few thoughts about her father and what he had said to her earlier that afternoon.

A couple of kids were murdered, here in the neighborhood.

They were about your age.

She realized now how heedless her regard had been of his concerns, and she immediately felt waves of guilt. Why hadn't she taken him more seriously? Her father was the best, a wonderful human being whose primary concern was her well-being—even though he could be a pain in the neck every now and then. Why couldn't she have just listened to him earlier? It would have made her feel all the better now. She felt herself longing for him, for his nurturing, realizing how little she'd seen him lately, how little she really listened to him when they were together, promising herself she'd make an effort to spend more time with him soon.

Then she wondered: *could the murder Dan mentioned be the same one Dad told me about? No. It couldn't be. City's too big, too much going on at once.*

She tried real hard to clear the unpleasant thought from her mind, that a student from her school, someone she might have *known*, had been murdered in her neighborhood. Too close to home. She continued, slightly dazed, passing the stairway leading down to the Q train subway station, now halfway to the math building.

Suddenly, someone—a man, or so it appeared from this distance—emerged from the cover of trees at the darkened corner of the math building. Something seemed strange about him—the way he just appeared from the darkness, as if he had been hiding, the way he was walking, steadfast and strong, determined. She looked around; although a few people were walking about in the distance, she was closest to the stranger.

Again she glanced forward. He appeared to be a tall man, but she couldn't see much more, as the shadow of the building shrouded his features. She could see that he was pacing quickly toward her. She slowed, squinting to get a better look, taking each step slowly, tentatively.

He passed through the amber glow of a lamp-post.

The dull gleam reflected dully off his bald head. And his sunglasses.

The student from her classroom.

She stopped in her tracks, heart slamming in her chest. She took an indecisive step backward, not sure if she should just ignore him and pass him by, or walk in another direction.

He continued at a hurried pace, passing under another street lamp.

The image she beheld as the light from the second street lamp showered the stranger with its ghostly yellow glow could be described in a million different ways, but at this terrifying moment her mind could not calculate a single solitary word. The horror was too excessive to comprehend. Her jaw slackened, her eyes bulged in her skull, a sharp, fear-induced agony probed her brain: clear warning signs that screamed *get away!*

She knew at that very moment that she had no choice but to trust her eyes, to believe in the shocking reality of what she had just witnessed, to accept it as real and not an illusion, to obey her instincts. If she didn't, there would be no time to escape with her life.

The bald student was holding an odd object in both hands—like that of the man in the subway.

It, his hands and forearms, were drenched in blood.

Jaimie found herself screaming, not because she wanted to—she certainly didn't want the bald student to realize that she had seen him—but because all the fear tormenting her mind demanded escape like an animal from a cage, and it did so, quite successfully—her terrified screams found their release.

The bald student started running after her, his black boots slapping the pavement like two great mallets. Jaimie panicked, spun around and darted into the subway entrance a few feet to her right, taking the steps leading down two at a time. She stumbled at the bottom, pressing her hands against the wall to break her fall.

She quickly glanced up and saw the bald student standing at the top of the steps, looking down at her. She stood paralyzed with fear for what seemed an eternity, gazing at him and the veiny lines of blood trickling down the black pants he wore. She was crying, staring, afraid to move.

He started coming down after her.

She let out another panicked scream, raced into the musty station, heart slamming against her rib cage, tears coursing down her face in an uncontrollable flow. Quickly she looked about. No police were in eyeshot—no people for that matter, other than an elderly MTA worker perched behind the bullet-proof barrier of the token booth. He stared blankly at her, with no compassion or concern for her tears.

Without hesitation, she leapt over the turnstile and sped down a second flight of steps, hearing a train screeching to a stop. She lunged down to the platform; a few passengers had dispersed from the now stationary train. Its doors rang, alerting passengers to prepare for departure. With a last burst of energy, she threw herself into the first car and fell to the floor.

The doors slammed shut.

And the bald student was there, banging at the doors, leaving smears of blood on the window, his mouth sealed shut and unmoving, all emotion drained from his face. It seemed as if his efforts at that terrifying moment were solely instinctual, animalistic.

She scampered to the opposite side of the train as it pulled away, leaving the man behind holding his strange object. Through the window, Jaimie could see a few people scurrying away from him, their eyes wide with fear at the sight of the blood on his hands and clothes.

She quickly looked around, fear still racing through her. A dozen people sat scattered within the car, looking in her direction. She stood up and gazed away, fearing that one of them might be a bald man with sunglasses. If so, she would have no choice but to break down and surrender.

She looked away, down to the floor, saw a flattened piece of chewing gum stuck there like an old gray nickel: something so insignificant, yet now a sharp symbol of pure, utter dread.

Shivering, she took a second, more careful glance around the car. A homeless man was stretched out across three seats. A few young women chatted in Spanish. An elderly black man was talking to himself.

But no bald men.

She looked out into the darkness of the tunnel beyond the window, wondering where the train was taking her.

At the moment it did not matter. As long as she was away from . . . *him.*

Run run, need to run . . .

The words had repeated themselves in David Traynor's mind, consuming his every thought, his every movement, just as they had earlier. He climbed the fire escape, not realizing until he finally made it onto the roof that the Harbinger had followed him to the apartment and was lurking nearby with the intention of stealing back the Atmosphere for himself.

David would rather die than allow that to happen.

When he finally found himself alone again with the wondrous object, only one objective occupied his mind: experiencing the true meaning of the Atmosphere, as quickly as possible, and with no interference. How amazing to realize that no other alternative existed! It was his destiny, his calling in life. It had finally come—and the Atmosphere had revealed it to him.

The Harbinger—Harold, he called himself—the selfish fuck had gotten in the way, tried to get in on his time with the Atmosphere. David had had no choice but to postpone everything until he knew for sure he could proceed uninterrupted, away from Harold's intrusion.

He had watched from the rooftop as Harold the Harbinger stumbled down the fire escape into the street, running wildly, arms flailing, calling out, "Supplier! Come back!" at the top of his lungs. When he finally disappeared, David's mind re-triggered his desire to run, and he followed its command. He went across the rooftop, down the fire escape on the opposite side of the building, through the alley and across 189th Street to the elevated subway platform three blocks away, where the Q express stopped every fifteen minutes.

Cease . . .

David stopped running, clouds of frozen breath spewing from his lips. He found himself fifty feet in the air atop the platform, the wind whipping restlessly at him. Staring out into the bleak emptiness surrounding him, he saw that nobody else was in sight.

He waited for guidance.

Commence . . .

He sat down on the cement platform, leaning back against a billboard. He placed his headphones on and pressed PLAY on the Walkman.

Music boomed forth, the beat repetitive and incessant, like the triggering cadence that had compelled him to run.

160

He waited an eternity, or so it seemed, until his mind finally told him to remove the Atmosphere from his pocket.

The train shook on, every passing minute feeling like an hour. Jaimie's mind wandered as she watched the bum sleeping on the seats in front of her. His body jerked as if roaches crawled under his clothing—not for one second did she rule out that possibility—or bad dreams floated inside his head. The odor emanating from his body introduced a roll of nausea in her, but she refused to move from her seat until the train came to a stop. She could then sneak out without anyone taking notice; she feared that the bald guy might have found a way onto the train and was trying to spot her moving through the glass windows in the doors separating the other cars. Or that maybe a different bald guy might come after her. After all, she had seen *two* of them. At this point, anything was possible.

She turned and looked out the window, cupping her palms around her eyes to block out the reflection. The train emerged from the tunnel and rose up onto an el, revealing a tight sweep of apartment buildings and warehouses. *Oh, no . . .* she was leaving Manhattan, entering the Bronx. Her intention had been to get out of the train, regardless of where she ended up, to find a phone and call the police if she didn't have the good fortune of spotting a cruiser or a cop nearby. But with all the goddamn trains in the city, the one waiting for her had had to be an express—to the *Bronx*, no less.

Count your blessings, Jame. If that train hadn't pulled in at that exact moment . . .

She continued to gaze out. The neighborhoods here were no place for a pretty young girl to walk around all by herself.

She felt the train slowing.

An anouncement blared through the speakers in the train's ceiling.

"Next stop, One Hundred Ninetieth Street."

Ecstasy, pure ecstasy, infinite orgasm, oh the colors, the beautiful colors, take me, dear Giver, take me, my blood, my semen, my fuel. It . . . is . . . yours . . .

The train slowed as it pulled into the 190th Street station. Jaimie peered out the window, trying to see if a cop or someone trustworthy in appearance waited on the platform. Billboards advertising the most recent movies flashed by, illuminated by amber halogens. Finally, the train ground to a stop.

She needed to make a decision, quickly.

The doors rang open. Cool air blew in.

She darted from the train.

The cold night air bit her cheeks. Behind, the doors of the train rang, sealing her from the warm, safe interior, abandoning her on the platform. She watched with dismay as the red taillights of the train's last car shrank into pinpoints, eventually disappearing into the night.

She turned and paced the length of the platform, her footsteps tapping atop the plastic-edged warning strip, echoing in the darkness. On the street below a car's tires screeched, the rev of its engine tearing into the night like a monster's roar. Jaimie clutched her slamming heart at the loud noise.

She felt a slight vibration under her feet. Turning, she saw a train in the far distance approaching from the opposite direction. A connection, back into Manhattan.

"Yes!" She pumped her fist and walked briskly to the enclosed overpass at the north end of the platform. She took the steps quickly, two at a time, up, over and then down. She could see the train's lights slowly growing from hints of illumination into widening searchlights.

She'd be on her way home in no time.

All of a sudden, she heard something odd. A groan—or so it seemed—emerging from behind the far side of a shelter ten feet away. She tried to see through the small Plexiglas structure, but posters advertising a remake of a classic movie shielded its surface. She stayed unmoving. The train, only a hundred or so yards from the station, would pull up to where she currently stood, making it unnecessary to move farther down the platform.

The groan rose again, riddled with choking, the effort of the gags sounding pained and anguished. Curious but tentative, she took a gentle step forward, craning her neck in an attempt to peer around the edges of the movie poster. She could barely make out what appeared to be the back of someone's head leaning against the Plexiglas wall. She thought she heard the tinny cadence of music radiating from headphones.

The person wailed again, louder, longer. Then came a series of sobs. She saw the person's head bob slightly.

She took another step. The small waiting area still shadowed the identity of the individual. Maybe it was a homeless person, hurt, sick, in need of care. Again she heard her father: *Stay away, worry only about yourself and not those around you.*

Good advice, but she could not listen to it at this moment. Someone could be hurt.

She stepped forward. "Hello?"

Another cough answered her, labored, strained.

The train began to pull into the station.

Feeling safe now that she would soon be on her way back into Manhattan, she took a deep breath and walked around to the other side of the shelter to investigate.

Jaimie's breath escaped her as the stark, horrifying image she beheld burned its way into her vision, into her mind. Nothing could convince her at that moment that a God existed, given the atrocious sight, and she subconsciously pinched herself over and over in the same mental spot, wishing it away. But the psychological pain she felt was real. And so was the horror before her.

It had taken her a few long seconds to feel the warmth of the blood seeping through her shoes, a river of it, pooling out into a semicircle five or six feet wide, dripping out onto the tracks. She tried to move but remained frozen in fear staring at this . . . *man* (that's what it appeared to be, or had been), disemboweled into a great crater that ran from sternum to thighs, as if a cannonball had been shot through him. His head gyrated wildly on his neck, his throat contracting with each revolution, producing the pained moans.

Yet, with the pain, with the torturous, ungodly affliction set upon this soul, the escaping life inside somehow managed to leave a smile on his face, the teeth clenched, the lips curled upward, pain and pleasure and death all combined to form the ultimate image of doom.

Again Jaimie tried to pull herself away and finally succeeded, her sneakers suctioning away from the gummy blood. The train pulled in, its braking steel wheels burning the blood spilled over the tracks.

The stench of heat and copper rose as the train stopped and its doors rang open.

Jaimie lunged forward, tripping over something in her path, something black, oddly shaped, something hard that hurt her toe and tumbled over the edge of the track to the street thirty feet below.

She fell into the car, tracking blood inside.

The doors shut behind her.

Breathing heavily, she looked up.

About twenty people were staring at her.

Chapter Fourteen

Harold had banged himself up pretty badly, and Frank figured the bald man had finally come to his senses and decided to surrender. It really seemed his only option at the moment. He lay kissing the ground, crying like a baby, wrists cuffed, face and hands showing some pretty nasty lacerations from the shattered glass. Above all, he had two guns poised six inches away from his brain. The once mysterious and formidable man now looked powerless, tears racing down his bloodied face.

Ernie continued pressing his knee into Harold's back while Hector busily removed a plastic tie from his belt to fetter the man's ankles. Frank held on to him too, contemplating the absurdity of the entire scene. Blood and glass everywhere, on Harold's face, his clothes, and on the tiled floor. It looked as if someone had dropped a huge glass pitcher of tomato juice.

A hot coppery odor filled the hall. A bulge of sickness formed in Frank's throat, and he had to choke back the urge to throw up. *Why had Harold done this to himself?* What evils motivated the man to perform so much intentional damage to his own body? Was attempted suicide his only alternative, given the situation?

As Frank pondered these and many other seemingly unanswerable questions, he noticed Harold's blood-spotted dome turning a juicy shade of red right before his eyes, like a ripening tomato caught by stop-action photography. He leaned forward to see whether he was witnessing a chameleonlike transition or if it had simply been a trick of the light reflecting off the blood.

The very moment he realized that it was indeed his skin flushing, Harold's red-soaked face twisted toward Frank and stared up at him, eyes wild and white and alive beneath his sleek mask of blood. His sudden and alarming stare contorted into a defiant scowl, a terribly angry look, and before Frank could warn his counterparts or back off himself, Harold bounded up with newfound stamina, quickly inflicting a swift and unanticipated wrestling flip on Ernie that sent him sprawling like a rag doll across the fragments of glass on the floor.

Frank and Hector staggered back, guns pointed, yelling "Freeze" again—to no avail. Harold vaulted up and once again started smashing his face into the bars. Sputters of jibberish—and fragments of teeth—dropped from his bloodied mouth. He struck himself again and again, this desperate attempt to launch himself through the bars in the window almost as puzzling as the larger mystery itself. The trio stood at bay at Hector's word—it became evident that Harold posed no threat to anyone other than himself—watching with dismay as Harold committed himself to this face-first attempt at escape (he *was* still cuffed), accomplishing no more than jarring loose one or two of the bars from their cement foundations, and a face full of shattered bones.

Harold's leaps had quickly turned to weak, instinctually driven body lobs, and the three cops tackled him once again to the floor.

He was no more than a lump of dead weight now, which made it much easier to immobilize him. Hector pressed his knees into Harold's calves, tied his ankles with the adjustable plastic restraint. Ernie reassumed his position, repeatedly digging his nightstick into the small of Harold's back. Frank lodged his knee into Harold's neck, the barrel of his pistol buried in his bloody broken nose.

At that moment, amid the high stress and confusion, Frank's personalities started doing battle. The irrational part of him tried to coerce him into blowing the bastard away, end this thing once and for all so he could go home and salvage the rest of his weekend. All he would have to do was pull the trigger and plant a hard one in his brain, although he doubted very much, outside of killing him, if a bullet would do much more damage to his face than Harold himself had already accomplished.

He felt his best alternative would be to listen to his sensible-detective personality and *not* shoot, as shooting him would be—as sick as it seemed—giving in to the maniac's wishes, granting him the pain and agony and death that he apparently so dearly desired. And giving Harold what he wanted was something that Detective Frank Ballaro didn't want to do, under any circumstances.

Frank gazed into Harold's tensed face, the horrible visage—eyes rolling, teeth clenched—sending shudders through his body. God, it really looked as if he had broken every bone in his face, the veneer of blood veiling the soupy, amorphous look it had aquired—as if his shattered bones were gently shifting under the skin.

From an outsider's point of view, the entire scene must've been quite a sight. A bloodied man, fettered at the wrists and ankles. Three grown men sitting on top of him, holding him down while he squirmed beneath them.

Frank would've bet a week's pay that given the chance, Harold would chew right through his own limbs in an effort to escape.

Frank dug the gun harder into his face. Harold grimaced. The pain must've been excruciating. "Why're you so desperate to get away, Gross, huh?"

"Need to die," he sputtered, a bloodied eyeball twisted up at Frank.

He stuck out his tongue and bit it off.

Frank grimaced and pulled his gun away as more of Harold's blood sprayed out on the floor. Harold buckled wildly, nearly lifting the three men off the ground, grunting and squealing like a pig snared in mid-slaughter. Hector and Ernie both yelled out, and Ernie slammed his club a half-dozen more times into Harold's lower back.

Finally, like a fish long out of water, Harold made an odd wheezing noise and stopped moving.

The sounds of their breaths echoed eerily in the hallway. "Don't let up," Hector yelled, heaving laboriously. "He might be playing dead."

"Jesus, how's he enduring all that pain?" Ernie was nearly in tears himself.

Frank, thinking the same thing, saw that an audience had gathered. A dozen or more of the floor's residents were crowded near the elevator, peeking over one another to get a glimpse of the action. Some laughed, others whispered. But all stayed back.

The elevators suddenly opened. For a fleeting moment Frank thought the residents of other floors were coming to investigate the fracas, but the onlookers—who were inching closer by the second—cowered back at the demand of the police rushing out onto the landing, at least a half-dozen uniforms and a few plainclothes officers spilling out like gumballs from a vending machine. A few more entered from the stairwell at the opposite end of the hall and started clearing the crowd.

Frank, Hector, and Ernie immediately surrendered their prisoner to four officers from the Bronx's Fifth-sixth Precinct. Frank felt a wave of dizziness and he had to lean against the wall a few feet away. He heard one cop calling for paramedics, another yelling at the looming onlookers to return to their apartments. The four cops crouching over Harold were shouting among themselves. Suddenly the hallway was alive with activity.

A few long minutes passed. Frank watched tiredly as a group of EMTs rushed in to work on Harold; it appeared that he had finally lost consciousness. Frank turned away from the grisly sight and walked a few feet farther down the hall, a hand on the wall for support.

"You okay?" Hector held a towel and was cleaning the blood from his hands. He offered it to Frank, who accepted it.

"A little winded. Been quite a day, huh?"

"We have a good many questions to answer."

"Last thing on my mind right now, Hect."

"I know. By the looks of it, you could use some sleep."

Frank smiled weakly, tossed the towel to the floor. "You said that about eighteen hours ago."

Hector peered around, observing the throng of activity. "We need to get ourselves out of here," he said, pressing. A few cops glanced at them curiously.

"What time is it?"

"About nine-thirty."

Frank looked around for Ernie but didn't see him. "How's Barba?"

"A little shook up, but he'll be fine. He's getting bandaged."

A man in his forties approached Frank and Hector. He wore gray cotton pants and a black sport coat. A gun bulged in his left jacket pocket. "Gentlemen, good evening. Sergeant Sid Clemens, Fifty-sixth precinct." He smiled thinly, as if making an effort at it. He did not offer a handshake; Frank and Hector still had some blood on their hands.

"I'm Captain Hector Rodriguez, from the Thirteenth, and this is—"

"Detective Ballaro," Frank interrupted.

"Yes, Frank Ballaro, from the Lindsay case. What're you doing out in the field so soon? Especially with the kid making bail."

Frank smiled. He didn't need the attention right now. He ignored the question. "Pleased to meet you."

"Not under these circumstances, I'm sure." He faced Hector. "I trust you'll be able to fill me in."

Hector stepped forward, stuck out his chest. Although in his late fifties, he still had an imposing air about him when it came to doing business, and he didn't appear too anxious to let anyone else get involved in this mystery right now, especially after all he'd been through over the last eighteen hours.

In a forceful yet professional manner, he pleaded his case to Clemens and requested that he take a step back and allow him to go about his business without any interference. "Sergeant Clemens, I've placed this man under arrest. The

172

details of the investigation we are working on in which this man is a primary suspect cannot be discussed at this time. I need to ask for your co-operation. After all on site medical treatments, I'd like him placed in the Strong Medical Center under clinical supervision. A Dr. Samuel Richards will be notified of his admission, and directions will be furnished to him as to how to proceed with the patient. It is crucial to the investigation that these instructions be carried out. Am I clear on this, Sergeant?"

Clemens pinched his brow. He seemed a bit perturbed. "Captain Rodriguez, with all due respect, why wasn't a notification put in regarding my district's potential involvement in this?" Clemens pointed to Harold, who was being lifted onto a stretcher. "Whatever *this* might be?"

"Time was of the essence, and circumstances didn't allow us a proper disclosure of matters." He placed a gentle yet commanding hand on Clemens's shoulder. "Right now isn't a very good time to divulge any details regarding this case."

In asking Clemens for a little time, Hector in essence was exercising his rank to elicit the sergeant's professional respect—an unspoken rule that existed among the cops in New York City. When a simple favor was needed, it would under almost all circumstances be granted as long as it didn't interfere with or adversely affect those sharing space.

"Fine," Clemens said. "But I'll need a statement from you both."

Frank rolled his eyes. Déjà vu all over again.

Hector nodded. "I'll be happy to fill you in on what I can. Give me a few days, okay?"

Clemens nodded.

Frank edged down the hall, his legs feeling like wet tea bags. If Clemens really knew the severity of the case they were working on, and the fact that most of their efforts since early this morning had been done covertly, he'd have a hemorrhage over Hector's request for clemency. *Gee,* Frank thought, *Hector has really let things slide by the wayside. No longer by the book, that Hect.*

Hector had a few more words with Clemens, then met Frank near the elevator, where the doors finally closed on Harold.

"What he say?"

"He wanted to know how Harold got all fucked up."

"What did you tell him?"

"The truth. That the guy tried to throw himself through a barred window."

"He believe you?"

"Not for a second." A police officer came over and handed Hector his cap. He hadn't even thought about retrieving it, much less realized he'd lost it.

Ernie sauntered over, smiled weakly. He looked as pale as snow, as if he'd been locked in a closet for a few years. Both his hands were bandaged. "Captain, I'm sorry to interrupt. Is there anything else you need right now? I'd like to get back to the precinct. I have some work to do, and I'm guessing you'll need me to file a report."

Frank was hoping that Hector wouldn't have Ernie so much as whisper anything until they discussed the matter further. He peered at Hector, who and must have read his mind, or simply felt the same way, because he said, "Ernie, you go home and have yourself a nice dinner. Take tomorrow off. I'll call you if there's anything that needs to be discussed. I'll see you first thing Monday." Improper procedure, but given the perplexity and sensitivity of the situation, a strategic and necessary move. Frank would've done the same thing.

Ernie nodded, then added, "Sergeant Clemens asked me to give a statement."

"Hold off. No word of this to anyone. Until my say so."

Ernie took the elevator down. Frank pointed toward Harold's apartment. The entrance had been taped across and cops were coming and going in the hall. "Hect—the money . . ."

"It's already been grabbed. Open door equals free bait." The elevator rang, and Hector placed a hand on Frank's shoulder. "Before we call it a night, let's discuss our next move over a cup of coffee."

"Better yet," Frank said, listening to the detective inside himself. "Let's get the coffee and then *make* our next move." He reached into his pocket and revealed a small piece of folded paper. He gently unfolded it.

A receipt. Village Clothing. He smiled thinly.

"When did you grab that?"

"After *you* dropped it."

Hector grinned, eyebrows raised in question. "What good will that do us?"

"Let's get out of here, and I'll explain."

The elevator opened and they rode down in anticipatory silence, Frank rethinking the last eighteen hours as if he'd just seen a movie.

Chapter Fifteen

The city's night dwellers had taken flight: theater- and concert-goers freshly dressed for the occasion; happy-hour attendees still in the day's work attire, stumbling from their watering holes of choice; denim- and leather-clad youths, grouped together with no direction in mind other than to venture from street to avenue.

The traffic had thinned out some since Frank and Hector had battled rush hour nearly three hours earlier. During their return Hector shrewdly hit the beacons to escape red lights at 104th Street and 91st Street, making the going all the faster and, of course, turning the heads of a few curious pedestrians who silently accused them of abusing their status. The return trip took about ten minutes, the time spent in unspoken silence until Frank pointed out a coffee shop on the corner of Seventy-eighth and Madison.

Frank's thoughts during the short journey had been intense and to the point, like the unnerving memories of a man barely escaping the path of a speeding car: fraught with troubling questions and worry. His three personalities fought to sum up the day's events and to evaluate any possible relationship between them. From the incident in the alley and Bobby Lindsay making bail to the discovery of Harold Gross and the other baldies in the police file. The interview with the Racines and the eventual capture of Gross. So much information and detail. Still, frustratingly, no answers sprang forth. Frank had difficulty recalling a similar experience, one where he had come across so many events in just one day—and was still not able to make any sense of them all.

And to think he'd *still* squeezed in six hours' sleep.

Frank returned to the cruiser with two coffees and a bag of cinnamon buns. They drove west up Seventy-eighth and pulled into a Kinney System parking garage where the attendant grudgingly let them borrow a spot—the grimace on his face attesting to the fact that he'd performed this service many more times in the past than he cared to. The city's parking garages were a common pit stop, providing a quiet place for the police to wind down, and this one gave Frank and Hector a few moments to discuss the situation at hand.

"Oh, that feels good," Frank said, sipping his coffee. He closed his eyes and let the warmth spread through his body. "I need this bad."

"Not bad for a coffee cart." Hector's eyes had a lot of sleep in them, dark and droopy.

Frank uncurled the bag and dug out a cinnamon bun. "You know, I'm never gonna be able to sleep tonight," he said, taking a bite. "Between obsessing about everything that's happened and trying to figure it all out, my mind is racing."

"Let the sand settle a bit. You've been bombarded. We both have." He bit into the bun Frank gave him, washed it down with coffee. "You said you wanted to tell me something about the receipt?"

Frank took a deep breath. He'd been thinking the whole time since they left the Bronx that revealing to Hector everything going through his mind might not be the best idea. First and foremost, he knew that Hector would have a hell of a time considering the validity of it all, unless, of course Frank could convince him; this was entirely possible but potentially exhausting, given his own lack of spirit, energy and belief in what clearly seemed outlandish. And, of course, Hector's bull-doggedness.

But with everything he'd seen and been through over the past eighteen hours, something inside—his detective identity—told him that his ideas could very well be valid, that somewhere, somehow, it all tied in, that it could really make sense to Hector if he just laid it out clearly. Frank *had* to tell Hector, at least the rudimentary facts as he saw them. Spell it out as clearly as possible and keep his fingers crossed.

Of course, if Hector bought his idea, then the

two of them would have to search for proof. That was another story altogether, and where Frank would really need Hector's assistance if they were to break any ground. But first things first.

"The receipt," Frank revealed, pulling the small piece of paper from his jacket pocket, "is really only a small part of everything that's rolling around in my head. I grabbed it because I thought—and still think—that a visit to the store might provide us with some additional information."

"About what?"

Frank shifted in his seat, his body squared toward Hector. "I truly believe that this whole thing with Harold Gross runs much deeper than what appears on the surface: that he's just some crazy lost soul, a sadomasochistic murderer running around preying on the penises of teenaged boys. I've been thinking about it over and over, and it just doesn't make any sense. Think about it: What in God's name could his motivation be? Sick pleasure? I don't buy that. He was too hell-bent on killing himself for what I guess is the fear of having to disclose some secret he's holding inside. Hect, there's more to this sick puppy than just his bark and bite."

"We'll have some answers tomorrow. I plan on questioning him myself."

Frank frowned, shook his head in dismay. "He's not gonna talk."

"We'll make him talk."

"How? By roughing him up? Besides, he has no tongue."

Hector nodded, a grin of truth confirming his thoughts. "So what are you thinking?"

"This afternoon, when Martin was going through all those sketches of bald men, I couldn't help but think of Bobby Lindsay. You remember seeing pictures of him in the paper? A few days before the murder he shaved his head completely bald and kept it that way all through the investigation."

Hector grinned, clearly skeptical but still attentive. "Go on."

"At every questioning, every time we came in contact with him until the day of his arrest, Lindsay wore black clothes and sunglasses. He'd been very defiant about removing his glasses when we questioned him. When he finally did, his eyes were like black orbs, the pupils wide and dilated. We already knew at the time that there weren't any drugs involved. He'd been tested. So we attributed it to shock."

Hector nodded, eyebrows raised in question.

"Hect, call me crazy, but I saw that same dark, blank look in Gross's eyes. His pupils—they took up all the color, just like Lindsay's."

"Are you trying to get me to believe that Gross and Lindsay are somehow connected?"

"I think it's a possibility."

Hector shook his head doubtfully, then took a sip of coffee. "Frank, I don't think this is a time to let your gut do the talking. You're tired and upset about what happened with Lindsay—"

"Wait, there's more." There was a pause in their conversation as a parking attendant drove by in a black Lexus. "Gross was wearing gloves when he appeared in the alley, when he committed *his* crimes. Lindsay had been wearing gloves when he committed *his* crimes. There weren't any fingerprints at the scene. It's in my report."

Hector looked at Frank, made a *hmph* sound.

"Also, I find it very hard to believe that all those bald men wearing sunglasses we saw in the police computer were involved in isolated crimes. Each sketch—what were there, twelve?"

"Something like that."

"Each had been of a man suspected in the disappearance of a number of young adult males, and each case had been covered up by the FBI. Remember the two men Martin researched after he'd done Gross?"

"Hilton and Farrell."

"Both were listed as suicides. Said so right in the report."

Hector leaned back, his brows aimed skyward in thought. "Hmm. That's interesting. Gross was hell-bent on killing himself."

"Yes, but he failed miserably. And another thing—Gross's victims were young males, like Hilton and Farrell's."

"So how does that tie in with Bobby Lindsay? He murdered his sister."

Frank shrugged his shoulders. "That much I haven't figured out yet. But all the other similarities are there."

"So why go to the clothing store?"

"If Gross, Hilton and Farrell are connected in any way, which I'll bet my left arm they are, and

Lindsay is too, then I'm guessing there's more of them out there."

"More of who? Bald men wearing sunglasses committing murders?"

"Yes, Hect. Absolutely. It's too coincidental to be overlooked. Something's going on, something very strange, cultish, and we're uncovering bits and pieces of it minute by minute. We have to check out every possibility. Not only whether Bobby Lindsay could have had a part in all this, but whether there are more. There almost has to be. I find it hard to believe that we know about *all* of them."

Hector took a sip of coffee, looking out at the cars parked in the spaces opposite them. He twirled his mustache, eyebrows lifted in thought. "If there actually is a *them.*"

Watch out for them . . .

"I'll almost guarantee it. It's a coverup. We already know that."

"So what now?"

Frank smiled, knowing Hector already knew the answer to this one. Once again, Frank convinced his man—at least enough to warrant a further investigation.

"Village Clothing."

"You know, I haven't bought any of this yet," Hector said, starting the car. "As far as I'm concerned, our work is done. We've got the man who committed the murders in the alley, in less than eighteen hours, no less."

"I'm not looking to sell you, Hect. I only want you to check it out with me. I hate to repeat myself, but this thing runs much deeper than just Harold Gross, and I'm prepared to prove it to you."

"You said that already."

Frank nodded and rolled his eyes. "Just to prepare you, there's much, much more—beyond what I've just told you."

"You got more theories, huh?"

"Care to hear me out?" Frank smiled. He'd built up momentum and was now willing to spill it all.

"One thing at a time, Smoky. Let's go to Village Clothing first and test your theory, see if it holds any water."

They pulled out of the parking garage, waving to the attendant (who elected not to return the friendly gesture), then headed downtown.

Chapter Sixteen

Bobby Lindsay sat silently brooding in the family dining room, his mother, stepfather, and lawyer sitting opposite him, each of them ineffective in coercing additional information regarding his involvement in Carrie's murder. They dug desperately and incessantly, like treasure hunters, seeking any response other than *I just don't remember doing it.*

When not trying to pry words from Bobby's lips, Jo-Beth Lindsay argued relentlessly with her husband, Jake, and Bobby's lawyer, Marvin Korn, their words shooting back and forth like volleys in a Ping-Pong game. For reasons still unexplained, Bobby had had a great deal of trouble making any sense of the English language since he'd been accused of the heinous crime, so their harried utterances sounded much like foreign words to him, garbled and unintelligible.

Bobby held his head in his hands as the three adults flung their frustrations back and forth in gunfire fashion. He rubbed the sweat from his palms into his dampened brow, staring through his sunglasses into the whorls of finished oak surfacing the dining room table. He tried hard to make sense of the conflicts consuming his thoughts—he still possessed the ability to communicate with himself inside his head and wanted nothing more than to understand what the hell was going on around him—at the same time trying desperately to block out his parents' painfully incomprehensible arguments. Their words went on and on, back and forth, blah blah blah eating at his brain. He realized he couldn't take it any longer: their voices, grating his spine, abrasive and cutting like long fingernails slowly scraping across the surface of a chalky blackboard. He rose from the table, ignoring their hails for him to return to his seat. He moved to the center of the living room, near the tapestry couch, leaning down to scratch an itch beneath the homing bracelet around his ankle, its heavy metallic grip chafing his skin, leaving a crusty redness at the point of contact.

When the itch was relieved, he slowly stepped to within a few feet of the front window. He peered outside, staying back just far enough to avoid being glimpsed by the hordes of media gathered behind the police barricade set up just across the street, and from the police who were providing surveillance around the clock.

The whole damn thing seemed so unreal. *He had been accused of murdering his sister!* It sounded so horrific. Unbelievable. Two days after her disappearance the police had searched the house, combing the place from Bobby's downstairs apartment all the way to the attic. When they finally revealed to the family that her mutilated body had been found in the hallway closet next to his parents' bedroom upstairs, Bobby felt as if he'd been struck in the heart with a great blow.

He refused to accept the loss of his sister, and had continued to not believe the dreadful truth: that Carrie had been horribly murdered, her body stuffed into his own suitcase like a slaughterhouse discard.

Apparently his vehement denial led the police to believe that it was he who had committed the crime, and they'd started hounding him, keeping tabs on him, watching his every move.

Finally they brought him in. During the first interrogation they thrust a long line of sickening crime scene photos under his nose, one after another, each one depicting a bloody and brutal scene, the unendurable process seeming never to end. It was the first he'd seen of Carrie since her disappearance, and he had prayed it would be the last.

He didn't understand why *he* was being accused of raping and killing her. Sure, things weren't right in his mind—the confusion, the amnesia—that much he realized, but he also knew he wasn't capable of such a heinous act: her innocence violated, her body beaten and sliced. *Murdered.* No, no, no, he could never do that.

And what evidence had the authorities uncovered that would lead them to believe that he was the guilty party? Throughout the investigation he knew they would be watching him closely. His parents too. They quickly turned their focus on him, questioning him, prodding him for answers.

Suddenly, inexplicably, at the onset of the interrogation, he lost his ability to understand much of what was said to him. He could no longer reply clearly or intelligibly. Words spoken to him sounded like something spoken in a strange foreign language, and all his responses escaped his throat in uncontrollable, nonsensical blurts. This behavior, combined with his amnesia, surely made it seem that he was hiding something, or feigning insanity, and he was immediately bludgeoned with accusations. He realized that he had no choice but to sit mum, as his ability to comprehend and answer their intense probes was gone, his memories of life prior to Carrie's murder now completely lost.

When they finally came to the house, slapped the cuffs on him and read him his rights, the paranoia he'd experienced all along gave way to a sickening feeling so intense that words could never express it.

Bobby's past hadn't been so wonderful. He spent a good part of his time hanging out with the wrong people, getting into trouble, involving himself in minor public disturbances and other small-time crimes. Bored rich-boy stuff. He'd been arrested once for tossing a brick through the windshield of a parked car—his most serious offense. But never under any circumstance had he considered hurting another human being, much less his little sister.

Staring out the window into the illuminated night, he felt the gaze of a single policeman pinning him, and he shied away. Damn! If only he could regain control of his crazed thoughts, remember something—*anything*—from the missing block of time in his mind, then perhaps he would be able to speak up and defend himself, maybe even solve the crime and exonerate himself.

He turned and walked back to the dining room table, his mother, stepfather, and lawyer facing him. Beads of sweat trickled down his spine.

"You ready to tell us something, Bobby? Mr. Korn can't defend you properly unless you tell him the truth."

Bobby felt his jaw clench in frustration, the proper words unable to spill from his tongue. His tensed-up muscles sent jolts of pain into his head. "Can't remember." It was still the only defense he could muster.

The three adults shook their heads, brows furrowed, their frustration as severe as Bobby's. Marvin Korn stood, arms stretched wide, his heavy-set torso pressing against the buttons of his shirt. "Bobby—"

"Going to sleep." A new utterance, a means of escape perhaps.

Jo-Beth Lindsay stood, placed an arm around Marvin's shoulder and squeezed. "That might be the best thing right now," she said, staring at Bobby. Her blond hair was still in place, despite all the harried events the day had brought. "Maybe when Bobby wakes up, he'll remember something." She looked at her son and smiled, though it was clearly weak and false.

Something about that smile doesn't seem right ...

Bobby nodded and walked slowly from the room, feeling a chill race down his spine, as if he had a gun pointed at his back. He opened the door leading to his downstairs apartment and took the flight one step at a time, careful not to allow his tired legs to buckle. He reached bottom and passed the alcove where the washer and drier leaned against the wall like a pair of modern igloos.

The peace and quiet the apartment offered gave him immediate escape from the cruel, persecuting world. He lay on his bed, in the dark, staring across the room to the door into the kitchen. A policeman stood in the drainage recess at the bottom of the cement steps outside, his grainy moonlit shadow gently swaying back and forth behind the closed curtains.

For the first time since coming home from the courthouse today, Bobby closed his eyes and attempted to allow his mind some ease. The month-long investigation had been hell, today being no exception, and he prayed for his mind to erase *that* affliction, just as it had cleared away his memories prior to Carrie's murder.

He thought about everything that had taken place this morning, his being led from the holding cell into the courtroom to face the judge. At the time he would have bet his inheritance that the rest of his natural life would be spent rotting away behind bars, the inmates strongly expressing their dissatisfaction with child-killers like himself. One could imagine the shocking relief he felt when the judge actually went ahead and set bail, and then when his mother plopped down the big-time dough—it was like a dream come true.

Riding home in silence, he pondered the confusing situation, trying to make sense of what had just occurred, his mother signing for the right to his freedom. It really bothered him, because he couldn't comprehend her motivation. Why would his mother put up a million dollars in cash when he had been accused of murdering her only other child?

Something about her smile tonight didn't seem right.

She was hiding something.

Staring into the darkness, his mind wandered, beyond today, beyond the interrogation—what was his name? Bolero? Balloro? Damn, if only he could remember something, anything from the missing time in his memory before the discovery of Carrie's body. *Think, Bobby, think. What's the last thing you remember doing before you found yourself being questioned about the murder?*

He rubbed his bald head. Although the apart-

191

ment was cool and comfortable, sweat smeared across his stubbled scalp.

Sweat. Suddenly he remembered something. He had been lying right here in bed, his body drenched in sweat. Sweat. And . . . he had been listening to the radio.

In an effort to retrace his actions, he leaned over and switched on the clock radio sitting to his right on the nightstand. Immediately static blared through the tinny speaker. The frequency indicator in front, now aglow, showed the station pointer set all the way to the right, past the 108 frequency on the FM dial. He fumbled at the small serrated dials fixed into the side of the clock radio, the surrounding darkness making it hard to distinguish the volume dial from the tuner. He found the edge of one and gently spun it away from him.

Volume. The static rose, sending twinges of discomfort through his ears.

He moved the dial back down to its previous position, then stopped and turned it back up a bit.

He heard something.

Nearly buried within the grainy hiss, a . . . *pulse* emanated, a deep, resonating beat emerging from the clock radio's speaker like a heartbeat heard through an ear pressed against a naked chest. Bobby moved closer, gently inching the tuner in search for a clearer signal. The radio's dial squeezed hard against the right side of the display, moving ever so slightly.

The static suddenly vanished, and the pulse loomed forth.

Thrumph . . . thrumph . . . thrumph; so eerie, like a heartbeat. Bobby placed his hands on the radio as if it gave off warmth, feeling the syncopated vibrations within its plastic shell. They felt wonderful, each magical throb stimulating all his senses, hearing, touch, smell. Suddenly he could see in the dark, even through the sunglasses. He could smell his mother's perfume through the ceiling. And he could *feel,* oh, yes he could feel something *wonderful,* a rush of euphoria tingling through his body, introducing him to a high even more potent than drugs or sex.

Mysteriously, though, as these pleasurable sensations carried him away from his misery, he began to recognize them. A familiarity told him he had felt this way before. And as each pulse brought about more and more pleasure, his memory resurrected itself little by little, each and every vibratory injection rebuilding bits of memory in his mind. Excited, he gripped the radio tighter, desperate to seek more from the deep mystery within its plastic shell. More vibrations. Holes appeared within the dark wall of lost time, engrams of recollection breaking out like fingers poking through a sheet of cellophane. He could feel it coming back to him.

All of a sudden a memory arose, more intense than anything he could recall in the last few weeks, and he had to control his immediate desire to yell out. So crystal clear, a particular word standing out at the forefront of his mind like a lone soldier perched atop a battlefield's highest hill.

Atmosphere.

His mind rolled in crazy circles, the word—the *word*—leaping out at him repeatedly like specters escaping a haunted house after years and years of haunting. Atmosphere . . . atmosphere, over and over again in his mind. But what could it mean?

As he still gripped the radio, his mind found a connection to the pulse, and he allowed the flow of the experience to consume him and take him to the plane of existence it had planned for him.

Now another memory. Something about the bed he was lying on. It held a secret. He concentrated as best as he could on the engram breaking through, a million tiny images coming together to form a single whole—a puzzle pieced together, revealing an answer.

Something about the bed. The bed . . .

Under the bed!

The voice yelled out at him—from within his head, he thought—loud and clear. Not *his* voice, but the deep stirring assertion of someone—something—else. Familiar.

Still holding the radio, he sat up, knees off the edge of the bed. He gently slid down and crouched next to the bed, head to the Oriental carpet. He peered underneath, the whole time careful not to unplug the radio. He was amazed at his remarkable ability to see in the dark. The environment beneath his bed came into view. It was stark, nearly empty except for the carpet and a small plastic bag perched amid its patterns, the end wrapped tightly around itself, looking like an insect turning its armor.

He flattened his body on the carpet and reached for the bag with his left hand. His fingers gently caressed a wrinkle in the plastic and locked on.

He pulled the bag from under the bed. Something was inside.

"Harbinger . . ."

The voice—*the voice*—called out to him again. But it did not come from his head. It came from the radio in his right hand.

Suddenly Bobby felt his entire body swimming with an intense sensitivity, a rippling of pleasure racing from head to toe that turned his skin to gooseflesh. He held the radio to his cheek, opening his mouth to speak. Involuntary words whispered out: "Yes . . . yes, *Giver* . . ."

"The Outsider who stopped you. Do you remember him?"

Bobby forced his mind to recall the individual in question, thinking back to only moments earlier when he tried to recall his name. "The cop," he replied to the voice in the radio. "Ballaro." This time the name slipped from his tongue with ease.

"You were programmed to kill all intervening Outsiders, Harbinger. Recognize failure."

Tears sprang from Bobby's eyes, and he began to sob like a scolded child, his emotions uncontrollable. "I . . . I . . ." Once again he couldn't find the words to express himself.

"You were programmed to kill yourself upon capture. Recognize failure."

Bobby pressed the radio harder against his face. It felt warm against his tears, and with each pulse he felt a further bond with the Giver.

"Harbinger, what is your purpose?"

Suddenly Bobby perceived an odd sensation in his head, as if a switch had been turned on to reveal the appropriate answer to the query. "To seek out Suppliers."

"Harbinger, what will you do if an Outsider discovers you?"

"Kill them."

"Harbinger, what will you do if an Outsider overcomes you or escapes?"

"Kill myself."

"Harbinger, take the unit. Seek out new Suppliers."

"Yes, Giver," he answered automatically, looking down at the black plastic bag in his hand.

The radio went dead, and Bobby nearly collapsed to the floor. The radio slipped from his grip and tumbled next to the base of the dresser, static blaring from its speaker.

He kneeled, still gripping the bag, adjusting his jarred sunglasses back to a firm fit. He looked around his room, at everything there: the furniture, mirror, lamps, bottles of cologne, stereo, CDs, tapes, television. Suddenly everything took on a different light, a realm of character that seemed just as it did during the missing time, which had now miraculously returned under the influence of the Giver.

Take the unit and seek out new Suppliers . . .

His memory had indeed returned. All of it. He remembered what happened when by chance Carrie found the Atmosphere under his bed. He remembered hearing her scream while he was making a sandwich in the upstairs kitchen, how he raced down two steps at a time into his room and found her sitting upright against the tub in his bathroom, holding the Atmosphere as it harvested from her. He remembered the appearance of her Walkman headphones dangling loosely from her neck, the smile on her face bright and wide, as if the pleasure of the experience could in no way be equaled.

And, of course, he remembered the blood, pooling out on the cold tiles.

As the memories of the experience finished surfacing, he could recall how he felt afterwards, his utter confusion at the whole scenario, wondering how it could be possible for Carrie to become a suitable candidate for supplying.

Now, with all these memories refreshed in his mind, he tried and tried but still could not fathom an answer to this conundrum: all Suppliers were male, and Carrie was a sixteen year-old girl.

Under the bed!

The voice returned. Bobby looked at the radio. It sat on its side, static still radiating from within it. Perhaps the voice had actually come from his head? Again he laid it facedown on the carpet, peered under the bed.

A section of the carpet maybe two feet across was rising up and down very slightly, as if breathing, up . . . down . . . up . . . down, like the naked stomach of a sleeping man. He could hear a faraway noise, something machinelike, a steady syncopation similar to a turbine engine.

Under the bed!

Again the voice, this time definitely from his head, a memory planted within. With newfound energy, Bobby scrambled up, placed the black bag atop the bed and gripped the bed frame, pulling with all the strength he could muster. The bed moved jaggedly across the Oriental carpet, leaving uneven impressions in the nap. He pulled it as far as he could until his back pressed against the wall. Then he crawled over the mattress to the other side, where the breathing section of carpet was exposed.

From upstairs, he heard the door to the stairs leading to his apartment opening. "Bobby, you all right down there?" His stepfather.

Bobby felt a wave of panic consume him. "Outsider . . ." he muttered under his breath, gripping the edge of the carpet and pulling. The small section came free. He gave the carpet a mighty yank, swinging it around like a bullfighter flashing his cape, tossing it across the room into the dresser, knocking over a few bottles of cologne and a candle holder.

"Something's up!" his stepfather shouted from upstairs. "Bobby, what are you doing?"

Fearful of the Outsider's imminent approach, Bobby wanted to take action but couldn't move as the sight before him had him frozen in indecision, had him standing motionless for what seemed a long period of time, completely blown away.

There was a massive hole in the floor, running nearly four feet across, jagged splints of hardwood jutting out at the edges. Tendrils of white smoke seeped out from the murky depths, crawling across the floor around his ankles like stage fog at a rock concert. Bobby leaned forward and gazed into the darkness of the hole, looking for an answer but finding only cold bursts of air rising up from deep within.

"Bobby? What are you doing down there?" his mother called from above, sounding worried. They were afraid of him, and chose to keep their distance. "Get the police!" she yelled. "Right out front!"

"Outsiders . . ." Again he muttered to himself, hearing the shuffling above. He needed to take action. He kneeled on one knee, grasping the homing device around his ankle. There were two small lights built into it. One was illuminated green, the other a lifeless red.

He gripped on it and pulled. Nothing. Of course. He stood back up and spotted the black plastic bag perched atop the bed. He quickly snatched it, tore it open.

He smiled.

The Atmosphere.

From upstairs, commotion, the footsteps and shouts of additional Outsiders.

He held the Atmosphere close to his heart, gently rubbing its smooth ebony spines, listening closely for guidance.

Seek out new Suppliers! Flee the Outsiders!

Gripping the Atmosphere tightly, Bobby stepped forward into the hole.

Chapter Seventeen

Lights abounded as Frank and Hector cruised into Times Square—on the streets, from cars and buildings—a sea of neon cascading over them in a deluge of illumination, as if a slice of Las Vegas's famous Strip had been cut out and fitted onto Broadway like a piece from a great jigsaw puzzle. Here the traffic was thick, and their progress slowed accordingly, but the sea of light gave them a much-needed distraction from the dark events of the day, and made the slow going much more tolerable.

"I like the lights," Frank said. "Never get tired of looking at them." They passed the *Newsday* building, where the famous ball was dropped every New Year's Eve. A stroboscopic burst of white light rose up the side of the building and exploded into a simulated fireworks display at the top, igniting every building within the cluster of streets as if a giant camera's flash had been set off.

"Gaudy, if you ask me." Apparently Hector's patience had taken a leave of absence, along with his energy. Frank chose to ignore his statement.

Escaping Times Square, they cruised downtown into Greenwich Village. *The tribes are out,* Frank thought, getting an eyeful of the environment's trendsetters. Didn't matter what day of the week it was. Once night assumed its mask, its tawdry children would crawl out of the woodwork to shed their energy on the entire collective—the stores, the street vendors, the bars, the galleries—known as Greenwich Village.

They turned left on Mulberry Street off Sixth Avenue and slid four blocks across town to Bleecker, where they made a right and "borrowed" another spot in a parking garage.

"They always make faces," Frank said, reaching into the back seat and grabbing the yellow manila envelope containing the sketch of Harold Gross.

"Who?" They exited the car and walked a slow pace from the garage.

"The parking attendants. They hate it when we take their spots."

Hector smiled. "They should thank us. No thief's gonna hit 'em up with a cruiser sitting a few feet away."

Just as Frank was about to agree, he spotted the boutique. "Hey—look." He pointed across the street to a small storefront squeezed between an import record store and a magazine stand. A small banner was draped across the wind-up awning, its once white cloth now aged brown. Yellow letters ran lazily across the hanging drop cloth like a happy birthday banner pinned to a basement wall: VILLAGE CLOTHING.

They shuffled across the street, brushing past a group of heavily pierced youths who had just left the record store. Their flamboyant androgyny gave Frank the creeps. "Do these kids have parents?" he thought aloud. Hector ignored him, his sights pinned on the boutique.

"Well, I'll be damned," Hector said, grinning and shaking his head in amusement as he stared at the display in the front window. Within the barrier of dusty glass, a variety of trendy clothing was splayed haphazardly. Hats, jeans, skirts, scarves, jackets, in every fabric imaginable, it seemed: denim, leather, cotton, lace.

Every article of clothing was black.

Frank smiled and sidled up next to Hector. "Shall we, boss?"

Hector peered at him from the corner of his eye, his leer rife with as much sarcasm as Frank's drawn-out invitation. "Yes, we *shall*. And I'm not your boss. Not anymore, anyway." He held the door open for Frank. "I don't need the headache."

A dry odor hit Frank at once, the waft of stale dust and cigarette smoke making him at once feel a sneeze blooming. Tweaking his nose, he stepped farther in and caught the aroma of incense burning from an unseen source, its stench competing with that of the cigarettes, making the environment barely fit for humans.

The inside of Village Clothing was much like any shop in Greenwich Village, cramped with fixtures and teeming with browsers, the latter all kids adorned with some parent's nightmare decoration—painted hair, tattooed skin, pierced extremities. Each and every one of them a sight to behold.

Funny, then, that they all turned and stared at Frank and Hector with openmouthed looks of wonder, as if Hector's uniform or Frank's khakis and sweater were an unspeakably outlandish choice of fashion. It could have been the smatterings of Harold's blood on their clothes, but Frank figured it was most likely the appearance of the law.

Frank led the way, mostly ignoring the clientele and peeking around at the seemingly endless variety of black clothing. Amazing, he thought, how they got it to all fit into such a small area, racks and rounders crammed with black vests, jeans and tops.

Techno music blared from hidden speakers, its incessant drone reminding Frank of the music he sometimes heard tearing up the walls in Jaimie's room. He also recalled the CDs lining the shelf in Patrick Racine's room. The dead boy's taste had clearly included this tedious music. Curious, Frank peered around, seeking the source of the music, and instead noticed a security camera hanging from a brace in the ceiling at the right rear corner of the store. Right below it a sign

read: DON'T TRY ANY FUNNY STUFF, WE'RE
WATCHING YOU.

"Help you, gentlemen?"

They turned and encountered an older, formidable version of the shoppers in the store: a man
in his mid-forties, smiling, his brownish teeth
playing hide-and-seek behind an overgrowth of
mustache concealing his upper lip. Hair ran amok
atop his head like a bale of tumbleweed, a tattoo
of a snake slithering down the left side of his face
all the way to his jaw.

"Good evening," Hector said. "I'm Captain
Rodriguez from the Thirteenth Precinct. This is
Detective Ballaro." The man introduced himself
as Judas and they exchanged handshakes. "Are
you the store proprietor?"

Judas furrowed his hands into his jeans pockets. "Yes, I own this place."

"May we have a moment of your time?"

Judas shrugged a friendly gesture. "Sure. Come
this way." Weaving away, he led Frank and Hector through the racks of clothing to the rear of
the store. They went through a door that had an
EMPLOYEES ONLY sign on it and entered a tiny
office.

Frank had to practically shield his eyes at the
colors abounding here.

The walls were inches deep in posters, mostly
music-oriented, psychedelic prints of guitars,
keyboards, lights and spaceships, the various
names of techno bands splayed across their
brightly hued surfaces like planets and suns in
some extraterrestrial astronomical chart. Ban-

dannas and scarves dangled from every dusty fixture in the place, like the shedded skins of rare tropical reptiles. Floor lamps, incense holders, beaded lampshades. Candelabras, their waxes long burned, coating the metal capsules in a milky, hardened ooze. It was all here, scattered and neglected in this graveyard of psychedelia. Whether nostalgic or just plain messy, Frank couldn't decide. Nevertheless, it was quite a sight.

Judas shoved aside a river of papers camouflaging an old metal desk and sat down on it, moccasined feet dangling.

Frank reached into his jacket pocket, removed the receipt he'd taken from Harold's apartment and handed it to Hector. Hector unfolded it and showed it to Judas. "Do you remember this particular purchase?"

Judas took the receipt, looked at it. Frank could see the veins at his temples throbbing, the one below the snake tattoo nearly sending the snake into motion. "What seems to be the problem?" Although Judas's appearance was more than unpleasant, his bearing seemed mannerly and cooperative.

"We're investigating a murder. One of the victims had this receipt in his pocket. We're hoping you might be able to tell us something about the person who might have purchased these clothes."

Judas ran a hand through his mustache. "This is dated two weeks ago. I see a lot of people come and go. I'd be lyin' if I had to pinpoint one particular guy, you know?"

"Who's J.P.?" Frank pointed to a small space on the receipt where the letters were written. "Is that the salesperson?"

"Jack. He's off today."

Frank opened the manila envelope, removed the police sketch of Harold Gross and handed it to Judas. "He look familiar?"

Judas's eyebrows searched the heavens, lines of intense thought carved deep into his forehead. "Yeah, he does." He kept his eyes pinned to the portrait of the bald sunglasses-wearing man. "He your murder suspect?"

"Could very well be," Hector said.

Judas hopped down from the desk, walked around and took a seat in the chair behind it. He opened a drawer and removed a remote control. "I have a security system set up that takes video snapshots of the store from the rear, to the left of the checkout desk. I had it installed two years ago after the store was held up. I stay open 'til midnight every night, and figured it was the least I could do, afford really, to prevent that type of thing from happening again. The camera's visible from almost anywhere in the store, and I think it does a good job at deterring shoplifters."

Frank nodded. "We saw it."

"Look." Judas pointed the remote toward a black-and-white surveillance monitor perched on a small cart to the side of his desk. The dust sheathing it was thick enough to write his name in. Frank and Hector edged around the side of the desk and saw a grainy video-cap of nearly three-quarters of the floor space in the shop. In

207

the foreground, several customers stood frozen in time; in the background, Frank and Hector were caught walking through the entrance. Judas pressed a button on the remote and a second shot flickered into view, showing the two cops having a conversation alongside a rounder of leather jackets, a few nearby customers eyeing them suspiciously.

"It's rigged to run three seconds of video every time the front door is opened; this way I get at least something of everyone who comes into the store. With all the traffic I get, I'm guaranteed to catch a few precious moments on all my customers."

"How come you run it only when the door is opened?" Frank asked. "Wouldn't it make more sense to keep it going at all times?"

Judas reached down beneath his desk and pulled out a cardboard box. Opening it, he revealed a dozen or more videotapes, each labeled with a month and year. "If I kept it running all the time, I'd use up two tapes a day. I couldn't afford that, and really, I'd have no place to store them all. This way, I change 'em once a month."

Frank felt a twinge of excitement. He looked at Hector, who was looking at his watch. *Good ol' Hect,* Frank thought. No doubt he was sorting the same thoughts through his head: that this surveillance system of Judas's could possibly prove Frank's theory. Finding Harold Gross on the tape would be an unimportant factor at this time, the conclusion having already been made that Harold Gross was indeed at this store.

But what if another one of . . . *them* had been here, making a purchase?

Frank let his eyes roam the cramped office. A poster on the wall caught his eye: VILLAGE CLOTHING! TECHNO-WEAR FOR EVERY MIND-BENDING OCCASION! The detective personality inside couldn't help but think of all the CDs in Patrick Racine's room.

"Frank?"

"Yes, Hect?"

"What do you think?"

"Judas, would you mind if we took a quick look through your videos from the last two months?"

"Sure. The tape that's in now has the last three weeks on it. Judging by the date on the receipt, your boy will be on it toward the beginning." Judas aimed the remote, and Frank noticed two VCRs stacked one on top of the other on the floor below the cart. One was rewinding the tape currently inside it.

The tape clicked to a stop, and Judas began flipping through a multitude of grainy, blurry frames.

A few minutes of silence passed, showing a multitude of youthful customers coming and going from the store. Finally Hector abruptly pointed to the screen. "There. Stop!"

Judas stopped the tape and Frank saw him at once. A man, completely bald, wearing sunglasses.

But it wasn't Harold Gross. Someone else had come into Village Clothing recently, someone shorter, stouter. Someone who looked eerily similar to Harold Gross.

Judas pressed a button on the remote. The next frame showed the bald customer perusing a rack of clothing. The third showed him at the checkout counter making a substantial purchase. When he advanced to the next frame, the bald customer was gone.

"That sure looks like your boy," Judas offered.

Frank rubbed his chin in thought, the drone of the music from out front pounding through the walls. He felt the slight stirring of a headache, perhaps caused by fatigue, and he suddenly hoped he wouldn't be here much longer. "Judas, would you mind going through this tape with us? I'd like to see how many guys fitting a similar description have come in over the last two weeks."

"No problem, Officer." He smiled, nodding. Clearly he was enjoying this little adventure.

So they went through the tape, stopping a total of seven times in order to get a closer glimpse of bald men, some with sunglasses, all of whom made purchases. The third one they saw was Harold Gross.

A half hour later, when they finally returned to the frames Frank and Hector appeared in, Frank asked Judas to put in a tape from last month, then pulled Hector aside. "Well, what do you think?"

"Weird—but so are a lot of the kids who come in here. We'd find a hundred of 'em wearing green hair and eyebrow rings."

"Yeah, but this is different, I just . . . well I just

know, Hect. C'mon, I haven't been wrong yet, have I?"

Hector closed his eyes and rubbed them, the dark semicircles beneath rising like cold shadows. "No, you haven't. Believe me, at this point I'm pretty amazed that there seems to be a bunch of bald guys wearing sunglasses running around committing crimes. More so that they actually seem to be coming to this store to buy black clothing, just as you said. But why *this* place?"

Frank leaned away from Hector. "Judas? Do you play that techno music here all day long?"

Judas nodded. "You bet. Most of the time, anyway. Kids love it."

"I have another theory regarding that. At least now I do."

Hector put up his hands. "Whoa, Ballaro, one thing at a time. You still haven't told me how your Bobby Lindsay fits in with all this."

"Gentlemen?"

Frank and Hector faced Judas. He was pointing to a frame of a bald male customer wearing sunglasses standing right below the scope of the camera's eye, staring straight into the lens.

Bobby Lindsay.

Chapter Eighteen

Shivering wildly, wracked with pain and nearly frozen in fear, Jaimie stumbled up the steps of the Sixth Street station, her sneakerless feet scraping against the concrete steps, glass and pebbles tearing holes through her socks, cutting her soles. At the top step she stubbed her toe and cried out. A number of folks passing by took brief notice of the straggle-haired girl but shuffled on their way, disinterested—which was fine with Jaimie. She simply wanted to get to the safety of her home as quickly as possible, into the warm, caring embrace of her father, where she would be safe.

She found it amazing how the people of New York just ignored those in distress. After staggering onto the train in the Bronx, her feet wet and bloody, trailing tacky footprints on the subway car floor, she pulled herself into a seat and closed her eyes, trying to block out the heavy stares of the twenty-odd riders scattered through the length of the car. In the darkness behind her closed eyes, she heard gentle footsteps approach, and then the voice of a male stranger, asking if she was all right, but she kept her eyes sealed in answer, fearful that the voice might belong to a mysterious bald man with sunglasses, or even the bloodied disemboweled cadaver from the subway platform, and she simply replied, "I'm fine," in a curt yet civilized manner, keeping her hands to her face, running them through her sweaty, matted hair, all the while trying to control her shakes.

The footsteps backed off, no additional questions were asked, and she sat utterly alone, trembling, feeling the multitude of cold stares penetrating her as the train slowly shook its way back into Manhattan. She felt an alarming warmth at her feet, the blood, seeping through her sneakers, through her socks, through her skin, perhaps into her very bloodstream, seemingly poisoning her with whatever horror it carried—the same one that had stricken the poor young man sitting amid his viscera on the subway platform.

The first stop came and the doors opened. Unable to withstand the inquisitive stares from the other passengers, or the bloody poison tainting her sneakers, she impulsively stood and darted from her seat out through the opened doors onto the elevated platform at the 178th Street Station, still in the Bronx. The doors quickly closed behind her and the train once again left her in solitude, elevated thirty feet in the cold nighttime air. Her concerns suddenly centered on ridding her body of the rotten sneakers, and she kicked them off onto the tracks. Then she ran to the farthest end of the platform and waited nearly twenty minutes until the next train pulled in. She took a seat in the sparsely filled car—still gathering some wary looks—and pulled her knees to her chest, her chin on her knees, her sneakerless feet at the edge of the seat. She stared out the window, watching the stops come and go for what seemed an eternity, all the way to the Sixth Street station in Manhattan, where she hurried off, lightheaded, stumbling up the steps like a drunkard after an all-night binge.

Jaimie escaped into the moonlit night, the cool air drying her sweat, sending bumpy chills from her scalp to her toes. Her head spun crazily, the night's horrifying events still so fresh in her mind, creating a surreal cloud around her like a nightmare too difficult to shake away upon waking.

She slowly and gently paced along the sidewalk, careful not to teeter from her dizziness or step on anything that might injure her feet. People brushed by her, mere shadows, her mind unable to spell out their absolute reality. She felt like a ghost trapped in the lucid world.

Jaimie was in shock.

She followed her instincts as they blindly led her through the downtown streets, past the diner where she ate burgers and fries with her friends from time to time, past the tavern where the bartender would set her up with a free beer every now and then, even though she wasn't old enough to drink. Past an alley where a police cruiser sat guarding the adjacent sidewalk, the entrance blocked off with yellow police line tape.

She turned the corner of Fourth Street and peered at the brick-faced apartment building across the street, about a quarter the way up the block.

Home.

Bobby Lindsay crawled through the maddeningly narrow tunnel, knees and fists caked with dirt and mud, bald head scraping along the roots escaping the low-lying ceiling. It smelled of shit and bugs and all things gone to rot down here, but the odors didn't faze him in the least, because he possessed only one desire: to press on, to let nothing stop him from standing before the Giver once again.

Although the tunnel held no light, he could still see quite well. This keen ability, which he greedily accepted, gave him the strength and desire to continue, and he followed the long, winding tunnel to what he felt would be his ultimate destiny, his very purpose.

He slowed for a brief moment to peer at the device around his ankle, the green light—once aglow—now gone, replaced by a blinking red one, warning him that he'd be pretty much fucked if one of those Outsiders got hold of him. He knew quite well that it would be best not to let that happen. The Giver forbade it.

The air was cold down here, and he shivered,

wearing only jeans and a sweatshirt (both black of course; the Giver wouldn't have it any other way). Without ample pockets, he had no choice but to keep a close grip on the Atmosphere, never once weakening his hold as he crawled along the passage. He continued at a feverish pace for a short while, then stopped, selfish desire suddenly consuming him.

He wanted to relish the pulse of the Atmosphere.

The glorious Atmosphere, the wonderful object with the smooth ebony skin, with the six perfectly proportioned tubular extremities. He handled it ever so carefully, so as not to disgrace it by getting it dirty. In his efforts not to tarnish its surface, another memory instantly returned, as if a bubble filled with thoughts had burst inside his mind and spilled its contents. The Atmosphere—it *had* been dirty once before. In the grasp of his sister Carrie. Clearly now he could remember standing at the threshold of his bathroom frozen with awe as the Atmosphere carried on with the filling process. He remembered finally retrieving it from Carrie's dead grasp, cleansing it of all the staining impurities in the tub, then cleaning the entire bathroom, the whole time telling himself that what had just happened with Carrie and the Atmosphere was a preordained event, that the Giver had wanted her to supply, and that he, Bobby Lindsay, would be adored in the eyes of the Giver for being there to make it happen.

But things hadn't turned out that way.

Bobby remembered wanting so badly to bring the Atmosphere to the Giver at that moment, to show him what he had done. But he thought otherwise, and suddenly found himself fighting the demands of the Giver, instead seeking further opportunities to harvest additional Suppliers. In his hasty efforts to do so, the Giver had deprived him of his memories a short time thereafter, and he instantly found himself lost like a young boy in the mall without his mother, standing in the bathroom with his dead, mutilated sister spread-eagled on the floor, blood at his feet and a strange object in his grasp. Frightened, he stuffed his sister into the suitcase and hid her from the world.

No, he didn't murder her; the Atmosphere did. Which was fine, as long as he was able to retain his memories and continue on with his duty as Harbinger.

Bobby heard a sound far ahead in the tunnel, approaching rapidly, a familiar enginelike hum growing louder and louder. He held the Atmosphere close, waiting in silence as the deep drone grew. The dirt walls around him began to resonate, above, below, on all sides. He pulled in his legs and sat squat, head touching the dirt wall above, rubbing his left elbow against the blinking bracelet on his ankle. He peered ahead, searching for a presence, fearful that the sound might be coming from the Outsiders—that they had found him.

But the growing tone materialized from ahead, not from behind. If the Outsiders had followed him, they would have approached from behind.

He felt his blood begin to race and he smiled, knowing that this couldn't be the approach of the Outsiders. It was the Giver, coming for him, just as it had weeks before in his room, when it first asked him to harvest.

Listening again, he heard a pulse—*the* pulse—making itself present in the background of the turbinelike resonation.

Then he saw the Giver.

Unable to coerce the strength to dig through her backpack and search out her keys, Jaimie rang the buzzer at the entrance of her building. She rang and rang, incessantly, but it went unanswered, so she reluctantly squirmed out of the backpack's binds and blindly rifled through her belongings until the keys jingled just past her grasp. She fished them out, her body shaking as much as the keys in her hand. The dozen or so keys all looked the same through her tears, and she was unable to immediately get the right one into the lock.

Finally one slipped in and she entered the building.

She approached the elevator and entered, pressing the button for the fourth floor. The doors shut and she rode up in silence, leaning against the rear wall, the elevator providing her a smooth, short, uninterrupted ride. The doors opened. Wiping her flowing tears with her sleeve, she moved down the hall to apartment 4F, her home. She battled with the keys again, not as long this time, finding the right one on the third try. She opened the door and staggered inside, making it to the center of the living room. She stood for a moment, confused, then the world went gray around her.

Her backpack fell from her hand and she fainted onto the carpet.

Breath exploded from his lungs in short, powerful bursts. Staying as still as an insect to avoid the prospect of becoming prey, Bobby Lindsay watched as the scaly black thing approached him. It looked like a snake in freshly shed skin, slick and wet, its length disappearing far into the dark tunnel ahead. Although it appeared to have no head, it still seemed to possess a sense of direction, the foremost tip ending in a pinpoint that swayed like an eel prowling from its lair.

It stopped in front of Bobby in an upright position, swaying hypnotically, flexing its probing end, sizing him up, not much unlike a cobra would a charmer's horn. Slowly it began crawling over him, like a giant poking finger, feeling him out, first his legs, then his body and soon his face, the roving appendage prodding and prodding, the pinpoint end opening into a suction-cup formation, seeming to taste him, leaving warm circles of moisture where it came in contact with his skin.

Bobby closed his eyes as the appendage performed its work, allowing himself to be encroached upon until it finally drew back. When he opened his eyes, the slithering appendage latched itself onto one of the tubular spines jutting from the surface of the Atmosphere. It abruptly tore the object from his grasp, the rapid action raising abrasions on his skin. He brought his pained hands to his face, bathing his wounds in his sweat, watching as the appendage swiftly whipped itself around the Atmosphere like a snake suffocating its prey. Wavelike ripples soon ran through the appendage.

As quickly and as hastily as it attacked the Atmosphere, it whipped away and detached itself, like a string from a spinning top, leaving the piece whirling in the dirt at Bobby's feet, spraying droplets of mud. Bobby leaned forward and retrieved it, his sights glued to the retreating appendage.

To the Giver.

He grabbed the Atmosphere and crawled after the appendage, its pinpoint end whipping up and down, side to side, widening the passage ever so slightly. Mud flew in a shower around Bobby, and he stayed back a bit, though careful to keep the appendage in his sight. The segmented extremity slowed as Bobby yielded, as if to allow the crawling boy to catch up, quickening its pace only when he came near. Blanketed in filth, Bobby followed along each mud-slicked turn, up, down, at intersections, all the way until an end finally came into view: a blue phosphorescent light appearing in the distance like the aura of something ghostly.

The appendage slipped from the tunnel into the light, its job apparently completed. Bobby reached the end and fell six feet onto the floor of a small black room. Coated in muddy filth, he looked up and found himself surrounded by the blue light, a ring of it encircling him like a great halo. Within it the pulse emanated. He felt its power in his veins, and he gratefully accepted its vital offering. At his ankle, the homing device had gone dead, its lights doused.

"Harbinger, what is your purpose?" The electronic voice startled him, its shrill monotone daunting. Just as suddenly, he again perceived a strange yet familiar sensation in his head, and an answer automatically came from his lips. "To seek out Suppliers."

"Harbinger, what will you do if an Outsider discovers you?"

"Kill him."

"Harbinger, what will you do if an Outsider overcomes you, or escapes?"

"Kill myself."

"Harbinger, take the unit. Seek out new Suppliers."

"Yes, Giver," he answered automatically, looking down at the Atmosphere in his hand. From the corner of his eye he saw the Giver's appendage slithering back into a hole in the wall—which sealed shut upon its complete withdrawal.

A light-filled door appeared opposite the hole from which he had fallen—which itself had mysteriously vanished, all traces of his entrance, including the mud he trailed behind himself, gone. He slowly walked through the oscillating door, the hall before him immediately dark and lustrous. He followed its path until he could go no farther and reached another hole just like the one he had fallen through. It led into a similar dirt tunnel. He crouched down and crawled through, following the passage for a lengthy amount of time until he came to an opening covered by a grate. He stopped momentarily, peering out toward a cement wall, thick cables tightly laced across its surface. He removed the grate, slid through and jumped down onto a cool soggy path with two parallel iron rails leading in both directions, left and right.

Subway.

He walked left, two priorities at once consuming him.

"Take the unit, seek out new Suppliers . . ."

"Kill the Outsider who discovers you . . ."

He thought back, quite clearly now, to the one who interfered, brought him down not too long ago and took him away from the Giver.

Ballaro.

In Jaimie's swoon, dreams came and went, each surrealistic episode never lasting more than a few minutes, or so it seemed. The illusionary worlds within her head encompassed endless seas of faceless people passing by, each and every one ignoring her existence, brushing her away with quick passes and cold shoulders. She cried and cried, her pleas unanswered, and she spun in circles at the center of the crowd, seeking just a moment's stability, feeling like an unseen spirit trapped in a world filled only with transient pedestrians en route to nowhere, ignoring her very existence. An unsettling feeling of déjà vu set in, and she tried her best to disregard it, pressing on to an unknown destination.

This is too easy, Bobby thought, entering the room. It was almost as if his arrival had been expected, and welcomed. Both doors had been open, granting him access not only to the building but to the apartment where *he* lived.

Ballaro.

And now, this. A woman, lying on her back on the floor, her head tilted to one side, a small puddle of drool leaking from her slack mouth, staining the carpet. He peered around cautiously. Furniture. Television. The gentle ticking of a clock in another room. But nothing else. Nothing.

At her side a backpack lay open, the contents spilled out. He kneeled next to her, put down the Atmosphere and grabbed the backpack by the bottom. He gently tugged, letting everything pour out. Notebooks, textbooks, a hairbrush, a makeup bag, a small wallet. He reached for the wallet and opened it, the girl's smiling face greeting him from a small clear window inside.

Fashion Institute of Technology
Student ID # 122–66–9856
Jaimie Ballaro

Bobby smiled. Ballaro. *Or the next best thing.*

Suddenly the phone rang. Heart racing, Bobby shot a harried glance at it but let it go unanswered.

He grabbed Jaimie and carried her like a bride from the apartment, leaving a trail of mud behind. He crossed the threshold just as the answering machine kicked in.

Chapter Nineteen

"Jame, if you're there, pick up . . ."

Frank turned and faced Hector, grimacing, the phone caught between his ear and his shoulder. The mustachioed captain was seated at his desk, gently tapping his fingers along the edge of the blotter as he waited for his computer to start up. Gloria Rodriguez, upon hearing the men, had risen from bed and was in the kitchen, preparing sandwiches and coffee.

"Jame? Last chance . . ." The eerie silence at the other end of the line sent a highly uncomfortable feeling creeping through his body, a feeling clearly brought on by his weak-rational personality, and even though it wasn't uncommon for his nineteen-year-old to spend her weekends out with friends until late hours, his worrying about her had always been the most difficult part of being a parent, and had always forced the submissive third of his personality to the forefront. He smiled weakly at Hector, attempting to mask his concern.

Hector spun his chair to face him, the computer's modem squelching. "Glad mine are all grown up." He offered a comforting smile, one that plainly said *been there, done that.*

Frank shrugged, feeling defeated, knowing there was nothing he could do at the moment. He left Jaimie a short message, explaining that he was at Hector Rodriguez's home working on something, along with the phone number in case she needed to reach him. Then he punched the message retrieval code on the keypad. The answering machine beeped and an electronic voice revealed that there were three messages. It beeped again and Neil Connor's voice spoke to him through the handset:

"Frank, Neil. Listen, something's up. I got a call at the precinct today from Bobby and Carrie Lindsay's father. Their real father, Jack Lindsay. Lives in California, but you know that already. Anyway, he insisted on speaking to you, said it was urgent. Something about the murder. He sounded really distraught, nervous, said something along the lines that it 'should've come out with the investigation, but it didn't.' I tried to get it out of him, but he kept mum, insisted on speaking to you. Can't imagine what it is, but it sounds like something big. He left his number, said for you to leave him a message and the number you'll be at, and he'll call you in the morning, first thing.

Give him a buzz, and let me know what's up. Okay?"

Frank pulled a pen from his shirt pocket and jotted down the number that followed on the pad next to the phone. He tore off the top piece of paper and placed it on the end table next to the couch.

Before he could guess what it was Jack Lindsay could want, the answering machine beeped again. Again it was Neil, this time in an obvious state of alarm:

"Frank, hold on to your pants, man, 'cause you're gonna shit 'em big time when you hear this. Bobby Lindsay's gone. Escaped. Just got the report. And you ain't gonna believe this. There's a big fucking hole in his bedroom floor, goes right into the ground. Way down too. Unbelievable. Don't know how the hell he did it. They had the whole fucking house surrounded, had him tagged and he just goes down and out. They've got some guys down in the hole now, saying the thing's at least twenty feet deep. You believe this shit? How in God's name did the kid dig a fucking tunnel in his room? Anyway, I hope you get this message soon. And let me know what's going on with the father. Think the guy knew about the escape? Let me know, all right? This has been a fuck of a night. Later."

Frank nearly dropped the phone, the shock of his partner's message hitting him hard. He held the phone just long enough to hear his own voice talking back to him from the tape, searching for Jaimie, before he let it hit the floor. He fell butt-first onto the couch, staring into space, his eyesight blurring the Rodriguez household into a surreal Dali-like environment.

"Frank, you okay? Frank?"

Frank shook his head, bringing the blurred images back into focus and finding Hector sitting on the couch next to him. "I just got a message from Neil. I . . . I don't know where to start."

Hector yelled for Gloria to bring a glass of water. She returned in seconds, her pink terry-cloth robe bundled around her, sashed at the waist, a tall glass filled with water in one hand, a cup of coffee in the other. "The beginning, start at the beginning. What'd he say?"

Frank took a sip of water and let the icy flow settle in his stomach. It heightened his senses, and at once he felt his lucidity returning. "Neil called. There were two messages from him. Bobby Lindsay's escaped."

"What the—"

"According to Connor, there was a big hole in his bedroom floor. A tunnel."

Hector's mouth dropped, and he sat back on the couch, shock obviously making its mark on him now. He looked at his wife, who read his expression—an expression she must've seen a thousand times before. She placed the cup of coffee on the end table next to Frank and quickly went into the kitchen, no questions asked. Hector leaned close to Frank, nearly whispering, "Frank, are you sure?"

Nodding, Frank said, "Neil's a bit of a baby, overreacts a lot. But he wouldn't exaggerate about something like this." Frank leaned back into the soft cushions of the couch, ran a hand through his hair. "You know, Hect, he doesn't know about Gross and all this shit we've been through."

"He will," Hector said. "It'll be in the papers tomorrow. The whole thing." He hesitated, took a deep breath and blew it out. "It's gonna be a long day tomorrow. With this thing out in the open, we're gonna have to report all our findings, everything we've been through today, which will slow our momentum big time. And our methodology ain't gonna look good on the commissioner's report. Damn, I should've known better than to let you—myself, for that matter—get involved. Oh, boy . . ."

Hector sounded worried now, for the first time since the whole thing started on Mason Street at four that morning. Again, Frank would have to convince Hector to let him continue with their work. "Hect, what we've uncovered in the last twenty hours is clearly the biggest thing I've ever been through, and I'd venture the same for you. This is huge—"

"That's exactly why we should report everything!" Hector looked away, in serious thought, worried and confused.

"Not yet, Hect. Please! We're on a major roll. Aren't you the least bit curious now to find out exactly what's going on?"

"What do you think?"

"So then, what's our next step?"

"Frank, please . . . I've been up for nearly twenty-four hours."

"Hect, I'm tired too. Spent. Too old for this shit. But I ain't stopping now. No one's gonna be able to pick up on our tracks. C'mon, you said it yourself. Something really fucked up is going down in the city, and you and I are the only ones who have any direction right now."

Hector yawned and ran a hand through his hair. "I was just going to check my email. If Martin found anything after we left the Twelfth this afternoon, it'll be there."

Frank placed his hands on his knees, a sudden burst of energy brought on by his ambitious detective personality. "Well, then, let's do it." *Good ol' Hect.*

Hector shook his head, in disbelief. "Let me get out of this uniform," he said, standing. "Have a sandwich, and I'll be right out." He walked down the hall into the bedroom, then stuck out his head. "Hey—Ballaro?"

Frank looked back at him, Gloria now at his side with a tray of food.

"You were right. I don't know how you knew, but you were right about Lindsay."

Frank smiled as Hector disappeared into his bedroom, thanking the detective personality inside for figuring it all out.

With sandwiches, pound cake and coffee in their stomachs, Frank and Hector were able to drum up some energy to continue their investigation— now from the comfort of Hector's living room.

"I've gotta get me one of these," Frank said, marveling at the magic of the computer's abilities. The screen showed a great big rainbow-striped mailbox that took up half the monitor's fifteen-inch display.

"I like the rainbows," Frank said in a mocking, effeminate voice. "It's so you."

"Piss off." Hector clicked the mouse cursor on the mailbox, and a big number three popped up on the screen.

"Testy. Haven't slept much?"

Ignoring Frank, Hector said, "Three messages. One from Martin, and it has an attached file. He must've found something."

He clicked on the mail entry from Martin and a letter came up on the monitor:

Captain Rodriguez:
I have a bit of interesting info regarding Harold Gross, James Hilton and Edward Farrell, and the disappearance of their supposed abductees. First off, yes, as discussed, Gross, Farrell and Hilton all had similar raps. What's interesting is that they're not the only ones I found. I went ahead and did the national search, and found something really interesting: 173 sketches of bald guys with sunglasses in the national database, most of whom had committed suicide after being pursued by authorities. Out of the total figure, 157 had been under surveillance by the FBI. The others were under scrutiny by local authorities but eventually vanished;

*all of the remaining sixteen baldies—gone
with the wind, just like their victims. All instances took place in one of four cities: Los
Angeles, San Francisco, Miami and New
York. Captain, I think you're on to something huge, something the boys in Washing-
ton don't want anybody else to know about.
My guess is that you hit the jackpot with
Gross. He's one of the few baldies the FBI
hadn't had a bead on.*

*As for Hilton, Farrell and Gross's victims:
I looked into the backgrounds of Andrew
Knowles and three other missing kids. Nothing much similar. Knowles was a problem
kid; a kid named Sutton had no problems,
good in school; one named Barrett was a
musician; the last, Tolson, an athlete. The
only likeness I could see other than what we
know already—age, Caucasian, etc.—was
that they were all big-time enthusiasts of
music, particularly techno. They all had fake
IDs and were frequenting dance clubs in
New York, and according to their parents,
spent way too much time listening to the
music, never leaving the house without a
pair of headphones attached to their heads.
Again, don't know if this means anything,
but it's all I could find out.*

Hope this helps. Talk to you tomorrow.
Phil.

"What do you think, Frank?"
"Want the truth?"

"Don't I always?"

"You remember Village Clothing, the music Judas had on?"

"That horrible shit? That was techno, right?"

Frank nodded. "Yep. And Pat Racine—when we were in his room, I happened to notice that his CD collection was almost exclusively techno music."

Hector shook his head, confusion mixing his fatigue and thoughts into a muddle. "So what does it all mean, Frank? Does it make sense?"

Frank made a real effort to smile, albeit a weak one. He looked at his watch; one A.M. was fast approaching. Gloria Rodriguez stepped from the kitchen at that moment, her hands nestled in her robe pockets. "Hector, I'm going back to bed. There's a pot of coffee on the stove. Please turn it off when you come to bed."

Hector offered his wife a smile comparable to Frank's feeble grin. " 'Night, hon." Gloria left the room and Hector looked back to the computer screen, speaking to Frank. "You know, I just thought of something we can do."

Frank, rubbing his eyes, groaned. "Good thing, 'cause Martin just beat me to my last theory. I'm fresh out now."

Hector rolled the mouse pointer over a globe icon and clicked it. He looked at Frank, eyelids drooping. "The World Wide Web."

Chapter Twenty

"I really gotta get me one of these things," Frank said, sipping his coffee, watching the computer screen as the results of Hector's searches on the Internet came up.

"Nothing of interest here," Hector said. In the forty-five minutes since they'd begun surfing the Web for information, they'd come up with very little that could help them with the investigation. Frank, being quite inexperienced with computers beyond the data entry and retrieval systems at the Twelfth Precinct, hadn't realized the extent to which the World Wide Web could be utilized. "It's complete chaos," Hector had explained. "Free speech run amok. If you need info, this is the place to go. My guess is that someone somewhere out there has all the info we need and is willing to share it with the world. All we have to do is find it."

Their searches were varied:

A query of BALD, SUNGLASSES, KIDNAPPING brought hundreds of meaningless sites pertaining to fashion, haircare, music, and beach attire. Hidden amid the fray, however, were a number of Los Angeles police beat reports revealing a bit of information regarding the facts they already had: the disappearances of a number of teenage boys from the local area, and profiles of the witnesses' accounts.

Another search they made consisted of KIDNAPPING, BALD, SUNGLASSES, and, at Frank's request, TECHNO. This spewed out a number of music sites delving into the city club scenes and the appropriate styles with which one could adorn themselves should they decide to partake in the lifestyle. A few additional police reports came up, though they did not offer any further information.

"Try this, Hect." Hector cleared the search engine's query space and readied himself to type. "Bald, sunglasses, techno and atmosphere."

Hector nodded and typed. "How come we didn't try that first?"

"We're both pretty tired, that's why."

Hector hit the search button and the computer's hard drive growled.

The screen displayed the following:

Query results: 6 hits.
1) North Pole's Hole in the Sky Caused by
Alien Invasion.

http://www.sanskrit.com/holeinsky
2) *Alien Invasion*
http://www.sanskrit.com/alieninvasion
3) *This Is Not Fiction! We Have Been Visited!*
http://www.sanskrit.com/nonfiction
4) *Alien Abduction: My Return From the Mother Ship*
http://www.sanskrit.com/abduction
5) *Alien Methodology Revealed: Binaural Beats Utilized To Manipulate Brain Wave Patterns.*
http://www.sanskrit.com/alienmethodology
6) *Beware the Men in Black: This Is No Joke!*
http://www.sanskrit.com/meninblack

An uncomfortable silence ran between them. Frank could hear Hector's heavy breathing, along with his own pounding heart, as they read the titles of the Web pages. Finally, Hector broke the silence. "All these pages have the same domain address, which means they've been authored by the same person or group."

"So somebody else knows something about what's going on, even more than we do, perhaps."

"Aliens? Don't get your hopes up, Jetson. It looks like the author has a highly active imagination. At first glance, that is. And besides, the keywords we searched for could very well be used in an entirely different context than the one we're looking for."

Frank inched his chair closer. "Let's check it out."

Hector clicked on the first title, *North Pole's Hole in the Sky Caused by Alien Invasion.*

An article came up, topped with a detailed sketch of the earth, looking down on the North Pole. A series of arrows pointed out the location of lower and higher ozone levels in the atmosphere. Below, a subtitle read: *Scientists covering up true cause of ozone hole.*

Hector read the article aloud:

The sky above the North Pole has developed an "ozone hole" in the atmosphere that is allowing extra amounts of cancer-causing ultraviolet rays to fall on the United States. The hole, which has been seen in the past two years, develops for brief periods early in the spring, when sunlight suddenly hits the clouds of ice particles in the atmosphere, liberating chlorine-based chemicals. These chemicals eat up ozone, which is important to life on Earth because it screens out much of the sun's harmful ultraviolet light.

Until now, the Northern Hemisphere hasn't been as vulnerable to ozone loss as the Southern Hemisphere, apparently because of differences in air temperatures and circulation. But in the past two years, air in the north has grown especially cold, and the ozone has thinned dramatically over most of North America.

Reports show that scientists have "struggled" to find a cause to the mysterious "hole" that appeared two years ago, and a reason for the build-up of chlorine in the atmosphere, which has exacerbated the loss of ozone. Falsified satellite measurements show an increase of nitrogen compounds in the lower atmosphere that have consequently fluctuated ozone concentrations. Due to the public's general disinterest in such ecological data, scientists have successfully deceived the curious, easily dissuading them to assume the simple explanation as a validity.

Of course, their explanations are utter falsehoods.

In or about the month of December 1996, a spacecraft of alien origin entered our atmosphere at the North Pole. Although visible to the naked eye, the craft remained stealthed to military personnel, exercising a nameless technology cloaking it from radar and satellite scans. The alien embodiment within anchored the craft deep within the arctic snow, spending a year or more there, scanning the Earth for particulars it could utilize for its own knowledge and subsistence, all the while manipulating the ozone layer above its position in an effort to simulate the chlorine-rich atmosphere found on their home world, wherever that may be.

It seemed that in time the alien body was unable to utilize the Earth's carbon-rich atmosphere to meet their immediate needs for survival, and opted for a different, more extreme course of action, one which serves some sort of acquisitive purpose. Although assumptions have been made, the true reason for their horrifically harsh methodology has yet to be determined. (The entire process will be examined more closely in a subsequent article.)

The powers that be, our almighty Government, have accomplished covering up this potentially ruinous crisis and have easily coerced the scientific community to create a whitewash of the alarming facts at hand.

If there is a God, let him help us should our Government fail in their measures to rid the planet of the alien virus.
Ruefully yours,
sanskrit@prs.com

"Quite a tale." The weakness in Hector's voice was most likely a result of fatigue, but it really sounded as if he were trying hard to shrug off the short article as a crude piece of fiction.

Frank stared at the words on the screen, his gaze unmoving, until the text blurred into a wash of black and white. "I find this interesting," he said, pointing to the words on the screen. "It talks of harsh methods and Government coverups. Haven't we seen a little of both today? Think about it: the kids in the alley, the weird object one of them held. That could pass as a harsh method, whatever it may be. And then the FBI's

239

Michael Laimo

efforts to keep the kidnappings under wraps. The person who wrote this knows something, Hect."

Hector grinned. "I don't know . . . I think what you've got here is another one of those Heaven's Gate–type kooks who's convinced that space aliens are waiting in the wings for them to jump aboard their spaceship to salvation."

Frank nodded. "Most likely. But this guy seems too smart. He ain't talking space gibberish. There's a lot of science here. It might not be aliens, but there's definitely something out of the ordinary going on, something big enough for the government not to want the public to know about."

"So you believe this stuff about the ozone layer and the hole in the sky?"

"Absolutely. Not necessarily the thing about the spaceship, but I do believe the hole in the ozone layer has been caused by something the big boys don't want us to know about."

"But what does it have to do with *our* mystery?"

"We'll find out now. Go back to the list of Web pages."

Hector hit the BACK button on the Web browser and brought up the previous page.

"Look at the last one."

Hector scrolled down: *Beware the Men in Black: This Is No Joke!*

"If his men in black are bald and wear shades, we're balls deep in alien ka-ka." Frank laughed aloud at his own humor but couldn't help but be spooked at the memory of the homeless man in

240

the lobby of Harold Gross's apartment building.

You come for the man in black?

Hector clicked on the domain address. The computer's hard drive made a series of grinding noises, and then the Web page came up.

A crude sketch of a bald man wearing sunglasses stared back at them.

Silence filled the room as the two cops read the caption beneath the picture:

This is a picture of a man in black. This is a picture of me, Sanskrit.

They continued to read:

> *If this man looks familiar, then you have perhaps seen one of the men in black. No, this isn't a secret government agent trying to whitewash alien existence from the public, like in the movies. Nor is it an alien itself. It is a simple human male, like myself, who has been taken hostage by the alien body through a simple yet powerful technique that cleverly utilizes binaural beats to gain control of the human mind (more on binaural beats in linked page #5).*
>
> *During their two-year presence here on the planet Earth, the alien body has continuously emitted an extremely powerful alpha wave pulse that, although inaudible to the human ear, is clearly heard through radio transmissions. Once the pulse connects with the correct type of mind (I have discovered*

that very few individuals have been affected by the pulse; those who have are physically strong males with similar interests and backgrounds that include a difficult childhood leading into an adult life most notably guided by a semi-aggressive, egotistical demeanor, a personality that has made it difficult for them to function with sound acceptance in society), the individual becomes entranced and falls into a state of Delta, an extreme form of unbreakable hypnosis (under almost all circumstances I would assume, mine being a unique case as far as I can tell) and becomes an all-answering slave forced to carry out the shocking demands of the alien body.

For what purpose these demands incur I have not the slightest notion, but it is a horrifying act that is necessitated, one that while in alien possession seems ecstatic, even orgasmic to those under the influence. From what I can gather, the alien body's embrace somehow triggers the pleasure center in the brain, forcing the captive to realize his actions as an act of pure, sexually animalistic promiscuity.

Which leads me to the real victims of their reign: the boys. The men in black are simply gophers (somehow the word "harbinger" comes to mind) for the alien body, seeking out the perfect subject for their puzzling needs.

The perfect subject retains personality

traits even more specific than those of the men in black: they are male, between the ages of fourteen and twenty, with—and this may sound strange, but it is explained as best as possible in linked page #5—a passionate taste for techno and ambient music. There are as far as I can gather, no additional commonalities. The sole purpose of the man in black is to seek out the aforementioned. The purpose of the boys is still unknown, but it is apparent that it fills a crucial need of the alien body, always, most unfortunately as I realize it now, resulting in violent death for the chosen subject.

Be wary of the men in black. They are easily spotted. Their hypnotic state compels them to act aberrantly: the skin and eyes become extremely photosensitive, hence sunglasses for the eyes; black clothing is worn, shrouding the body sans the scalp from the sun's ultraviolet rays (ironic, isn't it, that the alien bodies themselves are solely responsible for the most recent dramatic increase of radioactive ultraviolet rays in our atmosphere; it is my assumption that this error in fact thwarted their efforts to modify the atmosphere for their own accessibility), the chosen color of black preferred to absorb heat from the sun. This conduct patterns that of the alien, whose habitat I assume to be quite dark and hot, the atmosphere rich in chlorine.

It is with great regret that I cannot ex-

pound further as to the intricacies of the alien embodiment and the systematic relationship between the men in black and the young abductees, as memories of my own abduction are somewhat vague, seemingly masked by some sort of post-hypnotic suggestion. However, upon recalling their ability to apply binaural beats to control the human mind, I have analyzed the subject in great detail, and describe them in linked page #5.
Ruefully yours,
sanskrit@prs.com

"You done reading?" Frank asked Hector.

"I am now." Hector leaned back in his chair, staring at the screen, squeezing his cheeks with one hand.

"What do you think?"

"Well, there are two questions that immediately come to mind. First: Is there a problem? You bet. And we're right in the middle of it. Second: Do I believe this shit? Of course not. It's Heaven's Gate material, right out of the cult handbook. What you've got is some underground cult of wackos spreading their word, blaming aliens from outer space for their extremist activities. They no doubt have a leader, this Sanskrit maybe, not unlike Heaven's Gate's Applewhite, who's got a bunch of hopeless soul-seeking degenerates—the Harold Grosses of the world—shaving their heads and wearing weirdo outfits, following him around like lost puppies and snatching up teenage boys for God knows what perversions their quote-unquote religion called for."

"But from what we can tell, they're actually killing the boys, not recruiting them."

"We've only got two dead for sure, as far as we know right now. The rest are missing. Regardless, it doesn't matter. Pure and simple, it's definitely a cult. And they're running around carrying out their sick rituals at will."

Frank allowed his three personalities to weigh Hector's assumption as a possibility. They all seemed to agree that he was right and that no logical alternative existed other than to go along with his immediate speculation: that all this time they'd been unearthing the doings of some nationwide cult. "It's really frightening."

"Very much so. Under most circumstances, extremist cults are dangerous only to themselves. But here? This seems to be a unique situation, Charles Manson meets Marshall Applewhite, to the tenth degree."

Frank's detective mind at once spotted a few details that didn't make sense. "You know, I was just thinking . . . Bobby Lindsay actually revealed to us that he was involved with a religious group. It was his excuse for the shaven head—"

"There you go."

"—but then, how come we never found any evidence outside of his confession and his appearance that there was any involvement?"

"You also never found the hole in his bedroom floor."

Frank nodded in silence. "Which I guess leads

me to my next question. That hole, tunnel, whatever they said was there in his room—it wasn't there, Hect. We turned the entire house upside down. And then there's the tunnel that Harold Gross slipped away through, in the courtyard."

"That was a cesspool duct; he plucked the manhole cover off it."

"But there was a tunnel leading away from it down below. You said yourself that it had been dug out somehow. And then—and don't keep denying this—but . . . that object the kid was holding in the alley. I still think it has some significance."

Hector sipped his coffee. "A religious icon."

Frank thought about that. People have been known to kill over their beliefs. So it seemed to make some sense that Gross, in a state of religious frenzy, would have risked his life over retrieving the odd statuette. "I agree that everything we've discovered today could easily fall into a case involving an extremist cult—except, of course, the presence of the tunnels. Until these can be explained, I have to keep alternate explanations under consideration."

Hector grinned incredulously. "What, like aliens burrowed out the tunnel?"

Hector didn't understand that Frank had three personalities doing battle at all times inside his head, that he possessed varying viewpoints on almost every subject placed in front of him. Did he really believe in the far-fetched alien theory? Not really. More evidence did indeed point to the existence of a cult. His weak yet rational personality believed in the cult, and so did the strong, truth-seeking detective—for the most part. But deep within his irrational-impulsive personality—the one who got him into trouble, the one who wanted to shoot the rat in the gutter—some doubts existed with respect to the obvious answers. It felt that somewhere deep down beneath the obvious, the real truth in the situation was cloaked. And since Frank remained faithful to all his personalities, he needed to accept this alternative as a possibility, however debatable it seemed, until he could convince himself with sound explanations of all possible questions.

"Frank?"

Frank shook away his thoughts. "Yes . . . I'm here."

"It's almost two; we ought to call it a night. There's a lot we have to do tomorrow."

"Wait. I want to see the rest of the Web pages, at least the one on the binaural beats."

"Okay, but this is it. I'm asleep at the wheel." Hector rolled the mouse, aiming the cursor over linked page #5: *Alien Methodology Revealed: Binaural Beats Utilized To Manipulate Brain Wave Patterns.*

Binaural Beats, Rhythms, Sounds, Entrainment
Rhythm is the true essence of the cosmos. Everything shifts to its own cadence, from the micro-orbits of electrons and protons to the macro-orbits of planets, stars and galaxies. In all organisms, rhythm is unmistak-

able, from the perpetual tempo of the heart to the intervals of inhalations and exhalations. The pulse of human beings is elaborately sewn into the web of planetary oscillations.

Sound waves are calculated in cycles per second (hertz or hz). Each cycle of a wave is in actuality a solitary flutter of frequency. The typical scope of listening for the human ear settles between 16,000 hz. and 20,000 hz. We retain no ability to hear extremely low frequencies (ELFs), but we can detect them as rhythmical pulses, and the alien body has cleverly utilized this function to their advantage.

Entrainment is the approach of coexistence, where the resonances of one target will necessitate the vibrations of another, causing both to undulate at similar rates. External cycles, such as those existent in ambient and techno music, can have an immediate consequence on the psychological and physiological state of the listener. Slower rhythms from 48–70 BPMs have been demonstrated to enfeeble the heart and respiratory rates, thereby diversifying the preeminent brainwave currents, directly affecting behavior.

Binaural beats are perpetual resonances of imperceptibly distinct tones—those most common in techno music—which are administered to each ear autonomously in stereo via headphones. For example, if the left speaker's frequency is 100 cycles per second and the right speaker's frequency is 108 cycles per second, the dissimilarity between them is 8 cycles per second. When these sounds are orchestrated they result in a fluttering tone that intensifies and ebbs in a "wah-wah" tempo, which in turn effectively seizes control of various parts of the brain, based on cyclical dissimilarities. Binaural beats are not a superficial sound; rather they are subsonic tones heard within the brain itself. These tones are conjured as both hemispheres work concurrently to ascertain noises that are diversely leveled by key mathematical interims. The brainwaves answer to these surging frequencies by pursuing them (entrainment). Soon both hemispheres begin to work in tandem. Disclosure between the two sides of the brain is parallel with moments of innovation, awareness and knowledge on some levels; pleasure, eroticism and primordial yearning on others.

The four primary brain wave patterns are Beta, Alpha, Theta and Delta. Each has a differentiating pattern and yields an unusual level of awareness. Beta waves (14 cycles per second and above) manage the normal waking state of consciousness when focus is implemented toward the outside world, and are initially optimized by the alien body process. Alpha waves (8–13 cycles per second) are administered while dreaming and in simple meditation when the eyes are shuttered, and

*are broadcast by the alien body in external
form through the use of radio frequencies.
Theta waves (4–7 cycles per second) even-
tuate during sleep and are prevalent in the
highest phase of meditation. In concentrated
meditation and deep sleep, Delta waves (.5–
3 cycles per second) occur. The choice level
for deep perception is in the realm of Theta.
When in Theta, the senses pull back from
the external world and focus on the inner
one. Delta waves deliver a complete evacu-
ation from outside awareness and furnish
the most effective feelings of peace. Ultimately, through the alien hypnosis, Delta
waves predominate, and are present during
all of the subject's activity.*

*By strategically calibrating and shifting
sounds around the head, the sounds are absorbed in introspective intervals. This can el-
evate and adjust the perceived experience of
them. Particularly potent when experienced
through headphones, these tones establish
descriptive bearings in three-dimensional
soundscapes. A determinate combination of
alien pulse and binaural beats associated
with techno music results in the attainment
of hypnosis suitable for carrying out the
alien body methodology (more on alien
methodology in linked page #4.*
Ruefully yours,
sanskrit@prs.com

Hector's eyes looked as if glass had been blown
across them; beneath were dark prunelike rings.

"I know you're very tired," Frank said, "but we do have to consider this as a possibility, Hect. We've seen all this today, and I'm guessing there are more similarities in his other pages. We need to read them."

"I don't think I can do that right now, Frank. I'm beat."

Frank rubbed his eyes. "Tomorrow, before we leave, can you print out the other articles out?"

"Sure." Hector moved the mouse, performed a few clicks. "There. I've saved them on my hard drive."

"Thanks," Frank said. He hesitated a moment, then rubbed his hands together. "So what's the plan for tomorrow?"

Hector turned off the computer and stood up. His bones made a cracking noise. "Ouch . . . let me sleep on that one, Frank. I'll let you know in the morning. I'll get you a pillow and a blanket. Try to get in a few hours, okay?"

Frank nodded, although he knew sleep would be hard to find. His body wanted it, but he wasn't sure his mind would allow it. "I'll try my best."

Hector left and returned with a white pillow and a large blue comforter.

"Thanks, Hect."

Hector retreated in silence, then turned and said, "Tomorrow's probably gonna be another long day."

Frank closed his eyes. *Dear God, I hope not.*

Chapter Twenty-one

The night was black, but far from silent.

Lester wandered the desolate west-end streets for what seemed like hours until he finally caught word of tonight's location. Talk on the streets had the site set in an abandoned warehouse bordering the docks near Eighteenth Street, but as it happened, last-minute arrangements had to be made when a band of undercover authorities performed a non-related drug sweep in the area, breaking up the start of the gathering and forcing the troops to reassemble twenty blocks north at Thirty-eighth Street behind an abandoned tenement, just west of Hell's Kitchen.

When Lester finally located the congregation, many had already gathered. He unconspicuously slithered in and around the site, easily blending in but still soliciting some measly, paranoid sneers from the others in attendance, their wild eyes rolling, with no direction in mind other than to provide alarm to those who ventured too near, or to seek guidance from the Leader.

Jyro.

Lester was anxious because he had news for Jyro, and had been seeking him ever since those cops came into the building looking for the man in black. He'd been following this particular man in black for a few days now, just as Jyro had instructed the troops to do, and was sheltering himself in the lobby when he heard the cops approach. He remembered exchanging a few choice words with them, careful not to reveal too much about the rebellion. He took off right away to inform the leader, as the great Jyro needed all activities—however slight—to be reported, especially if the clash upon ... *them* was to succeed.

Flames pranced from garbage-can fires situated about the site, each offering warmth to four or five homeless men huddling close to escape the frigid night air. Wild howls flew back and forth amid the tiny groups—guttural discharges, profanities, senseless shouts—each serving no purpose other than to dispense aggressions in anticipation of the approaching festivities.

Slowly, Lester wound in and about the homeless cliques throughout the camp, until he could go no farther, finding himself at the entrance of a small tent made from a blue tarpaulin. Two large black men stood at the flapping entrance, muscles swelling, each gripping a formidable-looking steel pipe that had been either ripped from a nearby awning or torn from a gutter. They wore tightly woven bandannas on their skulls and sneered at Lester's approach, as if he were trespassing on sacred ground, which, in this obscure little world, probably was true.

One of the guards stepped forward and abruptly wielded his pipe across Lester's path, like a medieval sentry stationed at a palace entrance. Lester stopped short, feeling the wind of the rapidly swung pipe on his filthy face. He caught his breath just in time to defend himself before being questioned.

"I-I have news for Jyro!" he bellowed, cowering as if expecting a blow.

The looming guard's eyebrows pointed into a dark *V*, "Address the Leader with respect."

Lester swallowed a lump in his throat, his glance nervously darting between the two scowling guards. "I have news for the Leader." His breaths were short and stagnant.

The guard pressed his steel pipe against Lester's chest, then peered at the second watchman as he stuck his head into the tent. He pulled out after a few moments, turned and nodded slightly.

The guard pulled back his pipe and placed his face inches from Lester's. His breath stank of whiskey and something rotten. "The Leader will see you, disheveler." Lester was quickly and forcefully guided into the tent.

The interior of the tent was much larger than it had seemed to Lester from outside. Actually, the tent itself served only as a drape to the entrance of an alley situated between an abandoned building and a chain-link fence. A few torn couches and mattresses sat haphazardly at the entrance of the alley in an apparent attempt at coziness. Three additional guards seated on the couches immediately stood upon Lester's entrance, two of them holding pipes, one a large kitchen knife, each making the passage past the scrappy furniture all the more daunting. He could feel their hot, rancid breath on his cheeks as he passed them by, their flexing muscles providing an additional threat en route to the Leader.

The guard ushering Lester gave him a sudden, sharp push from behind. "Move along," he shouted, and Lester fell forward past the thugs, tripping over his own feet, landing on his knees.

"Good man," a dark gravelly voice issued, hushing everyone within. "Kneel before your Leader."

Lester peered up and saw him, the Leader, the great black man, seated on a fairly new reclining chair—clearly stolen—his presence alone holding strict command over all those in the room. He was dressed in torn jeans, a black T-shirt, and a brown leather jacket that looked as if it had been through more battles than a championship prizefighter. His head was shaved bald, a glistening sheen of sweat reflecting the torch flames set at either side of his throne. He wore sunglasses, and when he smiled at Lester, a gold tooth shone from within his mouth. "Well, well. I haven't seen your ugly face before."

Lester peered up at the impressive man. The story of Jyro was a familiar one among the ranks of the homeless. He had been a professional wrestler once, did the WWF circuit for three years before overdosing on some bad steroids. He lost half his mind, and it became impossible to negotiate a contract with him, much less have him get all his theatrical moves down. But Jyro had been extremely popular with the fans, a real money-maker, and with the promoters investing big bucks in him, he was forced to continue his participation in the circuit.

He hit rock bottom in a championship bout with Killer Kalhoun. The prearranged scenario was that Killer Kalhoun would win the fight in the eighth round, pinning Jyro to the canvas after performing a triple twist flip on him about two minutes into the round. But Jyro, after blowing a number of serious moves that had Kalhoun fiercely angered, decided to take matters into his own hands and force an upset. The 320-pound man caught Kalhoun off guard as he tried to perform a double back clothesline drop and ducked down, slamming him in the nuts with his shoulder as he passed over him. Kalhoun went down in a convulsion. The maddened Jyro immediately dove down and sunk his teeth into the champ's jugular, which created quite a spectacle, not to mention a great deal of blood. The frenzied crowd assumed it was fake all along.

When WWF security finally pried Jyro away from Kalhoun—they had to give him a damn good beating with their nightsticks—the downed wrestler had lost two quarts of blood, nearly a quart of which the out-of-control Jyro vomited back up on the security guards as they tried to restrain him. It was at that moment that the crowd quieted a bit, finally realizing that something had gone clearly wrong, and by the time the paramedics arrived, the entire arena had been silenced in shock. They ended up watching their two heroes being escorted away, one on a stretcher, one in handcuffs.

Killer Kalhoun survived the ordeal, but retired immediately after and spent the next seven years performing charity work for children with AIDS. Jyro, on the other hand, spent three years in prison, resigning himself, on his release, to a life in New York City's streets as a tyrant in the homeless community, providing leadership to all those lost souls willing to follow his command. Most were afraid not to.

"I-I . . ." Lester stammered. He peered down and saw two filthy white women, prostitutes perhaps, down on their haunches at either side of the recliner. They could have been sisters, each possessing hair once blond but now brown with soot, straggled and unruly. Their eyes were dull to lifeless gray circles sitting lazily in their sockets, seemingly propped up by the blackened crescents underneath like two dead babies nestled in charred cradles. Measly threads for clothes hung forlornly on their emaciated bodies, heroin tracks racing up their naked arms like parades of army ants. They sneered at Lester as he spoke, and he thought that any minute snakes would sprout from their heads.

"I saw a man in black today," he finally managed.

Jyro rose from his throne, flexing his muscles. He stepped forward, bald head skimming the top of the tent nearly seven feet high. Lester squinted, fearing the worst, that Jyro would bite into his head and devour his blood just like he did to Killer Kalhoun seven years earlier. "What is your name, disheveler?"

"Lester." He was shaking badly.

"Lester—what did you see today?"

"The cops; they took one away."

Jyro smiled. "Good. That's one less we'll have to deal with." Jyro leaned down close to Lester. "The rebellion is tomorrow, Lester. You up for it?"

"Y-yes, my Leader." He trembled like a frightened cat.

Jyro spun around and stood before his chair, one foot up on the armrest. "We meet tomorrow at midnight!" he shouted, raising his arms triumphantly in the air. The dozen or so people sharing space inside the tent shouted in return, one of the guards darting outside to spread the news. At once shouts emanated from the hundreds gathered at the site, the clamor growing by the second as word shot around the camp. The great black man looked down at the cowering Lester and smiled. "The rebellion has begun, Lester. Good job. Now take him away!" he shouted, the smile disappearing from his face.

Lester was forcibly ushered outside into the din of the night, into the growing crowd, where plans for the rebellion had taken flight.

Chapter Twenty-two

Pain wracked Jaimie's body when she awoke, cramps darting from joint to muscle to tendon as if electric prods had been lanced into her body, making it nearly impossible for her to move. She tried to remember what had happened, and as her tired mind searched for a recollection, she felt a terrible headache loom. She tried to twist her body, felt a hard floor through the pain, and realized with dismay that she was not at home; all the floors in her house were carpeted.

The subway, perhaps? She remembered being there. Suddenly everything started to come back to her, a nightmarish flash of events hitting her like some weird movie: the bloody bald man chasing her across campus, escaping into the subway, riding to the Bronx, the terribly injured man on the platform. Then her return to Manhattan, trying to find her way home, the whole time struggling to keep herself conscious. Finally, making it home.

So where was she now? Not in the subway. She made an effort to open her eyes, though it hurt to do so, tiny jolts of pain pinching the skin around them. At once a cobalt illumination doused her vision like a splash of ocean water, and she tried to raise an arm to shield her eyes. But she could barely move her arm, the pain of the slight motion far worse than the neon pain in her eyes, and she could only twitch her eyelids until her pupils managed to adjust to the strange light.

Finally her surroundings came into view. She had never been here before. Gazing warily about, she saw no details, just a black glossy sea racing away beneath her to an infinite horizon, as if she were floating in space. Looking up, she saw a distant ceiling, perhaps a hundred feet high, its surface as smooth and as lustrous as the floor. Wispy streaks of blue neon floated above her like clouds, their source unknown in this place of darkness. A sudden popping noise resounded within her head and she became aware of an odd, a deep hum like that of a great engine operating in the distance. She quickly realized that her pain felt too real for this to be some extravagant dream. Fear enveloped her like a sharp gust of wind, masking some of her pain, enabling her to resume control of her muscles. She forced herself to sit up and a great wave of dizziness washed over her, nearly pulling her back to the floor, but she managed to brace herself with her hands, keeping still until the spinning subsided.

She heard footsteps approaching. A hot flash melted over her, her wet fingers pressing against the smooth floor. She was soaked in sweat, her shirt matted to her body, her jeans itching her skin, sticking to her legs. Dirt was caked in her skin and clothes; she could feel the dried tightness of it. The footsteps grew louder, nearer. She stayed put, trying desperately to see through the wavy blue luminescence of the black room, but she could not make out where the footsteps were coming from.

"Who's there?" she tried to call, but it came out only as a whisper, the enveloping hum that filled the room overpowering her ability to hear her own pained voice.

Then a hand clasped down on her shoulder. She startled and turned, sending intense pain through her entire body.

She saw him and a gorge of fear rose in her throat. Bald. Sunglasses. Bathed in filth.

And smiling.

Chapter Twenty-three

For the second night in a row, the babies invaded Frank's dreams. Again they stood in a procession for as long as his eyes could see, an ocean of tiny bald heads disappearing into a neon blue horizon, a textured carpet of pink flesh laid out so close together that he, as their leader, could virtually step out and walk atop them. Mouthless, noseless, they stared up at him, their glowing eyes big and black and wet, suddenly full of leering hatred. The eyes . . . they looked like . . . like sunglasses. Suddenly he felt not like their leader, but like their prisoner. He tried to move his arms but could not. His wrists were tethered behind his back. His ankles too, shackled to the raised flooring on which he had stood so proudly only moments before. Now he cowered, scared, crying like a baby—not like one of these babies, but like a normal one. Like Jaimie had been years before. *No*, he said to himself, *these babies don't cry*. No reason to. They had everything they wanted. Again he tried to move but could not, and he felt great pain.

Then in the distance he heard a cry, perhaps from one of the babies after all. He looked out across the sea of textured flesh and saw a single baby on its back, floating across the expanse of heads, coming toward him legs first. A single baby, unlike the rest, the body small, pink, naked, but the head, although bald, fully grown, with bright blue eyes and freckles. *Jaimie*. Her eyes rolled up into their sockets, exposing the whites, her hands grasping at the sea of flesh, seeking his help, calling "Daddy! Daddy!" just as she did when she was young and needed him when she awoke from a nightmare.

Frank awoke, nearly leaping from the couch. Hector was clutching his shoulder. "Whoa, Frank, you okay? You were moaning out loud."

Frank gazed at Hector's looming face, the fatigue gone from his eyes, a few crumbs of toast lodged in the coarse hairs of his mustache. The aroma of coffee and eggs wafted in from the kitchen. Frank rubbed his eyes with his forearm. "I-I think I was dreaming," he said, the image of the bald Jaimie riding the sea of baby Harold Grosses still frighteningly clear in his mind.

"Why don't you take a quick shower," Hector said, "then have some breakfast? I called the precinct this morning. There was a message from Sam Richards at Strong Medical. He's got Gross

263

under heavy sedation and wants to see me first thing this morning."

Frank sat up on the couch. The small gust from the blanket blew a piece of paper from the end table onto the carpet. A phone number in his handwriting met his gaze. "Oh, no," he moaned, retrieving the paper. "Lindsay's father. I forgot to leave a message for him last night." The sound of bacon spattering came in from the kitchen, the aroma making Frank's stomach grumble.

"Why don't you get cleaned up, have something to eat and we'll start our day?"

Frank nodded, then moved to the bathroom. He dared not glance into the mirror, at least until he could wash away some of the morning wrinkles on his face. He showered, used one of Hector's disposable razors to shave, then came out to the kitchen, where Hector and Gloria were seated sipping coffee in front of two empty plates.

"Gee, you couldn't wait for me?"

Hector and Gloria smiled, both wishing him a good morning. A *good* morning it really wasn't, though. The few hours of broken sleep he'd managed hadn't been enough, and his body ached pretty badly from it. The day before had brought too much activity for a cop only two years away from retirement. He inhaled his food and tossed down two cups of coffee in silence while Hector read the paper and Gloria cleaned up.

Wiping his mouth with a napkin, Frank finally broke the silence. "What time is it, anyway?"

Hector glanced at the digital LED on the microwave. "Seven A.M., sharp."

Frank took another sip. "I'd like to call Lindsay's father now."

"It's four in the morning in L.A."

"That means he'll be home."

Before Frank could excuse himself, Hector tossed the *Daily News* in front of him. It had been folded open to reveal a page-seven blurb: BOBBY LINDSAY OUT ON BAIL.

Frank grabbed the paper and read the short story in silence. It told of how Jo-Beth Lindsay and her husband had put up a million dollars in cash for his release, and how Bobby was under high security electronic surveillance. Then it went on to give a few details of the murder, which Frank skipped over. It mentioned nothing of his escape.

"It's a small story," Frank said, dropping the paper on the table. "No hindrance to us."

"There's also no mention of the escape Neil told us about, nor of Racine and the events in the alley. We're good for now. Seems to me the precinct is trying to keep as much of this out of the press as they can until they get a grasp on everything."

"Which they won't really be able to do," Frank said, "knowing what we already know."

"Frank, go ahead and call Lindsay's father while I help Gloria clean up."

Frank nodded and moved to the living room. He figured that Hector's intention would be to continue this thing to the very end, which pleased him very much. Good ol' Hect, tried and true. He picked up the telephone and dialed the California number. It rang maybe eight times, and Frank was going to give it to ten before a tired-sounding man answered. "Ballaro?"

"How did you know it was me?"

"I turned off my machine because I had a feeling you would call at some ungodly hour." He sounded terse, and his slurred words didn't make much sense to Frank. It seemed sleep still had the man in its grasp.

"My apologies, Mr. Lindsay. Detectives work ungodly hours."

"And I thought you were off. At least that's what your partner said."

"Well, I'm supposed to be, but your boy got out on bail and that put things off a bit." Frank decided not to mention Bobby's breakout. He wanted to see what the elder Lindsay had to say first; although Frank doubted it, maybe Jack knew something about the strange escape, as Neil had surmised.

"Detective, I really don't want to get involved, and I think I've done a pretty good job of keeping my distance up until now. But I can't believe the truth hasn't gotten out about Carrie."

"What about Carrie?" Frank felt his heart throb with anticipation.

"You mean you don't know?"

"Know about what?"

"Detective Ballaro . . ." A pause filtered through the phone. He took a deep breath and continued, slowly, "My daughter, Carrie, C-A-R-R-I-E, was originally born Carey, C-A-R-E-Y. *She* is really a *he*. Carey is my *son*."

"*What?*" Frank wasn't sure he understood him correctly. "Are you trying to say that Carrie Lindsay was actually a boy?"

"Born on June sixth."

"Mr. Lindsay, with all due respect—"

"Ballaro, I'll only say this once. Jo-Beth has never been the most stable person. She wanted a daughter more than anything in the world. When we had another son, and decided on the name Carey, she immediately insisted from on raising the child as a girl, dresses, pigtails, even changing the spelling of his name. I had no say in the matter. Jo-Beth had all the money, an inheritance, and threatened me with it, really went nuts on me day in and day out until I had no choice but to leave eight months later and forgo the dough. Her life revolved around keeping Carey a girl, and I couldn't take it any more. No amount of money is worth what I went through after our second son was born. Anyway, I never really knew what became of my family after I left. I moved as far away as I could and started a new life. You could imagine my shock when I heard about the murder."

"Then what about the autopsies? The coroner's report said she'd been raped."

"You want my educated guess? Money talks, and Jo-Beth has a lot of it. Bobby is the only other person who knows that Carrie is really a boy. He was three at the time of his birth, and I know he remembers because I used to talk to him about it. I know how Jo-Beth thinks. She probably threatened to disinherit him if he ever revealed

267

the truth about Carrie—which I'm sure he would do if he was locked up for life. It would act as a kind of revenge if his mother didn't bail him out. He'd have nothing to lose. And as far as the autopsy goes—well, it's my guess that the coroner is a much richer man now than he was before the murder."

Frank's mouth fell open. Hector came over, holding a few sheets of paper, and sat down next to Frank. Frank held up an index finger, asking Hector to give him another minute. "Are you trying to say that Jo-Beth bribed the coroner to falsify reports?"

"Why don't you ask him yourself? I've said enough."

"Wait . . ." Frank started, but Jack Lindsay hung up. Frank thought about redialing but placed the handset into its cradle.

"What? What is it?" Hector licked his lips in anticipation.

"You won't believe it. What are those?" Frank nodded to the papers Hector held.

"The other three articles from Sanskrit. What did Lindsay say?"

"I'll tell you on the way to Strong Medical. We have someone else to see there besides Harold Gross."

Chapter Twenty-four

Bobby Lindsay threw the girl to the floor. She squirmed a bit but remained in place, and that was good because the Giver didn't have any tolerance for disorder. *The Giver better appreciate this gift,* Bobby thought. It had really been a nuisance getting her here; his shoulders still ached from carrying the dead weight of her body.

Snatching her from the apartment hadn't been so difficult; heck, the door was *open*. And with the early morning hours still providing cover, he'd carried her from the building mostly unseen all the way to the courtyard by the taped-off alley where the Giver had burrowed a tunnel some time ago. Only one person spotted him—a homeless guy.

An appendage slithered up from the bowels of the tunnel, lending him support as he slid to the

269

bottom. It cleared the way for him, providing guidance for the two-plus hours it took him to drag the girl to one of the Giver's blue rooms, closing up the tunnels behind him to conceal his path.

He waited here with the girl until the pulse finally emerged, its colors swirling on the walls like a giant kaleidoscope display. The Giver spoke, its voice the usual electronic monotone, echoing throughout the room. *"Harbinger, do you have the unit?"*

A great fear suddenly consumed Bobby. The unit, the glorious Atmosphere. It . . . it was *gone. Fuck! What did I do with it? The apartment! I put it on the floor in the cop's apartment when I took the girl.*

Bobby stood before the swirling lights on the wall, chest out in an attempt to cover up for his error. "I brought you something else, Giver."

From beneath the lights a small doorway materialized in the black wall, and the appendage appeared, slithering forth, its segmented chitinous exterior clicking on the smooth floor. It stopped at Bobby's feet, seemingly in wait for its prize, though there was none.

Bobby ran over to where Jaimie lay and dragged her across the smooth floor to the flittering appendage. He pushed her down and she groaned incoherently. "Here, Giver, a prize for you."

The appendage poked Jaimie's body, first her chest then her crotch, where it hesitated momentarily, prodded, then pulled away. The voice returned. *"Subject insufficient for harvesting. Harbinger, do you have the unit?"*

Bobby hesitated, then solemnly spoke. "No."

"Recognize failure." The appendage whipped back to its place in the wall.

Bobby strangely felt no love lost for the missing Atmosphere, not like he had when he first obtained it, not even as much as when he toyed with it in the tunnel just prior to abducting Jaimie. He felt only the need for revenge, revenge against the one who intervened and disrupted his relationship with the Giver. The Giver held no respect for him as a Harbinger, had called him a failure. It seemed to be cutting its ties with him, opting not to accept the girl.

"Harbinger, what is your purpose?"

Bobby felt a familiar clicking sensation in his head. An answer to the question sprang forth. "To seek out Suppliers."

"Harbinger, what will you do if an Outsider discovers you?"

"Kill them." He knew, unequivocally.

"Harbinger, what will you do if an Outsider overcomes you, or escapes?"

"Kill myself."

"Harbinger, find the unit. Seek out new Suppliers." A door appeared at the opposite end of the room, granting him an exit.

Bobby felt a sudden need to obey the Giver's command, but also felt compelled to act otherwise. Perhaps it was the fact that he knew he could not return to the Ballaro apartment and

271

successfully retrieve the Atmosphere. Outsiders might be there.

As he decided his next move, something unforeseen happened.

The girl abruptly rose from the floor and darted across the room to the exit. Bobby pursued, but she had him by at least ten strides and disappeared through the door the Giver had provided. By the time Bobby reached the exit and moved down the hall, she had vanished through one of the many break-offs that intersected the hall near its end. He cursed inside, knowing that the Giver would never approve of this.

Then again, now he had a new purpose: to find the girl. She was his only link to the cop who'd brought him down.

His only hope of revenge.

Chapter Twenty-five

Eight in the morning approached, a morning drizzle sifted from the sky and a naked overweight cook named Harry Porter—who had left work just an hour earlier—propelled himself headfirst at a rat scuttling across the alley floor.

He seized it with both hands just as it made a desperate attempt to disappear beneath a heap of sodden cardboard. The rodent wriggled wildly in his grasp, squealing frantically, almost in syncopation to the beat of the music emanating from Harry's Walkman headphones.

Harry wailed triumphantly, then opened his mouth and crammed the rat in, tail first, pushing it as far as it would go until only its little vermin face emerged, fidgeting from his jaws.

Harry bit down, his front teeth breaking the rat's back. The rat shuddered, its black-bead eyes popping from their sockets like tiny yo-yo's. Then Harry pressed the head in with his fingers and chewed and chewed with great pleasure, buoyantly working his jaws up and down on the rodent's tiny bones. It tasted wonderful: as succulent and appetizing as anything he'd ever prepared in his days as head cook at Frankie's All-Night Diner.

When the rat's bulk finally slipped down into his gullet, he scooted to the back of the alley and leaned against a Dumpster. He found an erection protruding from somewhere beneath his fat stomach. Feverishly, he gripped it, stroking it in a wild fit, the gristle on his hands lubricating his efforts and bringing him to a state of shivering orgasm in mere moments, and he slumped like a discarded hand puppet, lethargy consuming his mind and muscles in a river of release.

He stayed in this quiet state, licking the blood and semen from his fingers with feline consideration. Tears of joy dampened his vision as he gazed at the strip of rainy night sky between the buildings that formed the alley. A cloaked sun forced its darkened beams upon him as he pondered the simplicity of his old life, and the thrill of his new one.

Things were so much better, now that he'd found the Atmosphere.

Mosquitoes and flies tickled his skin to the point where he again felt himself getting hard. Rejuvenation seeping in, he scurried on all fours with animal-like finesse to the spot in the alley where he had hidden the Atmosphere—behind a wooden crate filled with rotting vegetables. He retrieved it and gazed at it, fascinated, garnering the same impassioned feelings as when he found it on his way home from work, under the subway on 190th Street.

Curiosity had been his only motive when he first beheld the Atmosphere, and he wondered if it had anything to do with all the police activity on the train platform thirty feet above his head. But in mere seconds he had become fixated on the oddly shaped black object, and he cradled it like a newborn, pacing the empty streets like a mouse in a maze, a man with no direction in mind other than to draw himself nearer to the heart of the intriguing object. It had felt so erotic, so stimulating to run his fingers across the six hollowed prongs that projected from it like thick black straws. It had felt so warm and soft at his touch, and made the music sound so damn good.

Atmosphere . . .

The deep voice resounded in his head like an echo shouted from a distant hilltop, and with unexplained urgency he needed to be alone with it, to be the only one to experience its special purpose. The alley had been the nearest place.

In just five minutes he was naked and feeding on the rat, food being his sole passion in life, the object, the *Atmosphere*, stimulating his devotion to levels previously unfelt in his years as a cook.

Harry scurried to the rear of the alley, crouched in the far corner, next to the Dumpster. Working his index finger around the lip of one of the prongs, he explored its smoothness with newfound intensity, allowing his instincts to take over. Abstract colors and shapes formed within his mind, their orgiastic flow sending out signals that only hinted at its further intentions. Yes, so much more was to be had from this thing called the Atmosphere, and he shivered with wild anticipation as all its other properties began to emerge. He moved his fingers quicker and harder across the ebony surface with unprecedented inspiration. He rocked his body to the pulse in his head. He had to—needed to—seek out the source of its desires for him.

One of the prongs on the Atmosphere suddenly widened, its end stretching open like a tiny mouth, a nozzle. It gently embraced the tip of his index finger, like suckling a nipple. Harry's heart slammed against his ribs at this sudden engagement and again he became erect.

As if the Atmosphere had somehow noticed this, a second prong extended from its surface, reaching down to his penis.

The pounding force of his heart reached the music in his ears, and instantly a unique feeling surged to all points in his body like bolts of lightning: fear, pleasure, pain, hunger, all intertwined, tempting his mind all at one intense moment. Harry shivered with joy. Yes, it was time.

The Atmosphere. It was going to reveal its true purpose to him.

The entire surface of the object began to pulse in his grip, like a heart freshly ripped from a body. It sweated a warm jellylike substance that lubricated Harry's delirious hands-on orgy with the growing black tubes. A faint light ignited from the heart of its body, and then it splayed out an incredible array of tints that danced gleefully over his hands like a blanket of fireflies. The flesh of his arms and hands turned transparent and he could see his veins and nerve endings glowing beneath his skin. Quickly and abruptly, the elongating tendrils around his finger and penis shifted into flat, shapeless forms. They swallowed the glowing ambience that irradiated his hands, and the light, that mesmerizing firefly light, was gone.

In its place: a pitch-black shadow.

And then there was pain.

The ecstasy that had held Harry quickly gave way to a blinding agony of sharp light. The hammering in his head turned pleasure into pain, doubling, tripling, and then his consciousness returned to acquaint him with the harsh real world where he was simply Harry Porter, head cook at Frankie's All-Night Diner.

A naked, bloody, filthy and quite confused Harry Porter.

The tube surrounding his penis stretched wide and swallowed his testicles like a hungry snake. Agonized, Harry fought back, trying to rip himself from the grasp of the alien object—the frothing amorphous lump of tar that was spreading over his wrists and groin like an oil slick on a rushing tide.

Grape-sized lumps swelled up on the surface of the growing object, each one pulsating with an apparent life of its own. It slithered over his forearms to his biceps, webbing across his lap like a blanket. Phosphorescent patches of purple and green glowed atop its gelatinous cover, as if those fireflies had been trapped beneath its surface. It seemed enraged, or ravenous, or simply savage, but regardless it grew larger and larger and convulsively thrust itself around his torso.

Harry finally found the wits to cry out, but his plea was short-lived, and he realized with great horror as he lost his voice and breath that the thing had ripped through his chest and filled his lungs.

The final sensation Harry Porter felt was darkness. Complete, utter darkness.

Chapter Twenty-six

The city streets held a throng of Saturday morning enthusiasts. Instead of men in business attire and women in heels pacing the sidewalks with briefcases looped over their shoulders, joggers bounced along in nylon track suits, bicyclists zoomed by, and residents walked their dogs, leashes in one hand, plastic-bag scoopers in the other. The tumult of weekday rush-hour traffic had given way to a more relaxed weekend environment. Hector piloted the cruiser through it all as Gloria Rodriguez's breakfast settled in their stomachs.

"It says here that Sanskrit spent a total of seventeen days as a Harbinger and harvested five Suppliers before escaping the mothership," Frank read from one of the three remaining articles Hector printed out that morning. "But it

279

still doesn't say anywhere what their reasons were."

"Whose reasons?"

Frank grinned. "The aliens." He'd spent their entire ride to Strong Medical Center reading the rest of Sanskrit's writings. One: trying to discover any additional similarities to their investigation, and two: to distract himself from the truth about Carrie Lindsay. He had relayed the story Lindsay's father told him as they left the house, and Hector had been clearly shocked, realizing now that they would have to approach the coroner at the hospital after they saw Sam Richards about Harold Gross.

"Frank, enough about aliens. Let's spend our energy getting to the *real* heart of the matter."

"I know, I know, I'm just trying to make some sense of this," he said, shaking the papers in his hand. "The whole alien theory, as wild as it seems—it's the only thing that pieces the entire puzzle together."

"Like it did at Roswell, right? Except the only thing we don't have is a weather balloon. Remember what Phil Martin said: If it seems too obvious, then it probably is. And nothing holds more truth right now. We're just missing something, a simple link that will explain everything. In the meantime, don't jump to any crazy conclusions."

Hector made a right turn into Strong Medical's garage and parked in one of three available spots reserved for doctors. They nodded to the attendant, who frowned back, and entered the hospital through the ground-floor employee entrance.

The hospital was as busy as ever. Even when the city found a few moments to nap in the early morning hours, Strong never rested. Nurses and doctors scurried back and forth, clipboards in hand, stethoscopes dangling like jewelry from their necks. A number of bedcarts were stationed in the hall, various noncrucial emergency room patients awaiting their turns for relief. A few nurses gossiped behind the circular desk Frank and Hector approached.

The nurses pretended they were invisible until Hector cleared his throat.

A middle-aged aide with reading glasses perched at the tip of her nose peered over her frames at them, the attached chain swaying on both sides. She said nothing.

"We're here to see Dr. Richards. He's expecting us." Hector added the latter just as the nurse moved her lips to ask. She nodded and paged him, and Sam Richards appeared moments later through a pair of swinging doors with the word *emergency* painted on them.

"Hector, glad you could come by. I've got a heck of a schedule this afternoon, and we have lots to talk about." Sam Richards had worked with the police department for over ten years, and he, along with a few other doctors at Strong, worked often with criminals who required psychiatric evaluation.

"A lot to talk about—what did you find out about Gross?"

Sam pushed through the swinging doors and

led Frank and Hector down a long hall. Frank always felt queasy when visiting hospitals, today being no exception. A combination of the institutionalized whiteness, sterilized odors and the thought of all those germs floating through the air spurred discomforting images of sickness. Things he wanted no part of unless he required treatment himself.

"Where did you find this guy, Hector?" Richards looked at Frank, but no introduction was made. He had dark circles beneath his puffy eyes and looked as tired as Hector.

"Police business."

Richards grinned. "As usual." He made a left, pushed through another set of doors and started down a flight of stairs to the basement. They walked to the end of the hallway where a security door closed them out of the psychiatric ward. Richards used a keycard from his pocket to gain entrance. The door buzzed, and the three of them went in.

The inside of the psychiatric ward had an air about it different from that of the rest of the hospital. Quieter, yet more foreboding, like evil under leash.

"We've still got your boy under heavy sedation. When they brought him in, he was out cold. Bloodied and out. He came around while some nurses were bandaging his wounds and all hell broke loose. It took three guards to hold him down until we managed to get him sedated. He's been out since, but it was a helluva scene. The

maniac tried to kill himself, grabbed a fallen scalpel and jammed it into his eye."

Richards stopped in front of a closed door and
slid open a small window at eye level. Frank
peeked in and saw a man lying on a steel gurney,
ankles and wrists bound tightly, bandages
shrouding his entire face, patchlets of blood seeping through. "That Gross?"

"Yep."

"So what's wrong with him?" Frank asked,
pulling away, allowing Hector to view the patient.

Richards retrieved a chart from a small box attached to the wall outside Gross's room and
handed it to Frank. "After Gross's sedation, I did
a routine check of motor functions, pupilary response, then had a brain scan done to check for
abnormalities. And we found some too. Quite
alarming, in fact. He had no reflex response. His
pupils, which were completely dilated, remained
open and nonresponsive to light. When the scans
came back, I couldn't believe what I was seeing."

He pointed to the scan of Harold's brain,
which was meaningless to Frank. "Here in this
area," Richards said, pointing to a white patch
with his pen, "is the temporal lobe, or pleasure
center of the brain. According to this readout,
this area alone is in a high flux of Delta, which
means that this man should be not only sleeping
but should be in a high state of swoon. Another
thing—all types of brain waves, when activated,
affect more than just one part of the brain, not

one isolated region, as it does here in the pleasure center."

"So what's that mean?" Frank asked.

"It means our boy is a walking orgasm, to put it bluntly. To him, nothing felt bad, only good. No matter the situation, it felt like sex. The scalpel in the eye? Orgasm."

"But *why'd* he try to kill himself?"

"That's something else altogether." Richards took the scan back from Frank and returned it to the folder. "Someone placed a suggestion in his mind, and I think it's making him take these harsh actions."

Hector leaned against the wall, arms folded. "Are you saying he's under hypnosis?"

Richards nodded. "Yes, and a very powerful form too, one that's got complete control of the pleasure center in his brain. I've never seen anything like it, and given the presence of Theta waves, I could safely guess that it's been mechanically induced. This is pretty sophisticated stuff we're dealing with here. And I can't get him out of it either, at least not right now. After he stabilizes, blood pressure, heart rate, we'll be able to send some mild electric shocks into his brain. That should disable the activity going on in there, and give him his own will back."

"Sounds like he's someone's zombie," Frank remarked.

"Could very well be. And if indeed that's how he's being used—well, that would be just amazing. It's a wicked form of mind control at its very best. Scary in the hands of the wrong person."

Frank's three personalities all agreed on that one, and they all played catch with different theories, mostly the cult one. It sort of made sense now, that perhaps a Marshall Applewhite–type leader was out there, a man who possessed the ability to control the minds of his subjects, only to have them carry out the deeds called for by the dogma of his religious beliefs. Maybe this Internet guru Sanskrit had never escaped the clutches of the cult after all. Could it be that his chatterings were merely post-hypnotic suggestions to cover up the true reality of the cults wrongdoings? Or maybe they were simply diversions? Regardless, it seemed most likely now that this whole mess was indeed the result of some hypnotic, alien-worshipping murderous cult.

That still leaves some things unexplained, Frank's detective personality pointed out. *Like the tunneling of holes in the ground. Big question mark there . . .*

"Frank?"

Again Frank had to rip his attention away from his deliberations. "Yeah, Hect?"

"You said you wanted to see the coroner?"

Frank turned from Hector and saw Richards standing there, looking a bit harried. "Yes, of course. Are we done here?"

"I think so," Hector said. "Not much more we can do until Sam hits Harold with some juice. In the meantime, we ought to go see what the coroner has to say for himself. What was his name?"

At first Frank's mind went blank. It had been some weeks now since the autopsy had been completed, and he couldn't remember the man's name. Then it came to him. "Latchman, or something like that. Dr. Latchman."

"Uh-oh." Richards turned his gaze away for a moment, and Frank saw that something was wrong. "Dr. Rene Lacheman. He resigned. Retired, actually. Said he was taking his family back to Canada."

"Damn!" Frank felt an emptiness in the pit of his stomach, as if he had just lost his girlfriend to his best friend. "Did he say anything about coming into money?"

Richards shook his head. "Don't know; can't say for sure. But it was strange the way he just picked up and left. No notice, no good-byes. Just picked up and disappeared. Heck, the guy worked here for fifteen years."

Frank and Hector locked gazes. Sickened gazes.

Jo-Beth Lindsay had paid off the coroner.

All of a sudden Hector's pager squawked. He plucked it from his belt and answered. He nodded once, then yelled, "Where?" eyes suddenly bulging. When he finished, he quickly put the pager away and looked at Frank.

"Another castrated kid was found. In the Bronx."

Chapter Twenty-seven

It was déjà vu all over again. First, the cold foreboding that had assumed control of her environment when she finally escaped the subway and found herself stumbling home, barefoot, her instincts guiding her the entire way. Then, from her dreams, the illusionary worlds within her head: endless seas of faceless people passing her by, every one of them ignoring her existence and brushing her away with quick passes and cold shoulders. She remembered crying out in those dreams, her pleas going unanswered. She remembered spinning in crazy circles amid the detached masses, seeking just a moment's stability.

Here in this foreign place she encountered the same feelings. They surrounded her as they had in her dream and she thought she might be dreaming again, but her pain was all too real, and although it seemed so fantastic in every aspect, she forced herself to assume it was real. Although *nothing* in her life lately seemed at all convincing.

Jaimie had successfully feigned unconsciousness as the bald guy—she had not yet decided whether this was the same bald guy from her class who had pursued her into the subway—spoke to the voice, that deep, otherworldly voice whose source she had chosen not to investigate. Peeking through squinting eyes, she waited until he was at a distance from her before breaking for the door that had somehow materialized in the wall. Of course his running footsteps quickly followed her, but luckily a maze of hallways appeared and she made her way through them, hoping that they would guide her out of this mysterious, dark place.

She eventually found an exit, but instead of leading her to the outside world, she found herself at the threshold of a large round room, its dark diameter perhaps a full hundred yards. Inside were a multitude of bald men in black clothing, all wearing sunglasses. They either ignored her or seemed not to see her as they worked feverishly on some type of project. Around the circumference of the room, a number of the workers were constructing platforms of some kind, each about four feet high and only a foot or so wide. Above ran a series of catwalks where the men had hoisted small boxlike fixtures made of glass or plastic. In one corner of the room a small glass structure sat quietly like a waiting animal, a series of dials and controls visible inside.

She gingerly approached it, surrounded by her enemy, glancing nervously about. Never had fear and trepidation consumed her as it did now, and if not for the experience in her dream, she knew she would not have had the nerve to go on. And remarkably enough, like the people in her dream, the men in the room left her untouched, continuing on with their project as if she did not exist. She peered up at the squarish fixtures. A flickering danced across the glassy surface of one. Lights? Then another flashed, and it seemed that indeed these were some kind of light fixtures. She took her time, pacing over to the small structure with the control panels inside. Here tiny lights flashed on a rack of what appeared at first glance to be stereo equipment: equalizers, CD players, power amps. Did this make sense? She looked over to the platforms again. They looked like . . . bars. Was she in a nightclub of some sort? If so, who were these bald men?

Confusion swirled around her like a great tornado, her thoughts muddled by fear. What in God's name was all this?

Suddenly a hand came down on her shoulder. She spun, her heart in her throat. It was *him*, the bald guy who had brought her here.

He smiled. "I'm different from the rest of these guys," he said, pointing. " 'Recognize failure.' " He removed his sunglasses and laughed, and Jaimie knew his face. She'd seen it a dozen times before in the newspaper.

Bobby Lindsay.

Once again, Jaimie fainted, this time right into his arms.

Chapter Twenty-eight

Jesus peeked over the edge of the Dumpster and saw the mutilated body. Then he stepped down and gazed at the blood splattered on the brick wall.

No matter, as long as he was able to keep this wonderfully strange object, the one he'd found minutes earlier on the alley floor.

Earlier, he hadn't been able to fathom why he had been drawn to the alley, but when he arrived there he knew—oh, yes, he knew unequivocally— it was this wondrous object he had come for. It was a remarkable piece, six equidistant prongs all shiny and black sticking from it like short magic wands. He held it close to his heart just like he would his very own daughter, Elise, then aimed his sights cautiously over his shoulder. He wanted to make certain that nobody saw him now, for if anyone spotted this marvelous beauty, they would undoubtedly attempt to snatch it away.

Gazing down, he started to massage it, gentle curiosity guiding his fingertips across the jet-black surface. In the back of his mind he could think of a dozen different things he should be doing, like getting home on time so Rosa could go to work and he could watch the baby. But he couldn't force himself to move. A strange pleasure paralyzed his body as his fingers moved across the smooth surface, distracting him from all that mattered—even the tide of blood just feet away.

A memory suddenly willed its way out from below the ecstatic feeling floating on the surface of his mind—from deep within his subconscious—and he remembered his duty: that Rosa would be leaving for work soon, that the baby would need to be fed.

Home?

Confused, he slid the object into his jacket pocket, keeping a tight hand on it. He left the alley, using only his instinct to guide him home through the quiet early morning streets.

It was only eight-thirty, and another long and arduous day was already in the works. Frank and Hector had completed their visit to the hospital and were now racing through the streets, lights ablaze, en route to the 190th Street station in the Bronx, where, according to Martin, another mutilated body had been discovered.

"One-eight-seven—Code Two . . . blood, blood everywhere!" Martin had said, relaying the shocking broadcast. A *187* meant a dead body. A *Code 2* meant come with no lights or sirens, an effort utilized to avoid drawing a crowd. Frank and Hector shut down the lights a few blocks from the scene.

They located the activity a block ahead, thirty feet up on an elevated platform. A horde of cops, detectives and forensics experts milled about on and below the platform. A number of squad cars sat alongside barriers arranged to block off the street to pedestrians, who had gathered in great numbers anyway. Hector pulled the car up next to a Fifty-seventh precinct cruiser.

Sure enough, just as Frank and Hector shut the car doors behind them, Sergeant Sid Clemens came thumping down the metal steps of the el, his hefty gut bouncing atop his belt. His approach seemed to bring a thin drizzle from the graying skies. Misery loves company, Frank thought, the cold rain a perfect match to Clemens's air of arrogance.

"Great—your timing is impeccable," Frank whispered to Hector. "You're on his shit list, Hect. You ain't never gonna get his cooperation on this one."

"Well," Clemens said, his face round with surprise as he stopped and greeted Frank and Hector. "Shouldn't you boys be checking up on your bald guy? I sent him off to Strong like you asked." His demeanor rang more of contempt than the desire to be of assistance.

Frank's irrational personality couldn't help but be irked at Clemens's clear lack of respect. "He called us *boys*, Hect." He stepped forward, pointing. "We've got more years in than you, *kiddo*."

Hector held up his hand, and Frank sealed his lips even though it maddened the irrational third of his personality to do so. "Sergeant Clemens, we believe that this particular murder may be related to the man we have in custody at Strong. If you'll simply allow us to take a quick look—"

"Captain Rodriguez, you know I can't, and frankly, I'm surprised you would even ask. Besides, I've got the area cleared of everyone except Forensics now."

Even though Frank thought he was a jerk, he clearly understood Clemens's position, and knew that Hector would too. "Fine," Hector said. "Let me just ask one question."

"Make it quick."

"Did you find anything unusual?"

Clemens's eyebrows arched. "Like what?"

Frank spoke up. "A strange-looking object, perhaps? Black in color, looks like a distributor cap, only roundish."

Clemens shook his head. "No. Why? Is there something I should know about?"

Frank looked at Hector and saw a spark of anger in his eyes. Clearly this wasn't the one question Hector had in mind. "No," Hector said. "Not really."

"Well, if you'll excuse me, gentlemen, I have some work to—"

"Sergeant, we've got another body!" The voice

came from a plainclothesman approaching from a small crowd of police who had magically appeared. Frank's ears perked up and he and Hector both sidled over to Clemens.

"Three blocks from here," the detective said, glancing at Frank and Hector.

"They're okay," Clemens said. Frank wasn't sure if the sergeant was actually throwing them a bone, or if he really couldn't care less if they listened. Probably the latter.

"An alley between One-hundred-ninety-third and Ninety-fourth. The body has similar injuries, based on the witness's description . . ."

Both Frank and Hector didn't stay to listen any further. They raced to the cruiser, slamming the doors behind them.

"I don't know why we're rushing, Frank. I mean, what else could we expect to find at this point?" He pulled the car away from the scene, lights twirling, trying to cut into the traffic that had built up around the closed street.

"I want one of those black things. With the points."

"And if you get one?"

"I don't know. But what other choice do we have at this point? We're gonna lose this thing if we don't break some serious ground soon. Then it's back to square one with the questioning, trying to come up with answers that make sense. In the meantime we've been able to keep most of what we've found out of the public eye, and our superiors', for that matter. Once it breaks, the cult—if that's what this really is all about—will go underground for a while until it finds a new city to terrorize. It's up to us, right here, right now, to put an end to it. We have no choice but to find some answers. Now. And I believe if we find one of those black things, it will provide them."

Hector remained silent, the siren howling at a line of cars gridlocked behind a red light. "You're right about one thing—we do have to solve this thing ourselves. And I agree, at this point we're the only ones who can do it. But I'm not sure what our next step should be, especially if we *don't* find one of those things."

"Haven't we been surprised time and time again over the past two days?"

Hector nodded. He finally managed to break through the traffic, a line of police cars following him through. "Are we being chased?"

"No. Escorted."

Atmosphere. Atmosphere.

Jesus repeated the word in his head, beat it into his subconscious. He reached into Elise's crib and tucked the covers under her chin. A sleeping angel, her breathing soft and hushed, her flesh as pink as rose powder.

He backed away and sat on the edge of his own bed, his eyes wandering to the strange object sitting on the dresser. He twisted his head to view its beauty from a new angle, then clutched his racing heart, at once struck with an immense determination to discover the true meaning of it.

Ah, and how beautiful it was.

Atmosphere . . .

The sleek voice in his head returned, louder than it had been before, helping him recall the overwhelming feelings that had swept over him when he first found it in the alley, feelings of love, hate, fear, excitement, hunger, all combined into one great emotion.

Suddenly one of the six prongs began to wiggle, like a tired worm on a fisherman's hook. The uncanny sight had Jesus rubbing his tired eyes with disbelief. He blew out an anxious breath, and when he removed his hands from his face the fading blackness revealed something extraordinary: all the little tubes, undulating to and fro, slowly and hypnotically, like six tiny charmed snakes.

He realized that this was his cue, that the Atmosphere was ready for him.

He stood and removed his clothing.

Naked, Jesus reached out his hand to it. All six tubes stopped moving, and Jesus froze along with it. The room became uncomfortably warm, sauna-alike, and sweat coated his body. The air around him suddenly felt thick, like syrup, and within it he could feel an electricity fraught with immense hunger and desire.

A single tube pointed at him. He stood like a soldier, arms outstretched, prepared to accept its offering. A few droplets of blood trickled out from the tip of the tube. He closed his eyes in ecstasy. "I am yours . . ." he muttered, and then the object spat a stream of blood at him.

Jesus relished the wet heat upon his chest, rivulets of crimson painting his torso and legs. He rubbed it into the skin on his chest, shoulders and face, kept at it until he was coated with blood.

Fulfill your desire, your hunger!

He turned and walked to the crib, bare feet streaking through the blood on the wood floor. For a brief moment he watched his daughter sleeping, then he picked her up and walked to the bed.

Frank and Hector raced into the alley, the first of the police to arrive. The first thing he saw was the blood, a remarkable puddling of crimson washed across the alley floor as if it had poured down from the sky in a violent storm. A pile of clothes came into view at the base of the Dumpster at the rear of the alley: a pair of trousers, tailored shirt, sport jacket, tie, shoes, underwear. It struck Frank that these clothes were the first evidence that all this carnage might have come from a human.

When he first laid eyes the mess, it looked like some kind of Santeria ritual had taken place, and that all the gore had come from a few slaughtered farm animals. Once, in the past, he had witnessed a horrific scene similar to this—blood and tatters of viscera strewn about like a sick piece of art, the result of fanatical animal sacrifice.

He walked over, Hector tailing him, stopping near the pile of clothing. Poking the pants with his foot, he noticed that the clothing had not been damaged in any way, which meant it had been removed prior to the murder. "See this? Show me a body and I'll show you a guy who spent his last moments as naked as a jaybird."

Hector walked around to the side of the Dumpster, placed a foot atop the crane hinge and stepped up. The grimace on his face told the story.

"He naked?" Frank asked, his detective personality already knowing the answer.

"What's left of him. His crotch is gone to the chest."

A flurry of activity ensued as a handful of police from the Fifty-seventh precinct ran into the alley. They suddenly stopped, the wide-eyed expressions on their faces a reflection of surprise, as they had just witnessed a very similar scene just a few blocks away at the 190th Street station.

A feeling of discomfort crept up on Frank, one that asked a very simple question: Why is all this happening?

Hector stepped down and another cop took his place, looking in at the carnage. "Looks like another poor bastard's been served up through a wood chipper," he remarked callously.

Frank focused on Hector as he walked over to him. His face was as white as sheepskin; it seemed Hector hadn't the knack for hiding his dismay. Frank offered a weak smile, then drew his gaze across the sticky pool of blood and internal organs.

Frank's detective personality pushed past the weak, timid one currently begging him to leave this mess for the other detectives to handle. It made him look back at the moment this whole damn thing started, when he got out of his car and stepped out into the puddle with the streaks of blood floating in it.

The blood. It had come all the way from the alley.

He tiptoed from the scene, eyes pointed to the littered ground. Tiny droplets of blood led away, out into the open, down the sidewalk. There were only a few, but they were there.

"Frank?"

He turned. Hector was in his face, breathing heavy, flushed. The sight he beheld in the Dumpster had really gotten to him. "Look, Hect." Frank pointed to the ground, trying not to make his discovery obvious. Eventually the other detectives would find this trail, but he did not want to give it away just yet.

"Déjà vu," Hector said.

Frank nodded. "All over again. Let's see where it leads."

Like a trail of bread crumbs, the tiny droplets of blood led Frank and Hector away three blocks, up the front steps of a brownstone and into a foyer past a pair of Victorian doors.

Frank and Hector entered the dull unlighted hall. After a quick inspection of the first floor, on which they found nothing, they moved upstairs.

The first door on the right had blood smeared on the knob.

Hector gave the door three loud raps with his fist. They waited. No answer.

"Again," Frank whispered. Hector banged the

door, louder. "Police," Frank yelled, pulling his gun. "Open up." He had to swallow a lump in his throat to get the words out.

"Let's go in."

Frank stepped back, picked up his right leg and gave the door a swift kick. It held. He kicked again, and again, sharp pain jolting the muscles in his leg. The fourth attempt proved successful and the door broke open, shards of wood splintering in all directions. Hector raced in, gun poised to the left, Frank gun-ready behind him. Instantly there was a rush of foul air. Cold, primal, dead. It made him shudder.

"*Frank . . . ?*" Hector's eyes were wide with apprehension.

In the silence they heard heavy breathing emanating from the apartment's only other room.

Frank and Hector stepped cautiously to the threshold of the other room. Frank could feel his eyes bulging, and his hand reached for his mouth to hold back the nausea caused by the thick, coppery odor issuing from within. He glanced at Hector. His face was white.

They readied their guns, hurriedly framed the opposite sides of the doorway. They gave each other nods of reassurance, then whirled in.

There was a moment's hesitation, and in that horrifying second Frank Ballaro had to question his sanity. "Dear . . . God . . ." he heard Hector say in a voice thick with nausea, and he at once tried to convince himself that insanity couldn't possibly be contagious, that the only madness in the room was within the man facing them.

A young Latino man, maybe twenty years old, if that, sat naked on the bed. His body was drenched in blood from head to toe, the mattress beneath him likewise saturated. He looked like some God-forsaken fetus newly emerged from a monstrous womb.

And then, the boy's face. A visage of the Devil himself: eyes wide and unblinking, the whites small pearl crescents floating in a crimson sea, the irises blackened like two charred wounds. And his mouth, smiling broadly, so happy, or so insane, or perhaps a perfect combination of the two. The scene was a sickening reminder of the unidentified boy from the alley yesterday morning, the only difference being that instead of a strange black object, this boy displayed a bawling infant in his hands, holding it out as if it were a generous offering to be graciously accepted by a willing hand.

And beneath it all, a bloodied erection stood tall.

Frank felt his face drip with icy sweat as he tried to make sense of the sight, but none of his personalities could come up with any form of rational explanation. "Don't move," he finally uttered, albeit weakly, gun shaking wildly, not sure if his words had been directed to the boy or to Hector.

Suddenly the man's teeth began to chatter, his head shaking wildly, like a ventriloquist's dummy possessed by some malevolent evil. Slithering whispers tremored from his lips, and Frank knew with little doubt that the soul of the young man inside was desperately trying to get out, trying to release itself from the evil that had him caged in his own body.

More tortured whispers. Almost words.

Frank twisted slightly toward Hector. "What's he saying?" he whispered.

"He's trying to tell us something."

Then one word slithered past his lips like a worm's last effort to escape a fish's mouth:

"Atmosphere . . ."

The room fell deadly silent. Not a breath was heard.

"Atmosphere," Frank repeated softly, as if to keep the baby from hearing.

All of a sudden the boy jerked up, legs wobbling in a grotesque dance. Crazily, Frank thought again of a marionette.

Through clenched teeth, Frank forced, "Whatever in God's name happens, don't kill him."

And at that moment the boy dashed in front of them, like a fleeting shadow in the night. There hadn't been enough time to even fix their eyes on him, much less try to stop him, before he dropped the baby and leaped through the only window in the room.

Glass rained everywhere. Frank shielded himself with his arms. Hector made a halfhearted coughing sound, and then there was a *crunch!* as the boy slammed into the sidewalk two stories down.

"I'm going down!" Hector yelled, speeding from the apartment. Frank ran to the bloody baby, checking for injuries; his quick examination showed that the blood had come from else-where. He carefully picked up the bawling infant, then scanned the red room. It looked like a slaughterhouse, blood and gore everywhere. Like the alley.

He heard a gathering of noise outside. He shuffled toward the window, then stopped.

Something sitting on the dresser grabbed his attention.

Chapter Twenty-nine

Fleeting visions came and went, like tiny bubbles of dreams bursting to reveal not quite visceral, yet clearly understandable images. His senses prevailed, remained acute, and amid the haze obscuring his consciousness, the visual smatterings of thought continued to flash in his mind's eye, maintaining his awareness of his true identity.

Harold Gross, Harbinger for the Giver.

In the past he had been only one or the other, Harold or Harbinger. But now? His feelings clearly spelled out an intermingling of the two personalities, partially retaining each of them, a perfect combination perhaps. Even now, in his coma, the ability to comprehend this newfound state of being seemed easy, clear and precise.

However, although his mind had seemed to keep up, the complication of his incapacitated body had him puzzled. Although he tried and tried for what seemed like hours, he could not force his limbs to move. So he lay dormant, for now at least, waiting in the dark in this strange room, concentrating on his mind and the growing wealth of lucidity seeping through. It seemed his only viable alternative.

Suddenly something else broke through to his cognitive mind, and he immediately cleared his psyche of all inner activity in an effort to concentrate only on the distant sound.

Oh yes . . . it was here.

The pulse. The Giver. It was coming for him.

Jaimie awoke, unsure how much time had passed. She lay in darkness, unbound yet mysteriously paralyzed. In the distance she heard the incessant beat of music, heavy bass drums, deep droning tones. Techno music. The sensation of it reverberated through the floor directly into her muscles and bones. It brought feeling back into her body and she tried to move. Pain darted through her in tiny jolts, each joint, every muscle hurting in its effort to find itself once again.

She remembered her passage through the strange nightclub, the sleek jet walls, the humid air and blue neon lights. And then the giant dance floor, its workers so intensely involved in their project that her presence had gone unnoticed.

Those workers. The bald men, black clothing, sunglasses, all a part of their facade. They could not simply be nightclub employees, could they? No. She had witnessed terrifying aspects of their mission. The hypnotic exchanges with other men, for instance, men unlike themselves, seemingly willing to be captured and taken away into their alien grasp. Was this perhaps a form of recruiting? And what of the one from her class who later emerged on the street drenched in blood?

Jaimie shuddered, realizing that her glimpses of these bald men were most likely small pieces of the puzzle, only hints of their true purpose. How many of them had there been in that room? A hundred? Maybe more. How many had had blood on their hands at one time? All of them, of course. Like Bobby Lindsay—and he was here.

Jaimie suddenly realized that her eyes had been closed, seeking light behind her lids. She opened them, but nothing changed. Darkness prevailed, and amid it her thoughts sought solace but found only anguish at the realization that she was a prisoner, here in the realm of some crazed cult of death.

The pulse grew louder, and with each passing beat, Harold's strength grew as well. He squirmed in his binds, wrists and ankles tied to the gurney on which he lay. Thrum . . . thrum . . . thrum . . . each three-second interval forcing energy into his muscles, erotic images of power and strength into his mind. He tugged and tugged at the bindings, more forcefully each time, his muscles screaming, lactic acid veining within, adrenaline flowing, blood pumping.

The pulse grew even louder. Now he could hear it rising from below, from deep within the earth

*but growing closer with each beat. Thrum ...
thrum ... thrum. Now he felt it just beneath him.
The gurney shook, and he pulled and pulled on
the belts, images of failure in the eyes of the Giver
threatening him with abandonment should he
not escape the Outsiders. Layers of skin ripped
away from his wrists against the edges of the re-
straints. Finally one hand broke free. He unfet-
tered himself from the belt on his other wrist,
then from those at his ankles.*

*The pulse grew louder and louder and
louder ...*

*He sat up, an all-consuming blanket of blue
light shrouding his mind's eye, and within his
thoughts he could see the same images the Giver
saw, images of the earth being chipped away at
from a variety of dark locations, a multitude of
limbs guided from one unified body, searching for
waves of modified life, for all those beyond the
confines of the body to return to the all-
empowering Giver, to take part in the greatest
event of all time.*

*Indeed, the time had come. Tonight all those
who had aided in the glories of the Giver would
unite to share in a mass prayer of sorts, to com-
bine forces and become part of the unified body.
Too bad, then, that those who had had the honor
of supplying would miss out on this great occasion. Perhaps it had been beneficial that he never
found a way to supply, despite all his strenuous
efforts. Now he could take part in the event itself!*

*The gurney shook turbulently, as if an earth-
quake approached. He leaped off and tossed it*

aside, his one good eye peeking out through the bandages masking his face. At first he looked to the security camera in the upper corner of the room, then to the crashing gurney and last to the buckling tiles in the floor. They rose up and down and up and down, finally shattering into pieces, cement and vinyl flooring flying up in a shower of pebbles and shards, dirt spraying the room. He shielded his face with his arms, peeking through as the appendage ripped through the floor of the hospital basement, twisting wildly like an angry snake, drilling away at the edges of the hole it created just for Harold.

The door flung open behind him and he turned to see a number of Outsiders gathered, staring with shock at the scene before them.

Unthreatened, he turned back and jumped into the hole. The appendage wrapped itself around him, guiding him down in a tight squeeze. He reached bottom and crawled away through the tunnels the Giver had created for him. The appendage led the way, then released its grip on him and stayed behind to obliterate the trail.

Again, Harold was free.

Jaimie stood up, grasping the darkness, pacing in circles but finding nothing, the floor warm beneath her bare feet. She moved and moved, crying, nearly wishing death upon herself, as it seemed her only alternative at the moment.

She leaned against the wall. Within, the beat went on, music vibrating in the walls, pulsing, *thrum . . . thrum . . . thrum*, synthesized drones seeping from the wall into her body, like the beads of sweat escaping the skin on her face.

Harold crawled and crawled, feverishly, dirt beneath his tattered nails, bloodied bandages dangling crazily from his face, on and on, forward, pressing, muscles screaming, bones aching. Suddenly, he no longer wanted to die. He wanted, needed to live, to experience the event within the domain of the Giver, to assist the others recruited to arrange for the perfect environment, to help establish the field for the ultimate harvest.

Then Harold saw the light at the end of the tunnel. Nearly out of control, he crawled to it, squeezing through the small entrance, falling into one of the blue rooms. Behind him, the hole immediately closed up. He stood, stretching his muscles, dirt falling from his body.

He glanced about the dark room and saw something odd.

A girl, in the room with him, standing just a few feet ahead, face, hands and body pressed against the wall. Crying.

Chapter Thirty

The afternoon lasted an eternity, and it seemed to Frank and Hector that all had been lost.

They had had a great deal of explaining to do. The two cops, out of jurisdiction, had found themselves in the middle of a suicide in which a father had nearly taken his infant with him. This of course didn't include the multitude of other events they had been involved in over the last thirty-six hours. Now, to their great misfortune, it all had to come out into the open.

It took the rest of the day to explain to officials from both the Thirteenth and Fifty-seventh precincts what they had found, how they'd gotten involved and where it all led to. From the incident in the alley to the discovery of Gross and the other bald men in the sketches. The interview with the Racines and the confrontation with

Gross. The receipt in Gross' apartment and how it led them to Village Clothing. Judas and the surveillance tape of Bobby Lindsay. They painstakingly detailed how they figured it all tied in, the murders, the prior kidnappings and the speculation of an FBI coverup. Then, finally, the cult theory, how Harold Gross, Bobby Lindsay and the others on file—James Hilton and Edward Farrell—might all have been involved.

Their story ended at the trail of blood leading to the apartment of the Latino man.

However, they left a few things out.

The day had been long enough, and to start delving into all the truly inexplicable issues would carry their interrogation well into the night. For one, the tunnels. Their existence had been common knowledge, yet no details other than some passing commentary had been voiced, their purpose seemingly shrugged off; good thing, as Frank could offer no revelations, either logical or far-fetched. It seemed none of the other cops could either.

They mentioned no word of their discovery on the Internet, leaving only their musings of cult practice on the table—a theory founded purely on intuition, of course. To reveal the alien babblings of Sanskrit as a lead to potential answers other than cults would only embarrass the cops.

And then the strange black object, the biggest enigma of all. At first its presence intrigued Frank, then it consumed him, driving him to seek out its function and its role in this entire mess. At first Hector had written it off to remote speculation on Frank's part, then labeled it a religious icon.

And now?

It had shown up at two of the crime scenes, in the alley early yesterday morning and now retrieved by Frank in the apartment of the Latino who'd nearly taken his baby out the window.

Now, with one of them in their possession, new theories would surely arise.

By the time Frank and Hector finally escaped the Fifty-seventh precinct in the Bronx, the sun had begun its descent behind the skyscrapers. They rode in silence back into the city to a parking garage on Fifty-sixth and Park. They located a diner a half block away and helped themselves to a booth in the rear, by the kitchen. The smallish, brightly lit restaurant housed mostly men, who probably, like Frank, had no one at home to prepare a warm meal for them at the end of the day. He rubbed his tired eyes and listened to the Spanish chatter of the cooks and waitresses behind the swinging doors that led into the kitchen.

A young waitress with long brown hair emerged. She took their orders—grilled cheese and tomato soup for Frank, a burger and fries for Hector. When she left, Frank fished the object from his jacket pocket and placed it on the table between them.

"I can't believe it," Hector said, shaking his head at the sight of the object. "You really had that thing in your pocket this whole time?"

Frank nodded. This was the first time he had had the chance to get a good long look at it since

pocketing it eight hours earlier, waiting for the
perfect moment to bring it out into the light and
examine it, feeling the need for privacy before
showing Hector his find. He stared and stared at
it, hardly believing that he, Frank Ballaro, had
finally taken possession of the most mysterious
object he had ever seen.

"So what in God's name is it?" Hector asked.

Frank shrugged. He suddenly felt as if he were
being hypnotized. In a trance he saw a strange,
wondrous place, a place of brilliant sunshine,
laughter and smiling faces, a place that catered
solely to lonely and desperate people, that
brought joy to the despondent. Frank considered
accepting its offer, the chance to relieve the lone-
liness tormenting his soul since Diane had left
him five years back. Perhaps all his answers lay
right here on the table before him . . .

"Sir?" The waitress returned with his dinner.
Through waves of confusion, Frank let his eyes
wander over her. Young, in her late teens, her
name tag scribbled in black pen: Sam.

"Oh, cool. Atmosphere."

Shock flooded Frank at her mention of the ominous word. What had been complete darkness in
his life at that moment exploded with a fire as big
and as bright as the sun. He thought briefly of the
Latino in the apartment, his child swathed in
blood; the harsh whisper that had leaked from
his mouth.

Atmosphere . . .

"What did you say?"

"That thing—Atmosphere. It looks like the

313

new nightclub that opens tonight. It's on all the signs. See?" Sam pointed through the window to a telephone pole outside. Frank could see a small poster stapled there.

"Pardon us." Frank nudged past Sam and rushed outside, Hector not far behind. He hunched his shoulder against the drizzle coming down, facing the small poster.

There it was, the object, a sketch of a building with six cylindrical columns on its roof. Above, words printed in ink as black as coal made an offer: EXPERIENCE ATMOSPHERE, SATURDAY NIGHT, OCTOBER 23. WEST SIDE TRAIN YARD.

"What do you think, Smoky?"

The answer was clear. "All three of me thinks we should go check out Atmosphere."

Hector grimaced in confusion but asked no questions. He agreed too.

Chapter Thirty-one

Frank and Hector sped back to Hector's house, lights and siren in full array. Hector quickly changed into plain clothes, while Frank placed a call home. He figured there would be a chance to catch Jaimie; usually around this time on Saturdays she would be getting ready to go out for the evening. But she did not answer. He left a message, then hung up to find Hector in a pair of khakis, a sport shirt and a long trenchcoat, giving Gloria an I-have-to-work-late story and telling her not to wait up. The frown on her face clearly stated that she would be up, regardless of how late he returned. This scenario was probably routine in the Rodriguez household, just as it had been during Frank's marriage to Diane.

They left just after ten, taking the cruiser through the streets at a moderate pace, giving themselves enough time to think about their options, and what they would do when they eventually arrived at Atmosphere.

"We'll have to let events unfold themselves," Frank muttered, staring at the poster he'd ripped from the telephone pole advertising the nightclub. "It's all worked out that way so far."

Hector glanced at the poster in Frank's hand. "If it weren't for the picture, I'd have to chalk up the name of the club to coincidence."

"But it *is* there. So what do you think?"

"I have no fucking idea."

"You know, it ties in to the whole music thing. The club, Sanskrit's article on binaural beats, the missing kids' interest in music, Village Clothing."

"I know, I know. I'm just having trouble swallowing it all."

"There's something else we haven't discussed. Something obvious." He looked over at Hector.

"Carrie?"

Frank nodded. "Her murder. Now it ties in. She was actually a boy. A young teenage male. Just like the rest."

Hector said nothing. Frank's all-knowing detective personality could tell that his former captain was as obsessed with this great mystery as he was. And his weaker rational self—well, it could tell that Hector was also scared—just like him.

He drove the car down Eleventh Avenue, parking at the curb in front of a strip of closed shops. A miserable drizzle fell from the muddy sky, coating them in a frigid chill. This section of town didn't just sleep at this time of night, it died, and not a soul or even a rat or pigeon seemed to venture out after sundown. There might have been some form of life here, but it stayed shuttered behind wretched doors. Frank shuddered at the thought of whatever unfortunates cowered beyond the stained walls of these dark buildings.

"Train yard's that way."

They paced through the night rain across Eleventh Avenue into the perimeter of the train yard. Frank felt for his gun, hoping to remain anonymous once inside the club, keeping his fingers crossed that there wouldn't be a metal detector, or that he wouldn't be frisked.

"Lots of open land here," Hector said, breaking the uncomfortable silence. "Perfect place for the Yanks to build a stadium."

Frank saw something ahead. He put a hand on Hector's arm, commanding him to stand still.

Two obscure shapes crossed the yard about a hundred yards ahead. They stepped over at least five sets of tracks, climbing through the connected cabs of those occupied by trains.

Frank and Hector moved forward, picking up the pace, careful not to trip over any rails. Reaching a lone passenger car, they stopped and leaned against it, eyes glued to the pair of bodies, the cold wetness soaking from the surface of the tempered steel through their jackets. The bodies they eyed shifted in and out of the shadows, over the last set of rails to a loading dock, where they climbed four steps to a landing bay door. One of the two people gave the door a few hard raps. The metal grate flew up and a large silhouette appeared. After a short exchange, they were admitted.

"Let's go," Frank said, stepping away from the train.

He only made it a step. The passenger train doors flew open and from within a group of men—ordinary-looking men, not bald, not teenagers, wearing jeans and sweatshirts—jumped down and abruptly grabbed hold of Frank and Hector.

They pointed guns at them.

"Come with us."

Frank and Hector were quickly led into the train. Once inside, they saw that the passenger car was not really part of a train; it held none of the things a train would house: seats, overhead storage racks, a bathroom. Instead, this lone car acted as a cover to something else, something top-secret, perhaps.

At least fifteen men were busy at work, seemingly keeping tabs on the goings-on around the train yard. A dozen or so computers sat atop as many desks, each one displaying information to a single occupant. Television monitors had been set up displaying what appeared to be a pinpointed area of the train yard. At the moment the monitors visible to Frank showed nothing but quiet, darkened landscapes, except one, which followed three young males pacing zombielike toward the loading dock.

A man dressed in jeans and a polo shirt confronted them.

Frank leaned over to Hector. "FBI," he whispered, eyes glued to the agent.

"Exactly," the man said, his voice deep and gravelly. "And you—police. So what do you gentlemen know about this nightclub?"

Hector was about to speak when Frank grabbed his arm, silencing him. "We were invited."

The FBI agent grinned. "I don't think they'd need *you* for anything."

Frank fought to ignore the jab. He was angered at this obvious coverup but made an effort to keep his emotions at bay.

"Let's keep this simple, gentlemen. Your path ends here."

Frank felt a chill run down his spine, as if someone had aimed a loaded weapon at him. Given the circumstances, he didn't doubt the possibility of being killed. "We were invited," he repeated, keeping his inflection as colorless as possible. He moved very slowly and deliberately to his pocket as not to let anyone think he might be reaching for a weapon. Then he pulled out the object, displaying it proudly yet cautiously to the FBI agents.

At the sight of it, their faces turned a pale shade of gray. The agent at the forefront stepped back, but only a inch, a thick vein in his forehead popping out. "Where did you get that?"

Frank put it back into his pocket. "The bald man gave it to me." He prayed this made sense to the agents, who Frank suddenly realized actually possessed the answers to the entire mystery he and Hector had been attempting to unearth for the past two days.

The agent remained silent and was about to speak when a slight stir broke out at one of the surveillance monitors. "Mullin—come look at this."

The agent questioning Frank turned around and walked briskly to the monitor.

"There're hundreds of them."

"Who the hell are they?" Mullin asked, the vein in his forehead growing bigger.

"No clue. They've got torches. They're coming this way."

Mullin raced to the rear of the train car and grabbed an assault rifle from behind a curtain draped across a storage area. "Get everybody together!" he yelled, storming about like a madman. Suddenly the place came alive, and Frank and Hector stood in the midst of it, confused, feeling as if they had suddenly become invisible.

Amid the fray of preparation, someone yelled, "What about the two cops?"

Mullin glanced carelessly toward them, clearly more occupied with the sudden emergency. "They have a unit. Let them go."

Magic words. The door they had entered flew open and Frank and Hector were pushed out. They fell down four feet to the rain-wet ground, their hands breaking their fall.

"Goddamn son-of-a-bitch!" Hector lay on his stomach, his head raised slightly. His cheeks had wet dirt on them.

"You all right?" Unhurt, Frank got to his knees

and checked on Hector. His ex-captain was mumbling a storm of profanity.

"I *hate* the FBI. Goddamned sons-of-bitches think they own the world."

"Keep your voice down. C'mon."

They stood and jogged from the trailer toward the loading dock, away from the brewing trouble.

"What did they see? He said *hundreds* of them." Hector was wiping his bruised palms on his trenchcoat.

Frank looked around but didn't see anything. He thought he heard a thunderous roar in the distance, and half expected to see a flash of lightning in the rainy sky but didn't. "You hear that?"

Hector nodded warily. "Sounds like a crowd."

"Let's not waste any more time."

They walked to the loading dock. To the entrance of Atmosphere.

They had assembled in great numbers. Lester gazed at the hundreds of homeless people standing around him in virtual prayer before the great leader of the troops, Jyro.

"We go in tonight!" Jyro screamed from his makeshift platform, constructed of milk crates and hemp. The troops returned the cry with a maniacal wail.

"We fight until death!"

"*Yah!*" The roar deafened Lester.

"We march and will not return until victory is ours!" He pointed behind him toward the train yard.

"*Yah!*"

Lester waited for the cue and then Jyro, in all his massive black glory, raised his arms up in the air and screamed, "The rebellion has begun!"

The troops marched forward, following their leader.

Frank and Hector climbed the four rusty grated steps to the platform of the loading dock. Frank's weak, passionless personality wanted so dearly to break out from the bonds holding it back, but his detective third and irrational third had joined forces, assuming control, creating a new, stronger will within him, a will that desired nothing more than to seek out the answers to this elusive mystery that had left him nearly lifeless, that wanted to destroy anything in his path until he unearthed the answers he sought.

They could hear a remote booming emanating from within the walls of the warehouse: a series of sounds too syncopated to be thunder, too synthetic to be anything created by nature. It was music, the droning of hard techno beats and ambient rhythms spilling out from within the walls of Atmosphere.

Just as the two nondescript figures had done, Frank walked up to the landing bay door with the word *Atmosphere* messily spray-painted upon it, raised a fist and knocked.

The door immediately slid skyward on its tracks and a man appeared.

Bald, dark sunglasses. But an unfamiliar man, this one possessing a tapestry of tattoos on his arms and a variety of face piercings. "You have an invite?" he asked in a monotonous, almost mechanical voice. The lenses of his dark sunglasses seemed to penetrate Frank, all the way to the bone, the look seeming to say, *what are you doing here, old man?*

Frank pawed the object from his pocket.

The bouncer stayed silent. Frank's heart pounded in syncopation with the muddied music. Then, stepping aside, the bouncer said, "Follow the arrows."

Frank slipped the object back into his pocket and entered, Hector glued to his back.

They entered an empty dark room, the reek of mold immediately assaulting them. A series of small iridescent green arrows ran across the cement floor and they followed them, one careful step at a time, their faint illumination the only source of light. Frank's timid personality squeezed through a bit, contriving terrifying horrors lurking in the darkness: the ghosts of the dead, the suicidal Latino boy, Patrick Racine and the other boy in the alley, their mouths gaping, black blood oozing from the torn holes in their naked bodies, each one crawling from the darkness with mangled arms and twisted legs . . .

They spotted a door in front of them, a glowing green arrow on it pointing the way. Frank looked at Hector, wanting to say, *We don't have to do this, we can turn back now, get the hell out of here and let those FBI boys handle it.* Hector pushed past him and groped for the handle.

The door pulled open.

And the building was there.

Surrounded by a link fence, the dome-shaped structure sat like a giant insect, six great spines on its back reaching to the night sky, its bulk the size of a small stadium. "Jesus . . ." was all Frank could manage. When had this structure been constructed? Who built it?

Music seeped from its black shell, pulsing, throbbing, mesmerizing; the ground beneath their feet vibrated, a booming bass. They walked across a combination of dirt and crumbled cement, through an opening in the link fence toward what appeared to be a door. Frank and Hector both reached their hands out at the same time and touched it, its vibrating surface as smooth and as black as the surface of the object in Frank's pocket. Frank grasped the handle on the door.

They entered Atmosphere.

Three more bald men stood in a small foyer, clad in leather and wearing sunglasses. Frank quickly displayed the object. The one in front nodded and stepped aside, permitting them access.

They followed the music down a short hall and through a curtain into a huge room. They stood there rooted, astounded at the amazing sight before them, a vast interior whose domed roof ran maybe a hundred feet high, like that of a planetarium, hundreds of lights, a multitude of colors, flashing from the ceiling in a brilliant stroboscopic storm, exploding intermittently amid one another—all seemingly dominated by the music. Six huge column supports stood interspersed throughout the room, towering to the ceiling like monolithic stalactites in some dark cave. Frank imagined them continuing on through the roof and into the air, forming the six towering stacks outside. At the ceiling, a single cobalt ring of neon encircled the top of the columns like halos, a shower of fog raining down the sides in dream-like cascades. Hundreds of young adults—young *men*—gyrated about the columns on the dance floor, their bodies thrashing in seizurelike motions, in rhythm to the pounding drums.

All of them: young men, pretzeled together in an orgy of dance.

Slowly and quietly, Frank and Hector paced around the perimeter of the dance floor, eyes peering and necks craning, trying, but mostly not succeeding, to avoid the wildly swinging arms and legs escaping the spasmodic horde.

"What do you make of this?" Hector finally yelled through the raging din.

Frank shrugged his shoulders, quite unsure himself.

So what do you make of this, Frank?

For the first time since he and Hector had joined forces nearly thirty-six hours earlier, Frank saw himself as the leader, the one in control. He was now guiding Hector, not the other way around. There would be no more discussions, no more persuading. He wouldn't have to convince his ex-captain of their next move, to try and sway him. This was *it*, and he would be in charge.

Throughout the investigation, Frank had clearly held the stronger insight, had had some crazy yet conceivable ideas. Yet he had allowed himself to be guided by Hector's reasoning, his by-the-book police logic. But now things would be different. It was *he*—or better yet, a new Frank who was half true detective and half compulsive-irrational—who held the upper hand, here in what he assumed was the domain of the . . . what? aliens? cult?

Whoever, whatever they were, only a continued investigation would reveal for certain, and this investigation would be Frank's.

He slipped through the crowd, guiding Hector toward the bar. They squeezed into a spot next to a young man with a trail of metal loops running along the entire edge of his ear.

Following the instinctive calling of his detective personality, Frank peered at the variety of men here, their bodies acting ahead of their minds. He reminded himself of what Sam Richards had said about Harold Gross acting under a severe hypnotic trance. Were all the men here captured by this hypnotic force?

He stepped from the bar and walked along the edge of the crowd, farther into the heart of the club. He found a set of steel stairs leading up and followed them, Hector in tow, passing two young men whose arms and tongues were tangled together in a knotted embrace.

He reached the top, but another bald and sunglassed bouncer blocked the way. The bouncer raised his hand in Frank's face. "You have a pass?" His voice was deep and phlegmy, monotonous.

Frank once again fished the object from his pocket.

The bouncer immediately stepped aside and let Frank pass, no questions asked. But he did not allow Hector through, stepping between them. "You have a pass?" His statement sounded identical to the first, so much so that it could have been a recording.

Frank peered back at his ex-captain, not wanting to speak for fear of alerting their non-hypnotic states to the bald men. Hector tossed a slight nod at Frank, then turned and headed back down the stairs. Mentally, Frank heard Hector say, *"Go ahead, Smoky, I'll be all right. You go and find out what the hell is going on here."*

Now, also for the first time since the investigation began, Frank Ballaro was alone.

He turned a corner to the right and found himself gazing down a long doorless hallway, cobalt wisps of illumination floating within like specters, seeming to emanate from no true source. The walls were glossy and black, like the exterior of the building. Like the object in his pocket.

He followed the hall for perhaps twenty-five feet, to an impasse. He stopped, twisted his neck and peered back. The bald bouncer stood there, sunglasses staring at him. At once Frank felt extremely uncomfortable, as if he were being set up; perhaps a gang of thugs were planning to leap out at him at any second to make him disappear. He took a deep breath, trying hard to keep his newfound combo personality from bowing down to fear.

When he faced forward again, the impasse had disappeared, giving way to an entrance.

Frank strained to see as the darkness ahead loomed. He stepped forward, and a great round room sucked him in, large but still smaller than that of the dance floor he'd left behind. The walls and floor were sleek and black like everything else, devoid of anything noticeable except for a series of gray screens encircling the perimeter.

"*Sit . . .*" The electronic voice startled Frank, its monotone frighteningly similar to that of the bouncers.

"What's this about? Who are you?" Frank yelled, his voice echoing in the chamber.

"*Sit.*"

Frank took a step forward. The screens lit up, a dull swirl of blue and silver moving with lava-like slowness upon them.

"*Sit.*"

The lights brightened as the word reverberated. Frank, seeking only the truth, finally complied and squatted on the floor. He slid his hand inside his jacket and sought the comfort of his gun, just in case. Fear ran in line with curiosity in this surrealistic world.

"*Place the object on the floor in front of you,*" the voice demanded.

With his free hand Frank fished it out. As uncommonly gratifying as it felt to have had it, he was equally eager to be rid of it. He placed it on the floor and again asked, "Who are you?"

A small slot formed beneath the screen directly in front of him and a black snakelike tube slithered out, wet and glistening yet strangely crustaceous, twisting like an eel as it approached.

Frank tightened his grip on the gun. Bile climbed to the back of his throat. His finger sweated on the trigger.

The appendage stopped at the object. Its puckered tip kissed the air. Frank watched as it weaved in and about the six spines on the top of the object before attaching itself to one of them. Suddenly the screens changed color, from red to blue to purple, and then a brilliant spectrum of colors spiraled about. He watched with fascination, his breath lost in a confusion of emotions and fear.

The colors quickly faded to gray. The tube detached itself and shot back into the wall like a recoiling tape measure. *"The unit has been evacuated. Harbinger, take the unit and seek out new Suppliers."*

Harbinger? Frank clamped his hand over his mouth in thought. Speak no evil. *"What* are you?" It was barely a whisper.

Another slot in the wall opened, this time above the screen. A blue laser burst out and washed over Frank's body from head to toe, then blinked out. It was as if he had been scanned . . .

"Subject lacks necessary chemical agent. Unsuitable for harvesting."

Frank stood. "Chemical agent? What in God's name is—"

A face appeared on the screen. Well, not so much a face as a blur. But the eyes were there, large, black, prominent orbs taking up almost half the oval head. It flickered slightly, and Frank could see a small blur of a mouth open as it spoke.

"How did you find us?"

"I'm a detective. I find things. What's going on here? Who are you?" Frank took a step forward, gazing up at the face on the screen, his fear giving way to curiosity. His wary third, hiding in the shadows, showed its face a bit, wondering if this whole scenario might all be some great show, if the mysterious object before him had been some sort of backstage pass, granting him access behind the scenes. But his stronger detective personality knew differently, knew, in fact, that this whole spectacle was some huge excursion into a previously unexplored world, a bizarre new world in which he had become an unwitting participant.

"Subject does not carry the necessary chemical agent."

"Chemical? What chemical?"

"Chemical agent is genetically preponderant in young aggressive males."

"What chemical agent?" Frank's heart slammed against his chest.

Silence.

Then: *"The naturally ocurring element testosterone is not unlike our fuel."*

Frank at once felt all three personalities experience a similar emotion: uncertain fear. All along he had pondered the alien theory, that somehow visitors from another planet might exist. Now, as the proof of this came to light, the reason for their extreme measures also spilled out. That they—whoever *they* were—were trapped here against their will, and that their only means of escape would be to refuel. According to the now feasible articles by Sanskrit, their initial efforts had been to modify the earth's atmosphere in an effort to create an environment suitable for their own existence. Their efforts had failed but their secondary goal had had some degree of success.

He stared up at the screen, legs starting to cramp from squatting. The surreal face melted away into colors and then back again, the entire effect a great swirling conglomeration of living, breathing tinctures. "Atmosphere," Frank said, not really knowing how to determine the significance of the word other than to simply utter it.

"It defines all understanding of the human race."

The human voice came from behind him, and Frank startled at its intrusion. He rose up, the face on the screen still swirling from nonexistent to barely solid, then spun around and immediately felt his stomach knot with loathing.

Bobby Lindsay.

Frank opened his mouth to speak but could only stammer.

Bobby Lindsay stepped forward, and for the first time since his arrest he wore no sunglasses and had a thin growth of stubble on his skull. "I could ask why you're here, but that much is obvious."

"Lindsay, what is all of this?" Although Frank's fear and anger tore him to shreds, his curiosity held him together. "What defines the human race?"

"*Understanding* of the human race. Don't misconstrue the truth, Ballaro." Lindsay paced a silent circle around Frank until he reached the glowing screen. He stood in front of it, the landscape of intermingling colors and shapes providing an evil tapestry behind him. He pointed to the screen. The strange entity appeared for a moment, then swirled away into an amorphous shape. "The Giver. His understanding of the human race. That object before you is an Atmosphere; but then again, everything here is."

"You're not making any sense, Bobby. You never did."

"Think about it, Ballaro. You must know a great deal about this place, about the Giver, to realize how significant the Atmosphere really is. The Giver came here through the Atmosphere, almost redefined it. It hid beneath it for a long time, using its scope to scan us and our language. Haven't you turned on your radio and heard the pulse? That pulse—it's all hearing, all knowing of our way of life. And it exists solely through the radio. And the radio—well, it's everywhere."

Frank thought about what he was saying, and even though Lindsay appeared mad, it made sense. If this Giver, as he called it, had initially scanned radio waves at its location beneath the hole it caused upon its entry into the atmosphere in an effort to learn about human culture, it most assuredly would have picked up a great deal of programming. Almost constant programming, in fact, and not just from public radio channels but also through short-wave communications from scientists who had eagerly moved to investigate the sudden phenomenon.

Frank placed a hand on his gun. The music in the walls grew louder.

"Don't move, Ballaro. This is my domain." Bobby stepped forward, inches from Frank. He leaned down and grabbed the Atmosphere from the floor. "I am your Harbinger, and you are my Supplier."

Frank watched in terror as the object that had once been in his pocket started to change shape. Bobby rubbed it feverishly, black eyes staring maniacally at Frank, the blackness upon it changing into a spectrum of liquefied colors like those upon the screen. The screen grew brighter, the face now gone, giving way to thicker, more vibrant hues. The object melted from Bobby's grip, dripped to the floor like spilled syrup and seeped onto Frank's legs, quickly ascending them to his crotch. He stood there, frozen, afraid to touch the slithering mess. A warmth spread into his penis and testicles, a sexual warmth that he hadn't felt in many years, ever since Diane last pleasured him.

But it had no stimulating effect on him.

Frank was impotent.

The voice of the Giver emanated, its electronic timbre echoing amid the muffled beat of the music. *"Subject is unsuitable for harvesting. Recognize failure."*

The mucky thing that had once been the black

object slid from Frank's crotch and flowed like a great blob of liquid mercury back into the hands of Bobby Lindsay. Frank watched in horror as the smile on Bobby's face, at first wide and proud, suddenly disappeared and gave way to a scowl of fear and pain. The object, still in its liquid form, started to spread over his hands and wrists. Bobby panicked, crazily shaking his hands up and down in an effort to loosen the growing lump. No good. It swallowed his forearms to the elbows. He rolled to the floor, screaming in pain, as if he was on fire, trying to douse the flames.

The colors on the screen swirled fantastically, the voice booming out. *"Subject is suitable for harvesting."*

Frank turned to run, had taken a few weakened steps when an exit suddenly appeared in the sleek jet wall. He quickened his pace toward it, stumbling, wanting to find Hector.

He heard another scream.

The scream of a girl.

Then he saw Harold Gross, first his bandaged head appearing through the ghostly doorway and then the upper half of his body, now clad in hospital garb. He seemed to be struggling with something. He looked toward Frank and smiled a wide, incredulous grin that clearly stated, *What the fuck are you doing here?*

Then he pulled her in, one hand in her hair, the other wrapped around her neck, clearly choking her.

Frank's heart dropped. In all his life nothing

had ever terrified him as this did: his daughter, Jaimie, his whole life, his very blood and soul, in this *place*, in the arms of a killer. Fleeting images filled his mind with terrible new mysteries: How in God's name had Harold Gross escaped the hospital? How had Jaimie ended up in his grasp? What did Jaimie know about this place? Why was she here?

As serious as those questions were, they needed to take a back seat to the immediate situation, and how he planned to save her. He prayed—not to God, but to his three personalities. Everything had had a way of unfolding to his benefit since the very beginning, and he prayed that it wouldn't stop now.

He kept his gaze glued to his daughter, her eyes tightened into tear-laden slits. He saw her mouth tremble in fear but could not hear her cries through Bobby Lindsay's tortured screams and the pounding music emanating from the walls. "Don't worry, baby!" he yelled, trying to reassure her and himself that everything would be okay.

Harold Gross stopped seemingly stunned at the sight behind Frank. Still holding Jaimie tight, he yelled in tongueless gibberish, "What the fuck is this?" then tramped forward, dragging the struggling girl with him. "I bring you a gift and you let *him* supply? *I* want to supply."

With no warning he threw Jaimie to the ground and ran toward Bobby Lindsay, who was now nearly shrouded in a gelatinous veil of black slime. He yelled something incoherent at the

Giver, its colors swirling frenziedly, then began to tear at the liquid Atmosphere surrounding the screaming Bobby, whose arms reached out from beneath the surface of black slime like tree branches lifting up from the surface of a tar pit. The Atmosphere responded, quickly sucking Harold into the fray. A loud slurping noise discharged, as if it were *drinking* him, and then a new set of screams followed.

Harold Gross finally got his wish: to supply.

Frank ran to Jaimie and held her in his arms, absorbing her sobs. Over her shoulder, he watched in horror as two siphonlike hoses formed from the body of the Atmosphere and encased the two men's abdomens, each lengthy tube whipping wildly about like eels out of water.

When the muffled screams beneath the Atmosphere finally stopped, it automatically snapped out of its gelatinous form back into the familiar object Frank had come to know: small, black, shiny, six perfect spines emerging from its rounded surface. It tottered on the floor's surface like a dropped lid, then came to a stop, two tattered bodies twitching on the floor next to it.

Beneath the screen the small aperture appeared again, and from within the appendage slithered out and attached itself to one of the spines emerging from the Atmosphere. A whining noise ensued, and when it stopped, the voice of the Giver echoed in the dark, blue-lit chamber.

"The unit has been evacuated. Take the unit, seek out new Suppliers."

"Fuck you," Frank said, then quickly ushered Jaimie from the room.

Outside the black walls of Atmosphere, another war of sorts manifested, a dozen or so men with guns opposing a few hundred wilding street people with torches and minds gone askew. Bullets flew, some hitting their mark, others soaring astray into the night. From the opposite direction, an arsenal of weapons struck their targets: flames, rocks, pipes, anything hard and within a hand's reach. In the end, when all had been said and done, many lay dead, even more injured. The street people had prevailed.

Lester was among the injured, a bullet weaving a charred path through his lungs. He lay gasping for air on the battlefield, looking peculiarly at a lone train car that had been upended. As it disappeared behind a wash of film across his sight, his life passed before his eyes. At that moment his illness escaped his mind, and in return it left memories of the Lester who had once been loved and had loved in return, a gentle, caring man who had had a family, a job, an appreciation for life and all it had to offer.

He also remembered a time long ago when he first entered this world with all hope of becoming a normal human being.

And with his last breath, he would leave it the very same way.

Frank and Jaimie fought corridor after corridor, each lengthy path identical to the next, its glossy black walls illuminated with a soft touch of blue. Instead of relying on sight, they followed their ears, listening to the music, using their hands to determine the vibrations in the walls. Finally a storm of dancing lights came into view at the end of one tunnel, and they raced out, finding themselves on a platform twenty-five feet above pure chaos.

At first the scene looked much like it had when Frank and Hector had first entered the club: dancers writhing about, heads bobbing crazily, arms and legs tangled in spasmodic furor. Sheets of blue laser light bulleted out from various locations in the walls, each one pinpointing a specific dancer in the fray. Frank remembered the light that had washed over his body in the room of the Giver and realized now that the dancers were also being scanned.

"Subject suitable for harvesting . . ."

Dear God, Frank thought. *It's a mass harvesting of testosterone for fuel.*

Then he saw beyond those dancing, who appeared oblivious to the carnage sharing the room with them. Bald sunglassed men, hundreds of them—the Giver's servants—mingled amid the crowd. Some held the vile black objects in their hands, blindly seeking partakers; others had already found their subjects and watched with rapturous contentment as the teens surrendered their testosterone—and their lives. Screams erupted, some of pleasure, some of pain, howls cutting through the incessant beat of the music. Blood coated the dance floor and continued to pool from those just beginning to supply, the dancers slipping and sliding through the sloppy surface, giant finger painting–like streaks forming beneath their feet, some losing their footing and splashing down into the gummy mess, unaware of the menace.

And then the objects: hundreds of them, it seemed, many in solid form within the hands of the bald men, others taking on new terrifying formations in the possession of the teens. Some ate through their stomachs, others encased entire bodies in black shrouds. They moved, bubbled, gurgled, dripped, all seeming to possess lives of their own, feeding on their victims.

From within the walls of the great room, a multitude of writhing cable-like appendages emerged, each one poking about the massacre to track those post-harvest objects reverting to original form, like animals seeking scraps of food. Once an object had been located, the appendages attached themselves to one of its six spines, collecting the prize.

Pressing Jaimie's face into his chest, Frank stared dumbfounded into the anarchy, trying to absorb it as a whole rather than itemizing each horrifying ingredient: bodies strewn everywhere, torsos shredded, blood, bile and gristle seeping, pools flowing into one another, a great sea formed in their marriage, steam rising, coppery odors, feces and urine commingling, a pure hell rising into a coagulation of rot and corruption, gurgling moans escaping throats gone dead, last breaths discharged from lungs now crushed, snakelike extremities prowling the cracks, slurping, sucking, swallowing.

Frank slowly creeped along the catwalk, Jaimie inching along with him, each keeping their gaze from the pit below. Frank could feel the dampness of his daughter's tears through his jacket, tears caused not just from fear but from the burning stench rising up from the pit. In this moment when life seemed so distant, when the gates of hell had granted them full access, Frank could listen to nothing but his heart. None of his personalities, the strong truth-seeking detective, the timid common man, or the irrationally impulsive tough guy, could ever prepare for such a hellish adventure. The man who now existed was pure Frank Ballaro, nothing more, nothing less, and it would be his heart alone that would protect his daughter.

They edged around nearly a quarter of the room's circumference, the whole time screams of savage pain and howls of triumph rising up to torment their ears. Soon a stairwell leading down came into view. A few feet from the bottom of the stairs, just beyond a pair of disemboweled bodies, hung the curtain that Frank and Hector had originally entered through.

Suddenly a great horror struck Frank.

Hector.

Frank led Jaimie to the top of the steps. "We have to go down now," he said as gently as he could, trying desperately not to let her hear the tremble in his voice.

Jaimie started to panic. She pulled her face

away from his chest, her cheeks red, wet, and swollen. "Please," she cried, her head fearfully shaking back and forth. "I can't, *I can't!*"

She tried to pull away from her father, but he held on for dear life, dragging her down the steps. She stumbled along, screaming, her tantrum an uncontrollable storm. They reached bottom. Here the stench of blood and shit was ten times worse, and Frank had to hold back the rising of his gorge. It was here that he also heard, through the raging din of music and hellish wails of pain and pleasure, the voice of the Giver. But not just one voice—many voices, a chorus of hundreds, it seemed, all the same evil monotone.

"*Subject sufficient for harvesting . . .*"

"*The unit is full . . .*"

"*Seek out new Suppliers . . .*"

Over and over and over, the voices continued, as if stuck in wicked, inescapable overload.

Frank eyed the curtain, still hanging and remarkably unblemished. He thought quickly of seeking out Hector in the fray but chose to rescue his daughter instead, praying the whole time that his ex-captain had had the sense to flee this godforsaken place.

He took a step toward the curtain, Jaimie hanging on his shoulder.

All of a sudden the curtain tore away and from beyond an army poured in, led by a great black man with a bandanna tied to his skull. He raised his arms and yelled in triumph, the throngs of homeless rushing around him like a swarm of ants past their stoic queen. Some carried pipes, others torches or baseball bats or anything else that would function as a weapon. They entered in a hypnotic frenzy of sorts, attacking anything in their way: bald men, unprepared for attack and primarily defenseless; injured teens, taken out of their misery; and then the appendages, slithering back behind the safety of the alien walls. More blood flew, bodies fell in a congested Armageddon, piling atop one another, most of whom were alive and slipping in the blood of the dead.

The Giver's voice boomed out, a new phrase now, over and over.

"Subject insufficient for harvesting. Recognize failure."

Finally the mob thinned at the entrance, and the only thing separating Frank and his freedom was the giant leader of the troops.

He struggled forward on weary legs, guided solely by instinct and his desire to save Jaimie's life.

The giant looked down on them, steadfast and cocky. Insane.

Frank remembered his gun, and would use it if he had to. Jaimie shuddered uncontrollably.

He put his hand on his weapon.

The black man leaned down, spoke softly in Frank's ear, breath hot and rancid. "Who is your god?"

Behind them, an explosion. A wall went up in flames at the far end of the dance floor.

Frank peered up at the great man, the ripeness

of his body evident despite the harsh odors filling the room. Behind, a cluster of screams erupted from the pit. "There is no god."

The giant laughed, displaying his gold tooth, running a gentle finger through Jaimie's hair. "For if there was a god, he would save you, my child." Then he stepped aside, granting them access to the exit. "Remember, old man, the one who spared your child's life," he exclaimed.

"Come on, Jame," Frank whispered, looking up as thankfully as he could given the circumstances. He pulled Jaimie forward, staggering past the giant through the corridor and finally outside beyond the walls of Atmosphere. They ran through the fence and into the dark warehouse. When they finally stepped foot on the loading dock they found a battlefield in the train yard, bodies strewn everywhere, the FBI surveillance vehicle on its side. In the distance, lights and sirens approached. Behind, another explosion.

Then, a shout. "Frank!"

Frank turned to see Hector approaching from the left, a wash of blood across his trenchcoat. "All hell broke loose and I had to get out. I'm sorry." He shot Jaimie a peculiar glance, the weary look on his face clearly conveying that his mind would accept just about anything at this point.

"Don't ask. Let's get out of here." Frank pulled Jaimie with him. "I would have done the same thing, Hect."

"Dear God, Frank—what is all of this?" Hector asked, nearly out of breath.

"There is no god." Then, "It was *them.*"

Suddenly a rat appeared, squeaking, blood dappling its whiskers. It stopped a few feet from the three of them, its tiny beady eyes staring up at them, seemingly saying, *"Come near my warm meal and I'll bite your fingers off."*

Frank pulled out his gun. "Fuck you."

This time he blew the rat away.

Nothing more was said. They hurried as briskly as their fatigued legs would take them, over the tracks and across the train yard, watching as a horde of police vehicles raced in. Lights, sirens, shouts.

They reached the street where Hector's cruiser was still parked. Nearly collapsing from exhaustion, they leaned against the car and watched the activity from this safer distance.

A series of explosions sounded, and then something incredible happened.

Atmosphere—the entire nightclub—rose up in the air, a great black pod with bolts of lightning darting about its surface, elevating to a multitude of lengthy tentaclelike strands trailed behind it, ripping out of the ground, dragging up clumps of earth and cement until they all came free and slithered back into the base of the great floating system.

And then the great ship *Atmosphere* slowly inverted completely until the six cylindrical spines faced downward toward the earth. The ends glowed a shade of luminous blue, and in a flash it disappeared into the heavens, a great bullet of light, taking away all those still trapped within.

Chapter Thirty-two

Frank sat at the desk in his bedroom, booted up his computer and waited until the monitor display gave him the okay to proceed. In this time he thumbed through the *Daily News* and found a picture of the mayor inside, the caption bragging about the recent diminishing of New York's homeless population being due in part to the work of his appointed charities.

Frank grinned. Anything for a vote.

"Dad, I'm going out."

Frank looked up. Jaimie smiled, as beautiful as ever. "Be careful, hon."

"Of course. I'll be home by eight." She held up the cell phone Frank had bought for her. "I'll call if I get held up."

"Have fun."

Jaimie stepped away, then stuck her head back through the door. "Dad?"

He looked up. "Back so soon?"

She smiled. "You've done nothing but play on that computer since you retired. I hope you're not working, because if you are, I'll have to call Neil up and tell him to come over and help you out." The grin on her face told Frank that she had pretty much recovered from the memories of her—their—experience six months before.

Frank rolled his eyes. "Get lost—"

"Unless you've got yourself an Internet girl-friend . . ."

"I wish!" he shouted as she giggled and walked away.

He faced the computer and signed on to the Internet. Once the squawk granted him access, he checked his e-mail.

Two Messages

He clicked on the first message:

> *Frank,*
> *Haven't heard anything as of yet. My lead yesterday came up empty, so I'm sorry to say we still have to go on what we have at the moment, which isn't much, but it's still something. Talk to you later.*
> *Hector*

He clicked on the second message:

FB,
We've got secondary reports coming in from
our eyes in Omaha. Three kids now missing.
Two separate witnesses have given reports of
what appear to be Harbingers. One of the
sketches is now circulating the Omaha area.
I've attached the file. I think this is our cue.
I think we ought to go to Omaha.

It would be nice to finally meet you, FB.
Let me know what you think.
Ruefully yours,
sanskrit@prs.com

Frank aimed the mouse pointer over the download button and pressed it.

The sketch came up.

Bald.

Sunglasses.

Frank opened his desk drawer and removed the black plastic bag inside. He unfolded it and took out the object—black, shiny, six spines—that had greeted him so spookily on his living room floor when he arrived home that fateful night six months before.

He kept it in a safe place, knowing that someday he would need it.

Frank saved the picture file on a disk, signed off, then phoned Hector, carefully placing the Atmosphere back into the bag.

"Hello?" Hector answered.

"Hect, we're going to Omaha."

DEEP IN THE DARKNESS
MICHAEL LAIMO

Dr. Michael Cayle wants the best for his wife and young daughter. That's why he moves the family from Manhattan to accept a private practice in the small New England town of Ashborough. Everything there seems so quaint and peaceful—at first. But Ashborough is a town with secrets. Unimaginable secrets.

Many of the townspeople are strangely nervous, and some speak quietly of legends that no sane person could believe. But what Michael discovers in the woods, drenched in blood, makes him wonder. Soon he will be forced to believe, when he learns the terrifying identity of the golden eyes that peer at him balefully from deep in the darkness.

FOUR ORIGINAL NOVELLAS BY

BENTLEY LITTLE
DOUGLAS CLEGG
CHRISTOPHER GOLDEN
TOM PICCIRILLI

FOUR DARK NIGHTS

The most horrifying things take place at night, when the moon rises and darkness descends, when fear takes control and terror grips the heart. The four
original novellas in this hardcover collection each take place during one chilling night, a night of shadows, a night of mystery—a night of horror. Each is
a blood-curdling vision of what waits in the darkness, told by one of horror's
modern masters. But as the sun sets and night falls, prepare yourself. Dawn
will be a long time coming, and you may not live to see it!

RED

JACK KETCHUM

Fans and critics alike hailed Jack Ketchum's previous novel, *The Lost*, for its power, its thrills and its gripping style, and recognized Ketchum as a master of suspense. Now Jack Ketchum is back to frighten us again with . . . *Red!*

It all starts with a simple act of brutality. Three boys shoot and kill an old man's dog. No reason, just plain meanness. But the dog was the best thing in the old man's world, and he isn't about to let the incident pass. He wants justice, and he'll make sure the kids pay for what they did. They picked the wrong old man to mess with. And as the fury and violence escalate, they're about to learn that . . . the hard way.

The
LOST
Jack Ketchum

It was the summer of 1965. Ray, Tim and Jennifer were just three teenage friends hanging out in the campgrounds, drinking a little. But Tim and Jennifer didn't know what their friend Ray had in mind. And if they'd known they wouldn't have thought he was serious. Then they saw what he did to the two girls at the neighboring campsite—and knew he was dead serious.

Four years later, the Sixties are drawing to a close. No one ever charged Ray with the murders in the campgrounds, but there is one cop determined to make him pay. Ray figures he is in the clear. Tim and Jennifer think the worst is behind them, that the horrors are all in the past. They are wrong. The worst is yet to come.

___4876-0 $6.99 US/$8.99 CAN

DOUGLAS CLEGG
THE ABANDONED

There is a dark and isolated mansion, boarded-up and avoided, on a hill just beyond the town of Watch Point in New York's Hudson Valley. It has been abandoned too long and fallen into disrepair. It is called Harrow and it does not like to be ignored. But a new caretaker has come to Harrow. He is fixing up the rooms and preparing the house for visitors....

What's been trapped inside the house has begun leaking like a poison into the village itself. A teenage girl sleeps too much, but when she awakens her nightmares will break loose. A little boy faces the ultimate fear when the house calls to him. A young woman must face the terror in her past to keep Harrow from destroying everything she loves. And somewhere within the house a demented child waits with teeth like knives.

CITY
OF THE DEAD
BRIAN KEENE

Where can you go when the dead are everywhere? Cities have become overrun with legions of the dead, all of them intent on destroying what's left of the living. Trapped inside a fortified skyscraper, a handful of survivors prepare to make their last stand against an unstoppable, undying enemy. With every hour their chances diminish and their numbers dwindle, while the numbers of the dead can only rise. Because sooner or later, everything dies. And then it comes back, ready to kill.

THE TRAVELING VAMPIRE SHOW
RICHARD LAYMON

It's a hot August morning in 1963. All over the rural town of Grandville, tacked to the power poles and trees, taped to store windows, flyers have appeared announcing the one-night-only performance of The Traveling Vampire Show. The promised highlight of the show is the gorgeous Valeria, the only living vampire in captivity.

For three local teenagers, two boys and a girl, this is a show they can't miss. Even though the flyers say no one under eighteen will be admitted, they're determined to find a way. What follows is a story of friendship and courage, temptation and terror, when three friends go where they shouldn't go, and find much more than they ever expected.

__4850-7 $7.99 US/$9.99 CAN

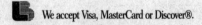